Praise for the novels of B.J. Daniels

"The new Powder River series is a must for Daniels fans and romantic suspense fans."
—*Fresh Fiction* on *Dark Side of the River*

"Filled with twists, danger, action, secrets, family dynamics, and romance."
—*Comfy Chair Books* on *Her Brand of Justice*

"Daniels is a perennial favorite, and I might go as far as to label her the cowboy whisperer." —*BookPage*

"Super read by an excellent writer. Recommended!"
—Linda Lael Miller, #1 *New York Times* bestselling author, on *Renegade's Pride*

"B.J. Daniels has [the] unique ability to astound with her mystery and suspense." —*Under the Covers Book Blog*

BJ DANIELS

RIVER
JUSTICE

CANARY STREET PRESS

CANARY
STREET
PRESS™

Recycling programs
for this product may
not exist in your area.

ISBN-13: 978-1-335-50815-7

River Justice

Canary Street Press
22 Adelaide St. West, 41st Floor
Toronto, Ontario M5H 4E3, Canada
CanaryStPress.com

Printed in U.S.A.

This book is dedicated to
my thirteen-year-old granddaughter Payton.
We recently spent hours at a bazaar together, visiting
and eating sweet treats her grams had made (not me).
Payton is an avid reader who loves books.
She reminds me of me when I was that age
in so many ways. This one is for you, Payton.

CHAPTER ONE

THE ENVELOPE LOOKED harmless enough. Plain, white, legal-size, with rancher Holden McKenna's name and address printed neatly in the center. No forwarding address. No stamp or postmark. But Holden didn't notice. His mind wasn't on the mail that Elaine, the family housekeeper, had picked up from the large mailbox a half mile up on the county road from the McKenna Ranch and brought unopened to the house as she did every weekday.

He'd found the pile stacked on his desk when he'd come back from his morning horseback ride. As usual, there was a lot of mail to deal with, all part of running a ranch the size of the McKenna spread in the Powder River Basin.

As he sliced through the envelope with his letter opener, he thought about the woman he'd lost but still loved, Charlotte Stafford, his neighboring rancher. The two of them had been estranged for years and often involved in all-out war. Still, this morning he felt something he hadn't in a very long time—hope. Because of that, he wasn't feeling his fifty-five years. He felt like that young buck who'd fallen head over heels for her when they were teenagers. The thought made him smile.

Part of his good mood could also have had something to do with the fact that it was finally summer in

Montana after a long, cold, snowy winter. An array of wildflowers bobbed in the breeze, birds warbled from the tops of the dark-leafed cottonwoods, and sunshine poured in the ranch house windows with a promise of warmth—at least for a while. After all, this was Montana, and summer was the shortest season of all.

But he knew that the main reason he was smiling was Lottie, as he'd always called Charlotte. The last time he'd seen her, she hadn't gone for her bullwhip or her gun when she saw him. True, she'd been grieving over her eldest son's arrest, but she'd let him hold her. He saw that as progress.

He wasn't completely delusional. He knew it was improbable that he and Lottie could ever find their way back to each other, but he could dream, couldn't he? Not that anyone in the town of Powder Crossing would bet on the two of them ever finding peace, let alone some kind of romantic bliss. Their rivalry was now carved deep in the basin's history because of his betrayal and Lottie's determination to hate him until she died.

"I'm going to pick up Holly Jo from school since they're getting out early today," his housekeeper said, sticking her head into his den and startling him out of his reverie. "Last day of school for the summer."

He blinked, uncomprehending for a moment. He'd been so lost in thought that he'd forgotten even the envelope he was holding in his hand—not to mention the stack of mail still sitting unopened.

"Holden?" Elaine said as she dropped her hand to her hip and gave him that chastising look he knew so well. A few years younger than him, she'd been with the ranch as far back as he could remember. Her mother had originally been in the ranch's employ, so Elaine had grown up here on the McKenna spread. She was much more than the housekeeper. He didn't know what he would do without her.

"Holden, seriously? You don't remember last night, the conversation at dinner about the big birthday trip? The one Holly Jo has been talking about for weeks? I guess you also don't remember that I'm picking her up from school and we're going shopping in Billings, staying at the Northern Hotel, making a weekend of it?"

"Right," he said as it came back to him. "Her promised thirteenth birthday present. She's redecorating her room." Before he'd brought the girl to the ranch, Elaine had done the then-twelve-year-old Holly Jo's room in pinks. A mistake. She'd hated it even more than the ranch. "I'd forgotten it was this weekend. Any idea what she's planning to do with the room? Given the way she dresses, I hate to think what her idea of decorating will be."

"She's thirteen going on thirty. You told her she could do anything she wanted," Elaine reminded him.

"I did, didn't I." He nodded, aware that he had no business raising a teenage girl at his age. But years ago, he'd promised her mother that if anything happened to her, he would take care of her daughter. Neither thought it would come to that. But after a bout with cancer, Holly Jo's mother had died, and he'd brought the city girl back to the ranch. She hadn't been happy about it any more than his grown children had.

Fortunately, Holly Jo had taken to the horses—at first planning to run away once she'd learned to ride. But later his son Cooper and friend and ranch hand Pickett Hanson had introduced her to trick riding, something even he could see she was excelling in. He hoped her wanting to redecorate her room was an indication that she was here to stay.

Elaine looked at the pile of mail he hadn't gotten through. "Is everything all right?"

"Just got caught up woolgathering," he said, not about to admit that he'd been thinking about Lottie. She was seldom far from his thoughts, but this morning more than ever.

"Uh-huh," Elaine said. Unfortunately, she knew him too well, so she'd probably guessed the path his thoughts had taken. She'd always encouraged him to try to mend his relationship with Lottie. He had tried over the years but to no avail. If Charlotte Stafford was anything, it was stubborn to a fault.

What he hated most was that because of him, his Lottie had become bitter, resentful and outright vindictive—not just about him but his entire family. Recently his son Cooper had fallen in love and married Lottie's eldest daughter, Tilly, throwing even more fuel on the fire.

Still standing in the doorway, Elaine looked worried about leaving him. "If you're sure you'll be all right without us."

"I'll be fine. It isn't like I'm here alone." The house was bursting at the seams right now. Cooper and Tilly were living in the huge, sprawling house while their home on the ranch was being finished. His sons Treyton and Duffy and daughter Bailey also lived in the house—though he hardly ever saw them—along with himself, Holly Jo and Elaine. As his children had grown, he'd added on, giving them all room to grow. The ranch manager had his own place closer to the stables and shop. The half-dozen ranch hands also living on the spread had a series of bunkhouses and cabins even farther from the house.

"We'll be back Sunday evening. You can call if you need me," Elaine said.

He would always need her. He'd often gone to her for advice as well as a good chewing out for something he'd done wrong. He loved Elaine in his way and suspected she did him as well. But for him, there had only been Lottie. There was only one woman he wanted. The one he might never have again.

"Go, have fun. And do your best to guide her choices," he said.

Elaine laughed at that. "Have you met this young woman?" Her expression turned serious again, as if still hesitant about leaving him, before she said, "Okay. See you Sunday, then."

Over the years, he'd given Elaine and his family cause for concern, he thought as he heard her drive away. He'd brought Holly Jo into their home with no real explanation, causing his eldest son, Treyton, to resent the girl and Bailey to simply ignore her. He'd done so many things wrong in his life, handled things poorly, and continued to make mistakes.

Glancing out the window at the beautiful early summer day, he felt a little of his hope slip away as he felt a chill. Like someone was walking across a grave? His second wife, Lulabelle, would have said it was an omen. But then again, if Lulabelle really could see the future like she claimed, then she would have never married him.

Still, he was eerily aware of how quiet this side of the big house was with his family all busy living their own lives. With a sigh, he returned to the envelope in his hand.

His thoughts scattered, he absently withdrew a sheet of paper. Unfolding it, he felt a jolt as he saw what was on it. For a moment, he could only stare in confusion. The words had been made from letters cut from a magazine and were all different sizes, shapes and colors.

Was this some kind of joke?

He struggled to read what it said. Then, in horror, he read it again. His hands trembled, the words blurring as his heart pounded, his mouth gone dry.

I Have Holly Jo
Will Contact
With Demands

CHAPTER TWO

BRAND STAFFORD STEPPED out of the shower and reached for a towel. His head swam, making him regret last night. How much had he drunk? He couldn't remember. Judging by how hungover and sick to his stomach he was, way too much.

What had possessed him? *Oh, that's right*, he thought, giving himself a mental forehead slap. *I found out that my whole life has been a lie.*

Not that he hadn't suspected as much. Little had he realized, though, that knowing the truth was so much worse than speculating. His own fault, he thought with a curse. If he'd never sent his DNA to be tested… It had been impulsive, something so not like him. He was the rational, calm, sensible, unemotional Stafford among a houseful of the opposite, he told himself.

Then, like kicking off an avalanche, he'd initiated something that he couldn't stop. Once he'd seen the results, he'd been determined to find out if his suspicions were true. The moment he did that, he opened a Pandora's box of secrets that could destroy his life and ruin others as well.

He swore as he wrapped a towel around his waist and stepped deeper into his bedroom suite. Like a lot of ranch homes, this house had been added on to as the family had grown. He had his own wing in the back of the house with a view of the mountains in the distance. Not that he noticed the view today. He was too busy mentally kicking himself for what he'd done.

For way too long, he'd pretended that he didn't want to know why he was so different from his siblings. Not only did he not want to buy into his suspicions, he definitely did not want to prove them. Then his sister Oakley, the rebel of the family, had gotten her DNA tested through one of the online labs. She'd gone on about how easy it was. "Just mail in a sample and the results are emailed to you."

When Oakley had mentioned what she'd done to their mother, Charlotte Stafford had thrown a fit. "Why would you do such a thing?" she'd demanded.

"I wanted to know who I am," Oakley had said, brushing it off as nothing. "DNA's amazing. Like if CJ, Brand, Ryder and Tilly all had theirs tested, even though we're siblings, the results would be different because we only share fifty percent of the same genes. Only identical twins share a hundred percent. Don't you find that interesting?"

Brand had. And he'd found their mother's overreaction even more curious. She'd been furious—and something even more telling. She'd been terrified. He'd seen it in her emerald green eyes and the way she wouldn't meet his blue-eyed gaze—the only blue eyes in the family.

He'd known right then that he had to have his DNA tested. He couldn't keep pretending. He had to know the truth. He'd sent for the kit, followed the instructions and mailed it in. Unlike Oakley, he'd had no intention of telling their mother. Even then, he was still hoping he was wrong.

But when it came back, he had proof that he wasn't Rake Stafford's son, because his results were nothing like the ones Oakley had left lying around in her room.

For years he'd heard the rumors about his mother and their ranch neighbor, Holden McKenna. His sister Tilly had married Cooper McKenna, so he figured he should be able to get a hair sample from Cooper's comb. It would be nice to cross off at least one suspect from his list—his main suspect.

With the DNA obtained from Cooper McKenna, he'd had another test done to compare with his own. That was when he'd confirmed it. He was the son of Charlotte Stafford and Holden McKenna—and he had a DNA report to prove it.

His mother and Holden—both married to others at the time—had gotten together and he was the result. He had the goods on both of them, which raised the question: Now what? He had proof, but what was he going to do with it? Confront his mother? Confront Holden? Did he want his father to admit it? His mother? Or should he bury what he'd learned and live with it just as he had for all these years?

Yesterday, after getting the results, he'd done what any red-blooded American cowboy would do—he'd gone drinking with friends in town. Something else he seldom did. He hadn't told anyone why he was drinking so much. But he'd consumed enough alcohol that one friend had insisted on driving him home while another friend followed in his pickup.

While he had a copy of the results in his jacket pocket, he hadn't even told his best friends.

They were worried about him before he'd done something even more out of character. On impulse, he'd had his friend stop at Holden McKenna's mailbox out on the county road. He'd scribbled Holden's name on the outside of the sheet of paper and dropped off the copy of the DNA report he'd been carrying around all night.

When he'd awakened just before noon today, he'd realized with a sickening roll of his stomach that there was no way to retrieve the report from the mailbox. By now, the mail would have been delivered, and someone from the McKenna Ranch would have taken it up to the house.

The thought of what he'd done made him more physically ill than the hangover. His timing couldn't have been worse. His mother's second husband's remains had recently been found in a well not that far from the ranch. It was no secret in the county that she was the number one suspect—if not the only one—because of her tumultuous relationship with her second husband, Dixon Malone, who had mysteriously disappeared years ago.

On top of that, his older brother CJ—and their mother's once favorite—was in jail awaiting trial on numerous felonies, including attempted murder and second-degree manslaughter. Their mother had already alienated both of his sisters, Tilly and Oakley, leaving only himself and his younger brother, Ryder, still at home on the ranch.

This was definitely not the time to drop his bombshell on her and the man she'd openly despised for years. Brand, clearly the product of a secret affair, didn't want this getting out. His family was the talk of the county enough as it was, one reason he and Ryder had always kept a low profile. They'd worked the ranch, avoiding the drama that was often going on up at the house— or in town.

As he started toward his bedroom closet, he caught a glimpse of movement outside. He stepped to his window in time to see a figure creeping along the side of the house, headed for the stables. Her back was to him, but as hungover as he was, he could still tell it was a young, shapely woman. Her head of long black hair fell almost to her shapely behind, a behind tucked nicely into a pair of jeans.

Clearly, she was sneaking around looking for something. He frowned, not sure he was up to dealing with a thief, given his hangover. But he realized he was probably the only one not off working somewhere on the ranch or in town today—other than this trespasser.

Given little choice, he pulled on jeans over his naked, still-damp lower body, going commando, and rushed barefoot to the door before she could get away. Time to find out what she was doing sneaking around the Stafford Ranch.

HOLDEN'S FIRST INSTINCT after reading the strange note was to call the sheriff. But he couldn't shake off the feeling that this was some kind of prank. A sick joke. He had to make sure that Holly Jo was missing. He tried Elaine's number. By now she would have reached the school.

His call went directly to voicemail. He left a message for her to call right away. He knew she wouldn't have turned off her phone, which meant she had to be on it. He tried not to panic as he chastised himself for not letting the girl get her own cell phone. He'd said she didn't need one, but right now he wished more than ever that he could call her. He just needed to hear her voice.

Holly Jo would think he was silly or senile when she heard his relief. He could just hear her. "Really, HH?" she would say. After she'd recently found out his middle name was Hank, she'd taken to calling him HH rather than Holden. "I'm fine. What did you think had happened to me?" she'd ask, laughing.

Just as he started to try Elaine again, his phone rang. With a flood of relief, he saw that she was calling him back.

"Tell me you have Holly Jo," he said before she could speak.

Those next few seconds waiting for her reply were interminable.

"She's not here, Holden. I can't find anyone who's even seen her. Her regular teacher was out sick and the substitute teacher didn't report it because of the short day at school." His heart dropped like an anvil from a plane. "The bus driver said she wasn't waiting at the end of the ranch road. I've been trying to call a classmate of hers who also wasn't in school today. Why would she skip school on a day when she knew I was picking her up early to go shopping in Billings? She's been looking forward to this for weeks, and now..."

"Elaine." She must have heard the anguish and fear in his voice, because she stopped talking abruptly. "I need to get off the phone to call the sheriff. I'm afraid Holly Jo's been kidnapped. I got a note. Please come home. We have to find her and get her back."

"No," Elaine said, her voice cracking. "Oh no."

He disconnected and made the call, silently praying to a God he'd abandoned years ago after his mother had died. "Stu," he said the moment the sheriff answered. Sheriff Stuart Layton and Holden's son Cooper had been friends since they were kids, spending endless hours on the ranch together. "Holly Jo's been taken."

"Holden? What do you mean *taken*?"

"*Kidnapped.* I got a note. Elaine went to pick her up at school, but she never arrived. She wasn't at the bus stop when the driver came by. No one has seen her."

"Sit tight. Don't touch the note again. I'm on my way."

As he disconnected, he saw his son Duffy standing in the doorway of his office.

"What's this about Holly Jo?" Duffy asked, looking worried.

He pointed to the note lying on his desk, and his son stepped into the room to read it. "Stu said not to touch it. He should be here soon." As Duffy scanned the oddly shaped words from a safe distance, Holden could see that, like he himself had originally, his son wanted to believe it was a sick joke.

"You're sure she's missing?"

"Elaine went to pick her up. She never made it to school." He saw his son's expression. *"What?"*

"There's this boy at school," Duffy said. "He's been giving her a hard time. Gus Gardner, Joe Gardner's kid from the Montgomery Ranch."

"Why is this the first time I've been hearing about this?" Holden demanded.

"I handled it. I talked to the boy."

"And?" he demanded.

"And nothing. Holly Jo got mad and took the bus home instead of riding with me. She said I embarrassed her. She also said that I didn't know anything. But it was clear to me that something was going on between them."

At the sound of a vehicle, Holden got up from his

desk and rushed to the door. He kept telling himself that this wasn't happening. Holly Jo would turn up. But what Duffy had told him made him even more worried. So much went on in a child's life that the parents never knew about. He hated to think of things he'd done that could have gotten him killed growing up that he'd never told his father about.

He'd made so many mistakes with his own children who were now adults. He had hoped that he could do better with Holly Jo. But he feared he might have already done something that was now jeopardizing her life.

"Duffy," he said as his son stormed toward the door. His youngest son didn't bother to look back as he rushed out, headed for his pickup. "Don't go off half-cocked and do something we'll all regret," he called after him. But if Duffy heard, he didn't respond as he roared off, no doubt headed for the Montgomery Ranch and Gus Gardner.

Holden swore as he watched Duffy swerve to miss the sheriff's patrol SUV now speeding toward the house.

As Brand sneaked around the side of the house, he saw the woman head for the stable. He frowned. What was she looking for? All of the hands must be out somewhere on the ranch, he thought as he ran barefoot to the back of the stable and carefully opened the door. Stepping into the cool semidarkness, he spotted her silhouetted in the open doorway at the other end of the structure. He couldn't wait to see the look on the young woman's face when he caught her.

He just wished he wasn't so hungover. His head ached, and he feared he might not be thinking clearly. He listened but could hear little over the sound of birds in the stand of dense cottonwoods that lined this side of the river. A cloudless deep blue sky hung over the mountains and river that formed the Powder River Basin. He breathed in the summer day, even though it was chilly here in the stable wearing only a pair of jeans and nothing else. He wished he had at least pulled on his boots.

She stood as if also listening. She didn't look as if she was here to rob them, especially all by herself.

On his way to the stable, he'd noted that his pickup was parked where his friend had left it last night. He couldn't see any other vehicles—let alone another person other than her on the premises. His head and stomach churned at the memory of all he'd had to drink last night—and what he'd done. He realized that from the moment he'd opened his eyes this morning, he'd been waiting for something bad to happen.

Given how he felt, maybe accosting a trespasser wasn't his best idea. The thought made him grin. Even hungover, he told himself he could handle this slightly built woman as she started to move away from the open stable doorway. He spotted a coiled lariat hanging on the wall, scooping it up as he moved soundlessly after her.

She must have sensed him, though, because as he cleared the doorway, she turned. He already had the loop in the lariat ready as she started to run. He'd spent a lifetime lassoing cattle and horses and fence posts. Throwing a loop over a slim young woman was child's play.

The moment the rope dropped over her, he pulled hard, bringing her to an abrupt stop. By then, he was stalking toward her, coiling the rope as he moved, ready to demand answers. He couldn't imagine what she was doing here, let alone what she might be looking for. But in a few moments, he would find out.

He wasn't sure what he'd expected when they finally came face-to-face with each other. If not fear, at least concern at being caught. Her wolf-gray eyes did widen a little. But the corner of her mouth turned up slightly as she cocked her head at him as if in amusement. It gave him a moment of pause, but not enough to make him stop closing the distance between them. Nor did he allow any slack in the rope. He had her. She wasn't getting away.

Yet the whole time, he was thinking that he was taken aback by how sweet and innocent she looked. Not beautiful by classical standards. Instead, cute from the button nose to the bow-shaped mouth. And those eyes, they seemed bottomless as fog, and yet there was a glint in them that made him wonder what he'd roped.

She hadn't struggled. Hadn't even tried to release herself from the rope now cinched around her slim waist. Nor had she tried to run or make any attempt to get away from him. Instead, she moved toward him.

Brand suddenly realized that he just might have roped in more than he could handle. But by then it was too late.

As Sheriff Stuart Layton pulled into the McKenna Ranch, he caught only a glimpse of the driver racing past toward the county road in one of the ranch trucks. Duffy? He'd been afraid it might be Holden taking matters into his own hands. He hated to think where the young McKenna might be headed or why. At least Holden hadn't left. With relief, he spotted the rancher waiting for him, standing on the front porch.

Patriarch Holden McKenna was a distinguished, large, physically fit man in his midfifties with salt-and-pepper hair and intense blue eyes. But as Stuart parked, he could see the weight of this scare already taking a toll on the bigger-than-life man.

Stuart had no idea what he was about to face. On the way to the ranch, he'd wondered if this wouldn't turn out to be something the girl had cooked up. He'd known that Holly Jo had tried to run away when she'd first been brought to the McKenna Ranch. His best friend, Cooper McKenna, had told him that the girl was smart as a whip and headstrong. He'd thought, though, that lately she'd been happier with the McKennas. Maybe he'd been wrong.

Kidnappings often ended up being family abductions where a member of the family took the child. But as far as the sheriff knew, Holly Jo didn't have any other family. That was why she'd come to live at the McKenna Ranch.

Her addition to the family hadn't gone over well with several members of the family, according to Cooper. That their father had brought the girl home without even an explanation hadn't helped. Had one of them taken her?

If a true kidnapping, the sheriff knew it could be a nonfamily abduction where an unknown person had seen an opportunity and run with it.

Until he knew what he was up against, Stuart tried not to speculate. It was just hard to believe that Holly Jo had been kidnapped. In all the years he'd lived in Powder Crossing, all the way back to when his father was sheriff, he'd never heard of a local kidnapping.

Crime in the Powder River Basin had been on the

rise, though, he reminded himself as he parked in front of the McKenna Ranch house and the man waiting there. Seeing the place still made him feel a little guilty. Growing up, he'd wanted his best friend Cooper's life. He'd imagined what it must be like to live in this house and be the son of the owner of this huge ranch. He'd always thought of it as being worry-free. As an adult, he knew better.

But he was still a little jealous. Stuart still lived in the same small house in town he'd grown up in. He'd always felt that he'd been dealt the wrong hand and had no choice but to play it out, fair or not. He was the son of the former sheriff and had followed in his footsteps. It seemed too late to change horses in the middle of the stream, as his father would have said. He didn't know anything else. Nor had he dreamed of being anything else—except being the son of Holden McKenna.

As he climbed out of his patrol SUV, he hoped to hell Holden was wrong about Holly Jo having been kidnapped. He was just a small-town sheriff who often questioned if he was up to the job—but never more than at this moment.

Even under all this stress, Holden still looked like the powerful man he was. Stuart couldn't believe that anyone in his right mind would mess with the ward of Holden McKenna. Not if they knew the family—let alone the patriarch. Holden was the kind of man who would track down the kidnapper himself and kill him without a second thought, Stuart realized.

As he walked toward the rancher, he reminded himself that maybe the kidnapper *did* know the family, did know Holden. Maybe this was personal. Stuart preferred that over the other, that someone outside the community had taken Holly Jo Robinson, a pretty young teen, to ransom her for money or worse.

There was another possibility, he reminded himself. With social media, Holly Jo wouldn't be the first young girl to get roped in by an online predator without realizing the danger she'd put herself in.

"I'm glad you're here," Holden said, motioning him inside. "We have to find her."

Stuart could only nod. There was no question that the girl had to be found as quickly as possible. The clock had been running since the moment she was last seen early this morning. He was familiar with the rancher's steel-hard determination. It was the fear he also recognized in the big man's face that worried him. He'd never seen Holden McKenna running scared before. He had a bad feeling it would make him all the more dangerous.

Stuart opened his mouth, started to reassure Holden, telling him that everything was going to be all right. They would find Holly Jo. She would be fine. She would be safe.

But he knew better than to lie to this man, so he only said, "Let me see the note," and let Holden lead him into his office.

CHAPTER THREE

ONE MOMENT BRAND STAFFORD was looking into those glinting gray eyes in that angelic face.

The next he was lying flat on his back in the dirt, and she was dropping his coiled lariat onto his bare chest as she stood over him. It happened so fast that he wasn't even sure how.

"Which one are you?" she demanded as she peered down at him.

He squinted up at her, the sun in his eyes as he tried to catch the breath she'd knocked out of him. "Which what?"

"Charlotte Stafford's sons. Or are you one of the hired hands?"

"What—" He started to get up.

"I wouldn't do that if I were you," she warned.

"Seriously?" He leaned back on his elbows. She wasn't honestly threatening him on his land, was she? He reminded himself that he'd just let this snip of a woman kick his butt. He blamed the hangover along with everything else he had going on right now for why he was finding himself in this situation.

He couldn't help sounding indignant as he said, "I'm Brand Stafford," and tossed the lariat aside. He got to his bare feet. She'd stepped back to let him rise, but there was still a challenge in her gaze. He met those gray eyes feeling as if they were locked in a standoff.

But it was the smile on her face that told him she'd known who he was all along. "Who are *you*?" he demanded. "And what are you doing trespassing on Stafford Ranch property?"

For a moment, she looked as if she didn't plan to answer. He debated what he would do if she took off running. Or whether he even wanted to try to stop her. She didn't appear to have stolen anything. He couldn't imagine what she'd been doing sneaking around the place, but he told himself she hadn't really done any harm—at least, not to anything but his ego.

He noticed that she was wearing a black T-shirt, designer jeans and a pair of new-looking cowboy boots. Everything about her looked expensive and well cared for. He was asking himself who this woman was when she decided to tell him.

"I'm Birdie Malone," she said, her chin rising and those gray eyes shining with open defiance. "My father was Dixon Malone, your mother's second husband, the man whose body was found in a well near here recently after he supposedly disappeared years ago."

She could have knocked him over with dandelion fluff. He had heard a private detective, hired by Dixon's daughter, had been around asking questions before the body was found. But the young woman standing before him was not what Brand would have expected.

"Which doesn't explain why you're trespassing on my ranch."

"Doesn't it?" She looked amused again. "If you were me, wouldn't you be curious about the woman who killed your father? Even curious about her...offspring,

Brand," she said, as if trying out his name and finding it distasteful. "My father told me about all of you, you especially. That's why I followed you last night from the bar. Nice of your friends to give you a lift home. You always drink like that?"

"No," he snapped, shocked to hear that she'd followed him. "Not that it is any of your business." He must have really been out of it last night not to have noticed her at the bar since she'd more than noticed him.

Given the way he felt, she really shouldn't be messing with him. A thought elbowed its way through his foggy brain. Frowning, he said, "Don't tell me that you've been here since last night."

"You really should lock your doors at night," she said. "Slept in the room next to yours. Are you aware that you snore when you drink? Your difficult childhood must have driven you to it," she said sarcastically.

He couldn't believe she'd been right next door last night in CJ's old room. "You don't know anything about me or my family."

"You might be surprised," she said with a flip of her hair. That shiny black wave cascaded over her shoulder before she swung it back. "Did you know I was going to come live here as soon as my father got some things settled with your mother? Apparently, whatever those things were, your mother decided to settle them permanently."

Brand didn't remember much about his mother's marriage to Dixon Malone. He'd been too young, and he figured his mother had been, too. But he'd heard through local scuttlebutt since then that the marriage had been the knock-down, drag-out variety. The man had spent a lot of time in town at the bar telling anyone who would listen what he thought of Charlotte Stafford. Not that most people in the county didn't know that she was hell on wheels.

"Just think, we would have met years ago if those things had worked out and your mother hadn't killed him," Birdie said. "My father was a big man. I'm just curious who helped her get him into that well. She had to have an accomplice. Any ideas?"

He stared at her. The thought had never crossed his mind. Until now.

"Okay," Birdie said. "I guess I'll be going, then, since you don't seem to be in any shape to provide those answers. Thanks for the accommodations last night, and no, I'm not leaving town until I see Charlotte Stafford behind bars—and her accomplice in the cell next to hers." She smiled as she held his gaze. "Don't worry. Our paths will cross again." She made it sound like a promise. Or a threat.

Turning her back on him, she started toward the stand of cottonwoods along the river. "By the way, Brand Stafford," she said over her shoulder, "you look like hell."

He watched her go, only a little surprised that she didn't seem concerned he might try to stop her again and have her arrested for trespassing. The way his life was going today, he felt no compunction to do so. Anyway, he didn't doubt he'd see her again.

Wiping dirt off himself as he walked back toward the house, he felt as if he'd been in a brawl. His head hurt, his stomach ached, and his pride was definitely bruised. Yet all he could think as he turned to see her disappear into the trees was, *that* was Dixon Malone's daughter?

His mother was definitely not going to like this. Normally, he would have felt sorry for anyone brash enough to take on Charlotte Stafford. But this time, he thought his mother might have met her match in Birdie Malone.

BIRDIE CLIMBED INTO her SUV parked on the county road, grinning to herself. She kept thinking about the expression on Brand Stafford's face when he found himself flat on his back on the ground. He'd underestimated her, something she should have been used to when it came to men. She'd expected more from one of the Stafford men, though.

Still, she couldn't help grinning. Earlier she'd pretended not to know who he was, but she'd known. One of his friends had called him by name when the men were playing pool at the back of the bar last night. She'd been curious about him long before that. Curious about his whole family, but maybe especially him because the two of them were about the same age.

She couldn't wait until their paths crossed again, only next time he'd be ready for her—and so would his family. Which was fine with her. She wanted them to know that she was coming for the Stafford matriarch. She wouldn't rest until her father's killer was behind bars doing the time Charlotte so richly deserved.

But she had to admit as she drove toward Powder Crossing, she hadn't expected her reaction to the Stafford Ranch, let alone Brand. The place was much more impressive than her father had described. That had been almost thirty years ago. The house had grown over that time as the Stafford children had.

Seeing it made her realize how large, how beautiful, how wonderful it would have been to grow up there. Her father had told her that once he was settled, she would have two older sisters and three brothers. Brand, because they were so close in age, had been her father's favorite. He used to talk about him a lot. She'd been excited, anxious to meet them, dreaming of her new life. He'd described them all as cute, but Brand was the cutest.

Brand was a whole lot more than cute. She could still smell the fresh-from-the-bath scent of him on her. His longish dark blond hair had still been wet, and he'd been half naked, his feet bare—like his muscled chest. Under other circumstances, she told herself, she might have flirted her way off the Stafford Ranch.

She reminded herself why she was in the Powder River Basin. Still, her thoughts shifted like the breeze, drifting back to Brand. His kind of handsome—even hungover—mixed with his Stafford confidence, had made her catch her breath. Not that she hadn't noticed the way his jeans fit him, or that broad, rock-hard chest of his.

But his blue eyes… With a start, she recalled that Charlotte had emerald green eyes, according to Jason Murdock, the PI she'd originally hired to find her father. Brand's siblings, she'd been told, had variations of green. Brand was the one outlier?

She had hoped that Murdock would find evidence she could use, but he hadn't. When her father's body had finally been found in an abandoned well on property near the Stafford Ranch, it had been quite by accident—and not by the PI.

If Dixon Malone's remains hadn't been found, everyone would have gone on believing that he'd simply disappeared, left in the middle of the night, deserting his new family the way he had left Birdie and her mother.

Everyone would have gone on believing a lie about her father, something she was determined to set straight. She didn't just want justice. She wanted everyone to know the kind of man he'd really been, a man who'd loved his daughter to the moon and back, as he used to say.

She swore that she would put him to rest—once she saw his killer in prison. Until then, she couldn't move on with her life.

HOLLY JO TRIED to open her eyes. Her lids felt too heavy. She could barely move, her numb cold limbs lying on the hard concrete floor on nothing but an old blanket. Prying her eyes open, she tried to make sense of where she was. Somewhere small and dark. Only slits of light slipped through the single boarded-up window—just enough that she could see it was still daylight.

She felt confused, her head groggy. What had happened? Why was she here? Struggling to remember, she pushed herself up into a sitting position. Her skull pounded, and she had an awful taste in her painfully dry mouth.

Glancing around, she found herself in a small room. There was a bucket nearby on the concrete floor and a plastic bottle of juice. There was only the one door. She got up on wobbly legs to try it. Locked. As she dropped back onto the blanket, memory forced its way into the dense fog in her brain. Her heart began to pound wildly as she remembered.

Stumbling to her feet again, she moved to the door and tried the knob again. Her pulse punched up another notch as she realized she was locked in and no one knew where she was.

"Hello?" she called, her voice raspy and low. "Someone?" Silence. Her legs felt too weak to hold her up. Her head began to swim. She felt sick to her stomach as she began to cry.

Her hands pummeled the door. She screamed for help until she could no longer stand, no longer shout or cry. Sliding down, she crawled over to the plastic bottle of juice and drank all of it before crawling back into the corner to her blanket. She closed her eyes and pressed her body against the wall to make herself as small as possible. She feared the man would be back. She was defenseless against him. But she also feared he wouldn't come back.

Her throat was so sore that she didn't want to cry again. "I want my mom," she whispered and felt hot tears stream down her cheeks. "Mama," she cried, even though she knew her mother couldn't hear her because she was dead. No one could hear her. Holly Jo was lost and alone and scared.

Close your eyes. Go back to sleep. She could feel exhaustion and something more dragging her down, feel herself falling into that deep dark well she'd awakened from. Blackness began to move in behind her eyelids, the emptiness filling her head.

She welcomed it. Anything so she didn't have to think the one thought that paralyzed her with fear.

What if no one ever found her?

CHAPTER FOUR

PULLING ON LATEX GLOVES, Stuart inspected what appeared to be a ransom note with growing concern. The message was short and to the point. The person who claimed to have taken Holly Jo said they would be contacting Holden with his or her demands. "How did you get this?"

Holden pointed at the open envelope on the desk. "Elaine found it in the mailbox this morning with the rest of the mail."

It hadn't come by US mail. No stamp, no postmark, no return address. Holden's name and that of the ranch had been printed on the envelope with exaggerated precision as if to hide the person's true handwriting.

"Do you have any idea why someone would take Holly Jo?" the sheriff asked.

Holden shook his head, but Stuart could see that he was worried it might be a personal grudge. Holden was a powerful and wealthy man with a huge ranch. He had made enemies over the years—not to mention the open war between him and Charlotte Stafford. Their offspring had gotten involved in the rivalry as well as their ranch staff.

He figured Chisum Jase "CJ" Stafford had often taken advantage of that rivalry for his own interests. But while he wouldn't have put kidnapping past CJ, Stuart didn't think this was his doing from behind bars.

But Holden also had a hotheaded older son who made no secret of his resentment of Holly Jo, according to what the sheriff had heard from his friend Cooper. Treyton McKenna and his father had been at odds for some time, but even more so after Holden had brought Holly Jo home to live with them. Treyton had also been vocal on how he felt about his brother Cooper marrying Tilly Stafford. But kidnapping the girl? What would he hope to gain?

"What are you going to do?" Holden demanded. "Holly Jo's been missing for hours. We have to find her."

"The first thing you need to do is make some calls," Stuart said as Elaine came rushing in, looking as upset as Holden. "Call anyone and everyone who might have seen Holly Jo since she left the house this morning. Neighbors, friends, family. Then I'm going to need a recent photo of her as well as her birth date, height, weight and a description of her and what she was wearing this morning when she left for school."

"I can write down that information as well as provide a photo," Elaine said, no doubt seeing that Holden apparently couldn't recall how his ward was dressed this morning, let alone other particulars.

"It appears from the note that she was kidnapped," Stuart said. "Once we get the alleged kidnapper's demands, we'll have a better idea of what we're up against. In the meantime, I need to search her room."

Elaine pointed him in the right direction, up the stairs and down the hallway. There was a *Keep Out!* sign taped to the door, the letters in black marker. Holly Jo had added a corral, mountains and a horse in the background.

The sheriff stared at the sign for a moment before he

opened the door, thinking about the girl who'd lost her mother and had been uprooted and brought here to live with strangers, *here* being in the middle of nowhere.

The room had been styled in pinks, which stood in direct contrast to the posters of horses, trick riders and rodeo cowgirls on the walls. A typical girl's room in rural Montana. The muddy cowboy boots accompanied by a pair of dirty jeans and a shirt near the door told the same story. This pink bedroom was at odds with the cowgirl who lived in it. Which explained the trip to Billings that Elaine said Holly Jo had been looking forward to.

He spotted the laptop computer on the desk but went to the closet instead. In one corner was an assortment of stuffed animals crowded into the dark, clearly exiled. Other than clothing, some hanging, some tossed on the floor, he saw nothing of interest.

But as he turned, he spotted a single tiny stuffed duck lying next to the pillow on the seemingly hurriedly made bed. He moved to it, picking it up as if it was made of glass. He studied the only plush toy that hadn't been relegated to the closet. The duck had a worn look, as if it had been handled a lot. A favorite? He pulled out an evidence bag and popped the palm-sized duck inside before pocketing it.

The computer required a password. He searched the desk but found nothing useful. As he looked around the room, doubt began to cloud everything. What he did over the next few hours could mean life or death for Holly Jo. So much was riding on him finding her quickly and returning her safely to her family—and bringing her kidnapper to justice. He had to do everything by the book and not make any mistakes while keeping Holden reined in.

It seemed an impossible task. He found himself going over the procedures he'd learned at the law enforcement academy for kidnapping cases, hoping there was nothing he was forgetting as he returned downstairs. Elaine looked even more distraught.

"Her friends haven't seen her?" he guessed.

She shook her head, clearly close to tears. "I just texted you her photo and the information you asked for. She doesn't have a lot of friends. But I talked to Pickett Hanson. He's been teaching Holly Jo riding tricks. No one down at the stables has seen her, and her horse isn't missing. I haven't found anyone who's been in touch with her. I don't know who else to call."

He nodded, impressed that she'd thought to check the stables. He turned expectantly to Holden, who'd gotten a call and had just now disconnected. "You talked to Cooper, Treyton and Bailey?"

"I spoke with Cooper. Couldn't reach either Bailey or Treyton, but I left a message for them to call. Cooper hasn't seen Holly Jo. He's out working on his new house. He wanted to come in, but I asked him not to. Instead, he's going to join our ranch hands to search our property for her."

"Is this birth date correct?" Stuart asked after perusing the information Elaine had given him. "Holly Jo's now thirteen?"

"Her birthday was a couple of weeks ago," Elaine said. "Does her age matter?"

"The FBI gets involved even if it isn't an interstate kidnapping for children twelve and under," the sheriff said. "They call it the Tender Years."

"Still, you can call them in to help, right?" Holden asked.

Stuart nodded. He didn't want to jump the gun. But there was no reason not to give the FBI a heads-up—just in case this was real. He made the call to notify the FBI and provide what information he had. If this turned out to be a real kidnapping, he would need the use of the FBI lab for what evidence he collected.

When he got off the call, he told Holden and Elaine, "The FBI will monitor the situation, and we'll be able to use their lab facilities. I'll get the note to their lab for possible prints." He sighed. "This will mean opening up everything in all of your lives."

"I don't give a damn," Holden said. "Just get Holly Jo back."

"I'm going to have any mail coming for you intercepted," Stuart told him. "I'll have a deputy watching your mailbox on the county road since that's how the note was delivered. We need to talk about how to handle any phone calls from the kidnapper. The FBI will monitor the landline. They'll try to trace the calls. I'll tell you what to say." He met Holden's gaze. "It's important not to lose your temper. We have to remain calm and do whatever the kidnapper asks. Once we get Holly Jo back—"

"The gloves come off," Holden said.

The sheriff didn't respond to that, knowing how hard it was going to be to keep the rancher from going rogue. Spotting the pile of mail sitting unopened on Holden's desk, he asked, "Do you mind if I look through that?"

Holden shook his head, appearing dazed as he dropped into a chair. Elaine stood by the door, thumbing through her phone. "I don't have hardly any photos of Holly Jo where she is smiling except ones on a horse. I sent you my favorite." Her eyes filled, and she quickly put away her phone. "Can I get either of you coffee? I could make a fresh pot?" she asked, as if she needed something to do.

Stuart was almost through the pile of mail when he found a sheet of paper that had been folded into thirds. At first it looked like a flyer someone had stuck in the mailbox since there was no address on the outside, no stamp, no postmark. All that was written on the outside was Holden's name.

As he unfolded it, he saw with relief that it was also not like the other note. There were no letters cut from magazines and formed into words. Nor had the sender written anything. It took him a moment to understand what he was holding in his hand.

It appeared to be a photocopy of DNA results.

"I'd love a cup of coffee," the sheriff said as he turned to Elaine, the DNA results in his hand. The moment she hurried off to the kitchen, he turned to Holden. "I think you'd better take a look at this before she comes back."

AFTER HIS ENCOUNTER with Birdie Malone, Brand went back into the house, feeling worse than when he'd awakened. The entire incident had left him shaken. Birdie was coming after his mother—and her alleged accomplice?

While that was nothing unexpected, given that she was Dixon's daughter, what she'd said about his mother having an accomplice was. Assuming his mother really had gotten rid of her husband, Birdie was right. She couldn't have done it alone.

Dixon's body was believed to have been dumped in the largest abandoned well in the county because of his size. Brand doubted even a single man could have accomplished the feat. He hated the trail his thoughts were taking. Who would his mother have gotten to help her with the body—if she really was guilty of his murder? Who could she trust to keep her secret? He hated to think.

Looking down, he noticed his dirty feet. He pulled off his jeans and hopped back into the shower. He wasn't sure what had surprised him the most—who the young woman snooping around the ranch had turned out to be, or how easily she'd taken him down. He was a good eight inches taller and seventy pounds heavier.

He blamed the hangover and the element of surprise—both giving her the advantage. He swore that the next time they crossed paths, it would be different. He was just glad that no one had seen what had happened. He'd never live it down if his brother Ryder had seen that slender woman put him on his back in the dirt—let alone if his older brother, CJ, had been around.

Stepping out of the shower, he realized that, his ego aside, Birdie Malone was going to be a problem. She'd said that she had come here to prove that his mother had killed her father—and expose her accomplice. He doubted their encounter earlier had dissuaded her from completing her quest.

As he dressed, he debated whether or not he should tell his mother about Birdie. He assumed she was in her wing of the house, though he'd hardly seen her—and only in passing. For a while, he'd forgotten about the DNA results—and the copy he'd sent to Holden McKenna. Would Holden contact Charlotte when he got the DNA results? He wouldn't if he already knew about the pregnancy. Brand frowned. His father did know, didn't he? How could he not?

He realized that even if Holden did tell Charlotte about the DNA results being sent to him, that didn't mean she would say anything. Brand was sure she would happily keep on pretending his conception with Holden had never happened—just as they had obviously done for years.

He'd never been impulsive and he regretted his recent impetuous behavior, as he told himself nothing would come of it. He had bigger things to worry about. Birdie Malone had followed him home last night. She'd also had the audacity to come into their house and sleep in one of their bedrooms.

He had a feeling that Birdie Malone was a loose cannon. Who knew what she would do next?

He decided that the best thing he could do was avoid her. Just give her a wide berth if and when he ever saw her again. No more drinking in town. He would just stay on the ranch, work and put all of this behind him.

Unfortunately, he reminded himself, he was also avoiding his mother. He had no idea what he wanted to say to her—if anything. But by now, she could have heard about the DNA results.

That was enough to convince him to leave the house. Wouldn't hurt to go into town and have some lunch. Wasn't the café having the pulled pork sandwich special today? He realized that Birdie was probably staying in town, maybe at the hotel. Maybe she'd rented a place, intending to stay as long as it took to find her father's killer.

Powder Crossing was so small, he was bound to run into her. He tried to scoff at the idea that Birdie could

find evidence after all this time that would implicate
his mother—let alone the person who'd helped her—if
she was indeed guilty. While certainly capable of murder, Charlotte Stafford might be innocent. Brand had
to believe that—even if no one else did.

Even though he'd just met the young woman, he was
pretty sure that nothing could convince Birdie Malone
she was wrong about his mother. Not that he had any
intention of trying. It wasn't like she'd found any proof
that his mother was a killer, right?

At least not yet, he thought with a groan.

He grabbed his jacket and headed for the door. Both
the DNA fiasco and Birdie Malone's threats would blow
over. In the meantime, he would keep his head down
and hope for the best.

It had been the way he'd survived growing up in this
family. No reason to change now—even if he could.

"WHAT IS IT?" Holden demanded, clearly having the
same trouble Stuart had understanding what was printed
on the sheet of paper—at first.

"It's DNA results," Stuart said as he watched the
rancher frown.

"I don't understand."

"It appears to be the DNA results for Brand Stafford and your son Cooper. Brand and Cooper share the
same DNA."

Holden's eyes widened.

"Brand's my son? That's what this DNA report says?"
Holden asked.

"It would indicate that, yes."

A variety of emotions swept across the rancher's

face. Confusion. Shock. Disappointment. And finally, disbelief followed quickly by anger.

"It's not possible." But even as Holden said it, Stuart saw realization dawn before the rancher swore.

"You didn't know," the sheriff said, stating the obvious. "I have to ask. Do you think this could have something to do with Holly Jo?"

The rancher looked up and frowned. "What? I can't see how one has anything to do with the other."

Neither could Stuart. But the timing bothered him.

The rancher threw down the report. "She never told me. Why would Charlotte keep something like this from me?" He looked up. "How could I have not known?"

The sheriff's cell phone rang. It was his office. Thinking it might be about Holly Jo, he took the call as Elaine returned with coffee for the two of them. He saw Holden pick up the DNA results again, fold the sheet and stuff the paper into his shirt pocket before accepting the cup of coffee. Elaine appeared to have sensed the tension in the room. She was studying Holden, looking even more worried.

Stuart watched the two of them as he listened to the dispatcher informing him that Joe Gardner was calling about a disturbance at his house on the Montgomery Ranch. He started to tell her to let a deputy handle it, when she mentioned it had something to do with Holly Jo and Duffy McKenna.

"Duffy?" Stuart said, making Holden look up expectantly. "That was Duffy I saw leaving on my way in, right?" he asked the rancher. All the McKenna offspring resembled each other, taking after their father.

The rancher nodded. "Duffy said some boy was giving Holly Jo a hard time at school. Gus Gardner."

"Put Joe through," the sheriff told the dispatcher. "Joe, what seems to be the problem?" he asked as he stepped out of the room. He listened for a few minutes, then said, "Put Duffy on the phone, please."

An obviously angry Duffy McKenna came on the line. "Listen to me," Stuart said, reminded of all the times Cooper's kid brother had tagged along, just being a pain in their asses. "You apologize and get the hell out of there before I have to arrest you for interfering in this investigation." Duffy started to argue. "Duffy, damn it, you have no idea what you're doing. We need you back here at the ranch. Now."

He disconnected and went back into Holden's office. "Duffy's on his way home. I'll talk to him. If there appears to be some connection to Holly Jo's abduction, I'll talk to Joe's son."

CHAPTER FIVE

BIRDIE MALONE SPRAWLED on the hotel room bed in Powder Crossing, staring up at the ceiling. There were moments when she questioned what she was doing here. It hadn't escaped her that her father's murder was a very cold case after all these years. What evidence there might have been was long gone.

And if she was right about Charlotte Stafford killing him and getting someone to help her dispose of his body, then the woman would have covered her tracks. Why was Birdie wasting her time and her grandmother's money here?

She'd been five when her father had left her and her mother. He'd come into her room late that night, crouched down next to her bed and taken her hand. She'd pretended to still be asleep, knowing he was leaving. She would cry and beg him not to go if she opened her eyes. She'd seen it coming after all the fighting with her mother, the woman he hadn't loved enough to marry. He'd stayed for his daughter until it became impossible. Birdie had seen other men go through the same thing before and after her father.

It had broken her heart when he'd left. She'd seen how hard the decision had been for him as he told her how much he loved her and begged her to forgive him, but he couldn't stay and he couldn't take her with him just yet. She'd felt his tears as he'd bent to kiss her cheek and said goodbye, promising to come for her soon.

Her mother never mentioned his name again after that, other than to say Birdie had been a mistake that she had no intention of making again. Men had always come and gone in her mother's life. One had stayed around and become her stepfather. He'd been kind and helped get her raised before he left, but it was Dixon Malone, her father, who'd always lived in her heart. When she was old enough, she took the Malone name, although her birth parents had never legally married.

Her grandmother on her father's side had been the one constant in her life, even though she lived in Texas. Nana had seen that Birdie went to college and took judo lessons so she could defend herself. Nana had taught her to dream. Her grandmother knew how much she missed her father.

The last time Nana had visited, she'd told Birdie that she was leaving her money and wanted her to use it to find Dixon, her only son, her only child. "I know he promised to come back for you, Birdie. He wouldn't have broken that promise unless something bad happened to him."

She'd sworn she would find him.

"And when the time comes, find yourself a good man. They do exist, no matter what you saw growing up with your mother, not to speak ill of the dead. You're too smart to follow in her footsteps. Remember that. And don't be too hard on your father, no matter what you find out. I know how much he loves you."

While she'd believed that her father wouldn't have broken his promise to her unless something had happened to him, she'd done as he'd always wanted her to do. She'd gone to college, graduated, gotten a job and started her career in business administration.

She'd known in her heart that he had to be dead. Otherwise, he would have come for her as promised. Yet her promise to her grandmother nagged at her. She hired a PI who had no luck finding him. When her father's body was found, she'd realized that if she wanted the truth, she was going to have to get it herself—and she couldn't wait any longer. She had to find out what had happened to him—even if what she discovered broke her heart.

However, now that she was here, she had to question her decision. What had she hoped to find following Brand from the bar in town all the way out to the Stafford Ranch—let alone helping herself to a room in the house for the night? It had seemed like a good idea at the time—and if she hadn't hung around this morning, she would have gotten away with it. No one would have been the wiser.

The problem was that it hadn't accomplished anything. Nothing she'd done so far was helping find evidence to bring her father's killer to justice.

She groaned, refusing to let her doubts derail her. Instead, she thought of her promise to her grandmother and concentrated on what to do next. She had to find a place to rent if she was going to stay in Powder Crossing or she would eventually run out of money. The idea of giving up wasn't in her.

"Sometimes you are exactly like your father," her mother used to say. "Stubborn as a mule and just as hardheaded."

She'd always liked to hear there were things about her that were like her father. He'd been her hero. She looked over at the photo on her bedside table. It was of

the two of them, taken on her fifth birthday. Her grandmother had framed it for her. It and a jewelry box he'd
given her were her most prized possessions.

Just the sight of them had made her mother furious.
"How can you idolize that man?" she would scream.
"He walked out on you as well as me. Stop thinking
he's coming back. He's not. He'll break your heart—
just as he did mine."

But he hadn't. He'd never really left her. For the year
after he'd moved out, he would stop by her school or
catch her on the way home to hug her and tell her how
much he loved her. He would bring her little treats,
and they would talk. She'd known he was sorry about
the way things had ended with her mother. She'd also
known that things weren't going well with the woman
he'd married, Charlotte Stafford.

"I'm coming to get you soon," he'd told her the last
time she saw him. He'd shown up at school on her sixth
birthday with a cupcake, candle and all. She'd told him
how much she missed him, crying in his arms. "I'm so
sorry, but I can't live with your mother. I'm not sure
she's the best thing for you as a mother either. I know
your grandmother is keeping an eye on you, so you're
safe until I can come get you."

He'd told her all about the ranchwoman, her children
and the grand house on a ranch where they all lived.

But that day he'd said no, her coming to the Stafford
Ranch wasn't going to work out. "Charlotte Stafford's no
more mother material than your mom and an even more
questionable wife. I need to work out a few things. But
trust me, we'll be together soon, my little bird." He'd
given her the jewelry box that day, making her promise
to keep it close always until they could be together again.

She'd kept the promise. It too sat on the hotel bedside table next to her.

That was the last time she saw her father. Her mother told her that he'd run out on the woman he'd married. Left in the middle of the night just like he'd done her.

Birdie had waited day after day. He wouldn't break his promise to her. He would be coming for her. After months went by, she'd known there could be only one explanation. Dixon Malone was dead.

Now everyone knew it. They even knew who'd killed him. All Birdie had to do was find a way to prove it.

She thought of Charlotte Stafford's son Brand. He might be a way for her to get closer to his mother and the truth. She almost felt sorry for him. It wouldn't be easy seeing his mother go to prison for murder, especially if he knew more than he was admitting.

Her stomach growled. She hadn't had breakfast, and now it was past lunchtime. Sitting up, she put thoughts of the Staffords aside and headed for the café.

AT THE SOUND of a vehicle, Stuart and the others seemed to flinch. "It's Duffy." They all three looked toward the front door as if hoping Duffy would come through it with Holly Jo. There was a chance that Duffy had found her walking down the road. That the girl had cooked this all up but now realized her mistake.

It felt as if the air was sucked out of the room as Duffy stormed in alone. His face was flushed, anger wafting off him like a bad smell. "I'm telling you, that kid, Gus Gardner, he knows something. His father's protecting him."

"What is that?" Stuart asked, his gaze going to what Duffy had in his hand—a leather work glove folded over what appeared to be a plain white envelope, which he thrust at the sheriff.

"Where did you get this?" Stuart demanded as he pulled on his latex gloves and took the envelope.

"I saw our mailbox door was hanging open, so I stopped," Duffy said. "I thought it might be from the kidnapper. I tried not to touch it any more than I had to."

Stuart gritted his teeth, telling himself this wasn't the time to get into it with Duffy, especially when he saw at once that the envelope looked much like the ransom one. But it also meant that his deputy hadn't gotten out here to keep a watch on the mailbox yet. If he had, he might have seen the alleged kidnapper.

He carefully sliced open the envelope and pulled out the folded sheet of paper. It resembled the first note, the words cut from a glossy magazine.

What was different was the message.

Tell the Truth.
Or the Girl Pays.
For your Lies.

All the color drained from the rancher's face as Stuart showed him the kidnapper's demand. There was no doubt now. This was about Holden. He watched the big man lower himself into a chair and drop his face into his hands.

Just as Stuart had feared, the kidnapper had something on the rancher, and Holly Jo was now being used as a pawn. He turned to Elaine. "Did Holly Jo by any chance keep a diary?"

"I don't know," she said, her gaze on Holden. She looked as shocked and upset as he did.

"I searched her room, but would you mind looking?"

Stuart said, needing to get both Elaine and Duffy out of the way. "Also, I'm going to need her computer brought down. If you don't know what her password is, please try to find it in her room." He turned to Duffy. "I need you to go into the dining room and write down everything about your confrontation with Gus Gardner. And please close the door behind you."

Duffy saw through the pretense but left as if he too was shocked by either the ransom demand or his father's reaction—or both.

With them gone, Stuart turned to Holden. "'*Tell the truth*'? If you know who has taken Holly Jo, you need to tell me now."

HOLDEN DIDN'T WANT to meet the sheriff's gaze. He had feared this was about him, and now he knew it was. He'd brought this on his family. He was risking Holly Jo's life, all because of something he'd done.

Tell the Truth.
Or the Girl Pays.
For your Lies.

His mind whirled, thoughts blowing past like trash in a strong wind.

"Holden, we need to find your ward as quickly as possible," Stu said. "If this is someone from your past with a grudge, as it seems, then Holly Jo wasn't abducted by a stranger or a possible online predator. The kidnapper is someone who isn't demanding money but for you to tell the truth. That seems to suggest that the person won't hurt Holly Jo, who is an innocent in all this. But we can't chance that. If you know who has her, you have to tell me now."

Did he? Who would take Holly Jo to force him to confess and apologize for something he did? He still felt it had to be about revenge.

He rubbed the back of his neck and tried to get his breathing under control, fighting to think clearly. There were so many truths, and even more lies. They blurred together in his mind. He'd rationalized so much of what he'd done over the years that he'd felt exonerated because no one had ever called him on it—except Charlotte.

But thinking he'd put it all behind him, that too had been a lie. He'd never truly been free of the people he had hurt. Hadn't he always known that there would be a reckoning and he would have to make amends that might threaten everything he'd built?

A clear thought fought its way to the surface. Why now? Why, after all this time, was someone demanding he pay for his past deeds?

"Holden?"

His mouth had gone dry. He swallowed and stood, hating to face the sheriff and admit the one truth he could no longer hide. "I have to make a list." He saw the flicker of surprise in the young sheriff's expression, could imagine it in the faces of his adult children if they found out. He considered all that he'd done as he moved to his desk, sat down and picked up a pen.

He didn't know where to start, so he began to write down names of not just people he'd wronged, but people who might hate him this much. When he slowed after a few names, he saw that the first name on the list was Charlotte Stafford. He started to scratch it off, telling himself Lottie would never use a child to get back at him, but Stuart stopped him. He watched the sheriff take the list from him, glancing at what he'd written, then up at him. Their gazes met.

Stuart pointed at his shirt pocket, where he'd hidden the DNA report. The sheriff gave him a look that sent a chill through him. "Brand's not at the top of the list?"

"Brand?" Holden said in surprise. "No, he wouldn't—"

"What are the chances you would get Brand's DNA report on the same day Holly Jo is kidnapped and all the kidnapper wants is the truth?"

He didn't want to believe it. Not his flesh and blood. But Brand might not understand that his father would have gladly told the truth if he had only known.

Holden felt as if the earth was dropping out from under him. "No," he said. He wanted to throttle Charlotte. How could she have kept this from him? If Brand had Holly Jo, then it was his mother's bitterness that had caused it. It was his mother's lies—and Holden's as well, he had to admit.

"I'm going to have Brand picked up for questioning," the sheriff was saying. "I need you to keep this quiet for now." He handed Holden the list of people.

Holden took the sheet of paper, leaving Charlotte's name at the top and adding their son Brand's, his hand trembling as he did.

"No one would blame you for being depressed, Charlotte."

She glared at her doctor. She'd known Dr. Joe Hammond all her life, long before he'd finally retired and moved to Billings. He'd delivered all her children—and delivered more than his share of advice over those years.

"You think I worry about what people think?" she demanded. "Now, that *is* depressing."

"Let me write you a prescription for something that might help."

She huffed as she pushed to her feet. "I'll let you know when I get that desperate."

"Charlotte," he said patiently. "It might be too late by the time you realize just how desperate you are."

"Joe, how many years have I been coming to you? Do you really think I would take my own life? If you do, then you don't know me very well."

"No, I can't see you hurting yourself that way, but maybe doing something almost as harmful to yourself?" She gave him a side-eye before he added, "I'm just trying to help you."

Charlotte felt herself soften a little. They were old friends. He'd been there when she'd needed a shoulder. He'd even once asked her to marry him, which made her think of the old expression *there is no fool like an old fool.* "I appreciate your concern, I really do, but I'm fine."

His hangdog expression said he didn't believe it. He might have semiretired and moved to Billings, but he still kept up on Powder Crossing gossip, she was sure. He knew how she'd felt about CJ, her eldest son, her favorite. Finding out about the kind of man he'd turned into had been devastating.

She still felt the crush of it pressing against her heart, making it hard to breathe as she awoke with it every morning, went to bed with it every night. It followed her even in her sleep, a nightmarish half sleep that often had her dragged awake to her own screams. She'd done her best to hide it from the world. Joe had now assured her that she'd failed miserably not just with CJ, but with the lies she'd been telling herself.

"You have a good lawyer, I'm sure," he said, still looking worried about her.

She realized that he wasn't referring to CJ, who was behind bars awaiting trial for so many felonies that she couldn't remember them all. She had refused to help him, leaving him to a court-appointed attorney, cutting him out of her life as if she had used a sharp blade like the one she felt he'd stabbed her with in the back.

"I didn't kill my husband." She hated that even Joe thought she was guilty. The moment Dixon Malone's remains had been found in a well near her ranch, everyone seemed to assume that she would be arrested for his murder. She figured they were all waiting for that to happen. "Joe, I didn't kill him."

He nodded but said nothing, as expected. Not even her old friend believed her. Sighing, she picked up her purse and cast him one final look. "You've been a good friend. I'm going to miss you, Doc."

"Retired or not, I'll always be available to you," he said. He sounded sad, as if he suspected they wouldn't see each other again. He was probably right. "Take care of yourself, Charlotte."

"You too, Joe." She turned and walked out, fighting the ache in her throat and the sting of tears. She'd never been a crier. Neither of her parents had been moved by tears. *Never let the bastards see weakness*, her mother used to say when she'd come home from school in tears over some mean girl. She'd learned to hold it in, ashamed when she showed fragility, and had taken care of her problems herself.

That was what made it so hard. Not only had she broken down after CJ had been arrested, but she'd also let Holden McKenna see that weakness when he'd found her down by the creek where they used to make love. She'd let him hold her that day while she sobbed out her heart, and she'd regretted it ever since. She hated that he'd seen her at her lowest, and she planned to never let it happen again.

She wiped furtively at her tears. In her fifty-three years, she'd done her best not to give anyone the satisfaction of seeing how wounded she was. And yet that was exactly what she'd done for years with her anger and bitterness over what Holden McKenna had done to her. She'd only been fooling herself. This man she hated and loved in equal parts knew her to her soul. She'd let him into her heart and had spent years trying to get him out before he destroyed her.

Straightening, she jutted out her chin and put on her sunglasses as she pushed through the door to exit the office. Once on the sidewalk, she stopped, suddenly aware of the blinding blue sky and warmth on the breeze. Summer. When had the seasons changed? It came as a shock, as if winter had ended, spring had come and gone in the blink of an eye, and here was summer, all while she'd been in with Doc.

She breathed in deeply and closed her eyes, wanting to stand there, taking in this day as if it were her last. She would get through this—just as she had everything else in her life. She would. She didn't need Joe Hammond's magic pills. She was Charlotte Carson Stafford.

Her cell phone rang. She let it ring two more times before she dug it out and checked to see who was calling. The sheriff? She let it ring a couple more times. Was this about CJ? Stuart knew she wasn't taking her son's calls. When he'd finally gone too far after trying to kill his sister, she'd become deaf to his pleas for help. He was now on his own.

Her phone stopped ringing, then began again almost at once. The same number indicated it was the Powder Crossing Sheriff's Department.

She told herself she had no choice but to answer. "Hello?"

"It's Sheriff Layton." Stuart? Why was he being so formal? She'd known him since he was a kid. "I've put a BOLO out on your son Brand for questioning. Do you know where he is?"

"What? Brand?" It was inconceivable. CJ, yes. Even Oakley. But Brand? This was the last thing she'd expected.

"I understand you're not at home. But if you know where he is, I need to speak with him. It's urgent."

"Urgent? About what?" she demanded.

"I'm going to need to question you as well. Where are you right now?"

"None of your business," she snapped. "Tell me what's going on, Stuart."

"Holly Jo, Holden McKenna's ward, is missing."

She couldn't imagine what one had to do with the other. "Why would you have any reason to question Brand—let alone me?"

"Charlotte, if you know anything about Holly Jo—"

"Obviously, I don't. I'm on my way home now. I'll come by your office with my lawyer."

"Good—that will save me a trip out to your ranch," the sheriff said.

The laugh rose up from deep inside her and burst

forth of its own volition. "If you think I would take Holden's ward—"

"I'll see you when you get here. I appreciate you coming to my office instead of making me find you."

She stared at her phone as she realized that he'd disconnected. "What in the world?" Her heart began to pound, the summer day forgotten as she headed for her vehicle.

CHAPTER SIX

AFTER HE DISCONNECTED, the sheriff studied the list of names Holden had given him. He and the rancher had stepped outside, away from the man's family. Elaine had not found Holly Jo's computer password or a handwritten diary. The computer would have to be turned over to the FBI. Duffy had written down everything he could remember about his argument with Joe Gardner.

Stuart was anxious to talk to Brand Stafford, but in the meantime, he would follow up with Gus Gardner. Even though he suspected the kidnapper was on the list Holden had given him, he couldn't discount the one person who probably knew more about Holly Jo's life than anyone—her nemesis, Gus Gardner, the boy Duffy suspected had been bullying her.

As he started to fold and pocket Holden's list, he had a bad feeling the names already on it were only the tip of the iceberg. With a jolt, he realized that one name in particular was missing. "Why isn't Holly Jo's father on here? I'd think he would be a prime suspect." It was a question he hadn't wanted to ask in front of the others because his friend Cooper had told him he didn't even know what his father's relationship to Holly Jo was or wasn't.

"He's dead. So is her mother," the rancher said.

"Dead?" Stuart had warned Holden that this was going to dig up dirt from every dark hole in his life. It especially would expose everything concerning his ward. "How was it that Holly Jo's mother asked you to take her?" He saw the rancher instantly begin to clam up. "Didn't she or Holly Jo's father have relatives that would have taken the girl?"

"No."

Stuart swore. "I know you're holding out on me, thinking it's none of my business, but you're wrong. If you want to get her back, then you must tell me *everything*. What is your relationship to Holly Jo?"

"I'm not her father, if that's what you're asking."

"Holden—"

The rancher cursed and stepped away a few yards to look toward the river. The Powder River, the lifeblood of those who lived here, passed right through the heart of the McKenna Ranch.

Many still claimed that the river was a mile wide and an inch deep and ran uphill. The joke was that it was too thick to drink and too thin to plow. Captain Clark of the Lewis and Clark expedition had named it Redstone River. But the Native Americans called it Powder River because the black shores reminded them of gunpowder, and that was the name that had stuck.

While Montana had prettier, deeper, wider and flashier rivers, the Powder seemed stubborn and steady as it began in Wyoming and traveled more than one hundred fifty miles to empty into the Yellowstone. In that way, the river had always reminded him of Holden McKenna.

"I rodeoed with her mother's husband," the rancher said finally. "I felt responsible for his death. Holly Jo's mother was pregnant with Holly Jo at the time. I owed her more than the money I sent each month to help them get by. It isn't something I'm proud of."

"How well did you know him?"

"Not well. Like I said, we both rodeoed. Can we just leave it at that?"

"No, I'm going to need his name."

The rancher cursed. "Robert 'Bobby' Robinson. He was from Roundup."

"Where did he die?"

"Billings. We were up on the band of rock cliffs above the city called The Rims. He and I…we'd been drinking and…arguing. He lunged at me, I stepped aside, and he went over. I was young. I panicked when I saw that he was dead on the rocks below. I ran, okay? I didn't report the accident."

"Was anyone else there?" He shook his head. "And you're positive that he died?" He nodded. "What were you arguing about?"

"I don't even remember. Like I said, we'd been drinking after a rodeo. Bobby was a bull rider. His wife was nagging him to quit. He was in a foul mood. After he died, Holly Jo's mother moved to Missoula and raised her daughter there."

Stuart nodded. "I'll see what I can find out about his family." Right now, he was anxious to talk to Holly Jo's classmate from school, Gus Gardner. Friend or foe, Gus might know if someone had been hanging around the school, watching Holly Jo. Or if someone had contacted her from her father's family.

"Stay here," the sheriff ordered after a deputy arrived to be with the family. Another deputy was keeping an eye on the mailbox down the road in case the kidnapper tried to contact Holden again. "Let me know if you hear anything, and I'll do the same."

Stuart felt the clock ticking. What made it all the more difficult was his small sheriff's department. Short-handed, he and his deputies had to cover the entire Powder River Basin. Two deputies from Yellowstone County had been brought in to help look for Brand Stafford after they'd checked the Stafford Ranch without finding him. Charlotte had gone to Billings for a doctor's appointment and was allegedly on her way back.

He knew from his law enforcement training that the first seventy-two hours of a kidnapping case were most crucial. But the first forty-eight hours were critical because that was when he had the best chance of following up leads while details were fresh in everyone's minds. The process had been compared to following a trail of breadcrumbs.

Right now those crumbs led to a boy named Gus Gardner, son of Joe Gardner and classmate of Holly Jo's. Duffy seemed to think that Gus had been bullying Holly Jo. He'd said that there had definitely been something going on between the two of them.

The moment Stuart drove up to the ranch hand's house, Joe Gardner came out. He was a string bean of a man, weathered and slightly bent for his age, having grown up as a ranch hand's son and becoming one himself after high school. In his forties, he looked tired as well as angry as the sheriff climbed out of his patrol SUV.

"Duffy McKenna has no business coming out here and accusing my son of anything," Joe began before Stuart reached the porch.

"He's upset because Holly Jo is missing," he said

calmly. "I'm sure we can clear this up quickly. I just need to talk to your son."

The man hesitated for a moment before he turned toward the screen door and called, "Gus!"

The door opened at once. Gus had no doubt been standing just inside, listening.

Stuart scaled the porch steps, taking in the boy as he did. Stocky, blond and moody-looking, Gus appeared guilty as well as nervous. But it was the abrasion on the side of the boy's face that caught the sheriff's attention. "I need to ask you about Holly Jo."

"We already told Duffy," Joe said. "We don't know anything about her."

"I'm still going to need to talk to Gus."

Stuart looked to Joe, who quickly said, "You're not talking to him without me."

"I wouldn't have it any other way," the sheriff said, although he doubted the boy would be forthcoming in front of his father. "Let's sit down here on the porch steps," he said to the boy.

Gus looked reluctant but took a seat, his father towering above them on the porch proper.

Stuart started with the easy questions. "When was the last time you saw Holly Jo?" No surprise that it had been in school the day before. "Are you friends?"

Gus shrugged and mumbled, "Not really."

"Have you been hassling her or bullying her?"

"What?" Joe demanded.

The boy's reaction was immediate. His head jerked up, his eyes wide as if he was shocked by the accusation, and he shook his head fiercely. As Joe started to object, Stuart waved him into silence.

"Do you like her?" He watched the boy swallow and

blush as he looked down at his boots and nodded reluctantly. "You know she's missing, right?" Another nod. "Is there someone who might want to harm her?" He watched the boy hesitate.

The words came out hesitantly. "There are these girls at school. Tana Westlake and her friends. They're mean to her. I told Holly Jo to stay clear of them, but she doesn't always."

He saw something in the boy's expression. "She stands up to them?"

Gus nodded and avoided eye contact again. "It only makes them meaner."

Stuart guessed, "You've taken up for her, and now these girls are after you as well." He watched Gus's mouth work, but no sound came out.

"Are you telling me you let a bunch of girls pick on you?" Joe demanded behind them.

Stuart shot him a warning look. Joe swore and stormed into the house, slamming the screen door behind him. But the sheriff knew he hadn't gone far and was still listening. "What happened to your face?"

The boy's hand went to the fresh abrasion on his cheek. "I fell down." It was a lie, but Stuart let it go.

"Have either you or Holly Jo told anyone at school about the bullying?"

"I wanted to, but Holly Jo wanted to handle it. I tried to talk her out of it."

"Do you know what she had planned?" he asked.

Gus shook his head. "She said it was better if I didn't know."

"When was this?"

"A few days ago." The boy kept his gaze down. "Do you think they did something to her?"

"I don't know, but I'm going to find out. Thank you for your help. Sounds like you're a good friend to Holly Jo. I'm sure she appreciates that."

Gus looked at his boots again as his father came out of the house and told him to get to his chores. "You make sure Duffy McKenna leaves my boy alone," Joe blustered.

"He won't be bothering Gus anymore," the sheriff assured him as he walked to his patrol SUV and climbed in.

On the way into town, the sheriff considered what he'd learned and what he would say when he got to the Westlake house. He knew this line of inquiry was getting him nowhere. But he had to follow up since there were little lies and big lies. When it came to kids, all lies seemed big.

Also, he'd once been a kid. He and Cooper and their friends had done irresponsible things that could have gotten someone hurt. The ransom notes with the letters cut from magazines seemed almost kid-like. Maybe the truth they wanted to come out was what Holly Jo had done to one of them—and had nothing to do with Holden's past. A long shot, but one Stuart had to take.

He was almost to the Westlake house when he got a call. Brand Stafford had been spotted in town. A deputy was on the way to check it out.

CHAPTER SEVEN

THERE WERE TWO kinds of families in the Powder River Basin. Ranch families and town families. Stuart knew from growing up here that the two were often miles apart economically—just as they were often at odds because of it.

Trying to survive in this town wasn't easy for those who lived and worked here. Jobs were scarce. Options were limited to service jobs in town. The men could find seasonal work on ranches while their wives worked as housekeepers at the hotel or waitstaff at the café or clerks at the feed store. Others drove more than an hour over the mountain to work in Miles City.

Amanda Westlake worked as a housekeeper at the Belle Creek Hotel in town. Divorced, she'd stayed, even though she'd originally come to Powder Crossing because of her husband's job as a deputy sheriff. Thad Westlake had long ago moved on, leaving town and Amanda. Now she and her daughter, Tana, lived in a trailer she rented on the other side of town. An older-model midsize sedan was parked out front.

Stuart parked beside it and got out. He figured Amanda wouldn't be expecting him, and he was right. On the way into town, he'd called the hotel to find out if she was working today. She wasn't.

He knocked on the trailer door and waited. He could

hear movement inside, one set of frantic footfalls accompanied by a "Mother!" and then the slamming of a door before the trailer's front door opened.

Amanda Westlake was a good-looking woman. He knew that local men, both single and married, had shown an interest in her. Just as he knew that she'd turned them all down, determined to get her daughter raised before getting involved with another man.

Her bottle-blond hair swung to one side as she cocked her head at him, waiting for an explanation as to why he was there. It was the response he often got in the Powder River Basin.

"I need to speak with your daughter, Tana."

Surprise registered in her expression before she said, "What for?"

"Sheriff's department business. May I come in, or would you rather we do this at my office?"

She seemed to consider that for a moment before she stepped back and he climbed the two steps into the trailer. It was nice inside. There were bright-colored pillows on the couch and flowers in a vase on the end table. From the doorway, he could see the kitchen. Clean, even though the air still held the scent of a recently cooked meal.

"Have a seat," Amanda said, openly studying him. "I'll get my daughter."

The girl who came into the room where Stuart had perched on the couch was small and slim. Her hair was long, threaded with blond highlights. She wore short shorts and a formfitting tank top. The look on her face was defiant. He wondered if that was her normal expression. He suspected it was.

"Please have a seat," he said to Tana and her mother. Neither sat.

"What's this about?" Amanda demanded.

He ignored her, keeping his gaze on the girl. "I want to ask you about Holly Jo Robinson."

She frowned but instantly looked guarded. "Who?"

"The classmate you and your friends have been bullying."

Tana laughed. "Seriously? She called the cops on us?"

Stuart hadn't expected the girl would admit it, let alone that quickly. "What do you have against her?"

She shrugged. "There's no law that says we have to like her."

"But there is a law against bullying."

Tana seemed surprised to hear that. "Seriously? You're going to arrest me?" She sounded excited about it, as if she couldn't wait to tell her friends.

"Have you seen her today?" he asked.

She shrugged, then shook her head. "I heard she skipped school."

He knew that if Tana had abducted Holly Jo, she couldn't have hidden her here in this trailer. "You have a car?" Tana mugged a face and shook her head again. "Your friends have cars?"

"What is going on?" Amanda said more forcefully.

"Their parents *bought* them cars and let them get their learner's permits early," Tana said and shot her mother a pointed look before turning to him again. "You going to arrest them, too?"

"Did Holly Jo do something to you?" he asked and immediately saw that she had.

Color rose to the girl's cheeks. "She's the one you should be arresting."

"What did she do to you?"

Tana's lips tightened like a vise.

It was her mother who answered. "Was that the girl who played the trick on you at school yesterday?" Amanda demanded. "It was Holly Jo, the girl from the McKenna Ranch? Why didn't you tell me?" She swung around to glare at Stuart. "Tana came home crying after that girl tricked her into sitting in some ketchup. She was wearing white pants. All the boys were laughing and making fun of her for..." She shook her head. "Everyone thought she'd started her period."

"Mother!" Tana looked near tears. "I can't believe you told him that!"

"So, what did you do to get back at her?" Stuart asked before the two began arguing.

"Nothing." Except the girl wouldn't look at him when she said it.

"I need to know what you did." He watched her, afraid and yet hopeful that this whole thing could be cleared up with one small confession. He could imagine the girls picking Holly Jo up before the bus got there. She would have been outnumbered. They could have tied her up and taken her somewhere. Maybe an old barn. There were plenty of those around. They would have just wanted to scare her, teach her a lesson. Maybe they planned to go rescue her later today.

Amanda was watching her daughter as well, worry in her expression as if she'd picked up the tension in his voice and knew that this was about more than bullying. "Answer him, Tana," she ordered, her voice breaking.

The girl glanced at her mother, then lifted her chin and settled her pale blue eyes on Stuart in a challenging glare. There was that defiance again. "I beat up her boyfriend."

"You what?" Amanda demanded.

He signaled her to be quiet. "What boyfriend?"

Tana gave him a look that said she thought he was pathetic if he didn't know. "Gus the wuss."

"What did you do to him?"

"I told you, I beat him up." He waited, his gaze locked with hers until she lost patience. "I pushed him down, jumped on him and ground his face into the dirt. I told him to tell his girlfriend not to mess with me again and to quit telling lies about me."

Stuart stared at the girl—just as her mother was doing. "You *assaulted* him. Are you aware you can be arrested for that? That his family can press charges and sue your mother?"

She tossed her head. "He wouldn't do that. His dad would find out, and—"

"Shut up, Tana," Amanda snapped, dropping her hand on her daughter's shoulder. The girl grimaced as her mother's grip tightened. "I've heard enough." She looked up at him. "Are you going to arrest her?"

"Do you have any magazines around the house?"

She looked at him in confusion. "Magazines?"

"How about your daughter? Does she have some magazines in her room?"

"No," Amanda said, shaking her head. "If you don't believe me, you're welcome to look."

He'd been watching Tana. Her friends could have magazines, because apparently their parents had more money. They could have made the ransom demand at one of their houses. He realized that the whole county would know soon about Holly Jo's disappearance, given the speed of the local grapevine. "Holly Jo is missing. If your daughter kidnapped her—"

Amanda let out a cry. *"Kidnapped?"* After hearing what her daughter had done to Gus Gardner, both of them knew the girl was capable of that or worse.

"If your daughter and her friends are holding her somewhere, Tana needs to tell me right now."

"We didn't do anything to her!" the girl cried, trying to turn to look at her mother. "Mother, I swear. I haven't seen her."

"What about your friends?" he asked.

"They don't do anything unless I tell them to," Tana told him, and then seemed to realize what she'd said. "Mother?" It came out a plea.

Amanda looked over her daughter's head at him. "I'll talk to her after you leave. If she was involved in something involving the missing girl, I'll call you."

He met her gaze. "Holly Jo's life is at stake." He didn't have to add what something like this could do to her own daughter's future if anything else happened to the missing girl.

"I promise I'll take care of this," Amanda said, her grip still firmly on her daughter's shoulder as he nodded and left.

As he closed the door, he heard Tana cry, "Mother! I didn't do it. Mother! You have to believe me."

As the sheriff climbed into his patrol SUV, a call came through from Deputy Terrance Dodson to tell him that he'd spotted Brand Stafford's pickup parked in front of the hotel.

"Bring him in for questioning, but, Deputy, make it clear that he isn't under arrest. We just need to ask him a few questions. I'm outside of town. I'll meet you at the office. Just don't go cowboy on him, Dodson. You hear me?"

"Ten-four, boss."

BRAND HAD DRIVEN into town, found a spot to park in front of the hotel and headed over to the Cattleman Café. He was still feeling rough and figured food might help the hangover. Back at the ranch, it was the housekeeper's day off, and he didn't feel well enough to rustle up some food for himself.

As he stepped into the café, though, he saw Birdie Malone was sitting at a table in the back. He started to turn around and leave, even as the smell of pulled pork made his stomach rumble. He hesitated. While he couldn't keep avoiding the woman if she was determined to stay in Powder Crossing, was he up to seeing her right now?

"Brand Stafford. You're late for our date," Birdie called out to him. What was she up to now? He turned back to see her smiling broadly. She motioned to the chair adjacent to her. "I ordered without you."

Everyone in the café was watching them with interest. This would have tongues wagging. The last thing he'd wanted to do was cause a scene in the café. He was the Stafford who didn't do those things.

He walked over to Birdie's table and pulled out the chair across from her. "Thanks a lot," he whispered.

She laughed. "Couldn't let you leave just because I'm here. You're not carrying a grudge about earlier, are you?"

"Nope. I'm used to women getting the best of me."

"I bet you are," she said, grinning as she leaned

across the table toward him. "And I thought I was the first. How disappointing."

Is she flirting with me? No doubt for the benefit of the diners still watching them with curiosity. He wondered how many of them knew who she was. They would soon enough, and when they did, they'd wonder what he was doing with Dixon Malone's daughter, given the latest discovery in the neighboring well. It was bound to get back to his mother, who he was already avoiding.

"Did you follow me here?" she asked and pretended to be touched by that.

"I was hungry, and today is the pulled pork sandwich special, my favorite."

"Really? Today's special is my favorite, too. It amazes me how much you and I have in common."

Brand shook his head, even though he thought he should try to mend some fences since they'd probably be running into each other again, as small as Powder Crossing was. "I feel as if we got off on the wrong foot," he said and flashed her a lopsided grin one girl had told him was killer. "Let me buy you lunch." He motioned to the waitress that he'd take the special.

"I can buy my own lunch," she said, openly studying him. "Seriously, what are you really doing here?"

"I told you. I was hungry, and I love their pulled pork."

"Uh-huh." She cocked her head at him. "You're not sure what to make of me, are you?" Her laugh was light and breezy like the summer day. She sat back and crossed her arms. "Why don't you just come out and ask. I'll tell you anything you want to know."

He thought about that for a moment. He realized he

wanted to know a whole lot more about Birdie Malone, but at the same time, all his instincts told him to keep his distance for obvious reasons. "I'm sorry about your father."

That seemed to surprise her. She uncrossed her arms and looked serious. "Do you remember him?"

He shook his head. "Not really. I was five when my mother married him. She had five kids in seven years and was busy running a ranch. We were raised by housekeeper-nanny types who came and went. Mostly went, because my mother didn't have much patience with the staff. I hardly saw my mother, let alone her husband." He stopped, realizing how much he'd told her. Birdie already had good reason to believe that Charlotte Stafford was a murderer. Now he'd also insinuated that she was a bad mother. "I shouldn't have said that. Mother..."

"It's all right," she said. "My mother didn't win any awards either, and she only had me to contend with. Fortunately, I had my father and his mother, my grandmother, my nana."

Their pulled pork sandwiches arrived, and seeing what she'd ordered made him smile. Not that he wanted to believe they had anything in common—other than their parents. "So, have you been in town for a while?"

"For a while," she said between bites. He watched her eat a fry before she said, "I'm sorry you didn't get to know my father. He was a good, kind, loving man. Go ahead and say it. Everyone does. Yes, he left my mother, but he always came back to see me. He loved me," she said simply. "He promised he would come for me soon the last time I saw him. He never broke a promise. That's how I knew that something awful had happened to him."

"You still saw him when he was married to my mother?"

"Every week. He told me about you and your brothers and sisters, about your house, your ranch…"

"And my mother." He could tell from her expression that Dixon Malone had told her a lot about his family, especially Charlotte.

She nodded. "You must have known that they argued a lot."

He really had little memory of his mother and Dixon. "I was probably busy protecting myself from my older brother and had more things to worry about than my mother and your father."

"CJ terrorized you?" she asked.

"He terrorized everyone," Brand said with a laugh. "We all learned to disappear when he was around or suffer the consequences. What made it worse was that our mother always believed him because he was the oldest. Her favorite."

"I can't imagine having siblings. I always thought it would be fun."

He scoffed at that. "Ryder's great, and my sisters are, too. CJ…?" He shook his head. "There was always a lot of drama in our house, which is why I spent as little time as possible there." He took a bite, thinking how much he was enjoying lunch—and Birdie.

They ate in a companionable silence for a few minutes. As different as they were, he was surprised they did have a lot in common. They were about the same age, had grown up with a distant mother and had lost their fathers at a young age. Except, he reminded himself with a jolt, his father was alive. For a while, he'd forgotten about the DNA test, the secret it exposed, and what he'd done with a copy of it.

When the café door opened, neither of them noticed the deputy walk in until he approached their table, another officer behind him.

"Brand Stafford? I'm going to need you to come with me," Deputy Dodson said.

"What's this about?" he asked in surprise.

"It's about you and what you were doing this morning when a student went missing."

"Who went missing? I don't know anything about—" He never got to finish what he was saying.

The deputy grabbed his arm and hauled him up from the table even as the other deputy said, "Dodson, the sheriff said not to—"

"Watch it!" Brand said as his chair tipped over backward and hit the floor with a bang. He lost his balance, shoving the deputy as he struggled to get his feet under him, only to have the law officer throw him face down on the table. Dishes went everywhere, his plate sliding off and breaking on the floor, as the deputy pulled back his arms and slapped cuffs on him.

"You're under arrest for assaulting a law enforcement officer and resisting arrest, as well as kidnapping," the deputy said.

"Kidnapping?" Brand cried.

The second deputy let out a groan as Deputy Dodson said, "Let's go," and dragged Brand toward the front door.

The last thing Brand saw as he was being perp-walked out of the café was Birdie Malone's face. Her expression said it all. What kind of family had her father married into? One that had gotten him killed.

Birdie sat in the café for a long time, staring after the patrol SUV that had taken Brand Stafford away. The café staff had cleaned up the mess.

"We'll bill Stafford Ranch for your meals and the broken dishes," the waitress told her. "You have any idea what that was about?"

"No." For a while, she and Brand had been bonding. She had let herself get seduced into thinking they were on the same side. That had things been different, they could have been friends. "I'll pay for my own meal."

She was nothing like Brand Stafford, she told herself. Were the whole bunch of the Staffords criminals? She warned herself not to trust any of them. Earlier, she'd let her defenses down. She should have known better.

How could she have thought that Charlotte had killed Dixon Malone and dumped his body into that nearby abandoned well and forget that Brand was her son? Not that he'd been the one who'd helped his mother get rid of the body. He'd been too young. But someone in this county knew what she'd done, because they'd helped her cover it up.

She reminded herself that her father had liked Brand when he was a boy. Had she let that color the way she saw the cowboy rancher? Clearly, she couldn't trust her own instincts since she'd found herself enjoying his company— before the law had come to arrest him. What had the deputy said they wanted him for? Kidnapping? Seriously?

With a start, Birdie recalled the deputy saying that whatever Brand was wanted for had happened this morning.

Maybe her instincts about him weren't wrong; maybe he wasn't like his family after all, because there was no way he did anything this morning since she'd been with him.

She paid her bill and left the café. They wanted to question him in regard to a missing person? A student, no less! It had to be more than just questioning. The deputy had taken him out of the café in cuffs, arresting him for assault of an officer and resisting arrest.

She didn't think either charge would stick, especially after she told them where Brand Stafford had been all morning. She could save him. Then maybe he'd help her find out the truth about her father's killer—and accomplice.

THE SHERIFF COULDN'T believe the mess he had back at the department.

"You need to cool down," Stuart told Brand as he ordered Dodson to take off the cuffs. "You're just being held for questioning," he said as he steered him into the cell, then closed and locked the door.

"You can't hold me without charging and booking me," Brand said.

"You really want me to charge you with assaulting Deputy Dodson and resisting arrest?"

"You know both those charges are bogus. I want to call a lawyer."

"Not necessary. I've already spoken to your mother. She's waiting in my office right now with her lawyer."

"You called my mother?" Brand demanded. "Why would you do that? I'm thirty-two, almost thirty-three years old!"

"I called her because I was looking for you and because I also need to speak with her. Once you calm down, I'll have you brought up so we can talk."

"How about telling me what's going on?" he called after him as Stuart walked away.

"Chill. I'll be back once I talk to your mother."

When he reached his office, Charlotte Stafford was pacing back and forth in the small space in front of his desk. Her attorney, Ian Drake, was sitting in one of the plastic chairs off to one side of Stuart's desk.

The moment Charlotte saw him, she stopped pacing and demanded, "You *arrested* Brand?"

"Yes and no. He was supposed to be brought in only for questioning. Please sit down," he said as he closed the door and calmly stepped past her to take his chair behind his desk.

"I demand to know—"

"Please sit down," he repeated. He was in no mood for her demands. "Brand is fine. He's cooling his heels in a cell right now while you and I talk." When she finally sat, it was on the edge of a chair as if she wasn't staying long. "As I told you on the phone, Holly Jo is missing. It appears she's been kidnapped. We need to find her as quickly as possible."

Charlotte looked shocked and even more upset.

"And you think Brand had something to do with it?" the attorney asked.

"The kidnapper isn't demanding money. He or she is asking for the truth."

Charlotte frowned, still clearly impatient with all of this. "What truth?"

"Possibly this." He leaned across his desk to hand her a copy of the DNA report. "It was left for Holden."

Charlotte barely looked at it. "What is this?"

"It shows that Brand shares some of the same genes as Holden's son Cooper. In other words, the DNA indicates that they are half brothers."

She blinked, then shook her head. He watched her swallow and look away as she sat back in the chair, gripping her purse, knuckles white against the leather.

"Were you aware that Brand is your son with Holden McKenna?" Her lips moved but no words came out. "If Brand kidnapped Holly Jo to force his father to acknowledge him—"

"That's ridiculous," she snapped as Drake advised her not to speak. "Kidnap a child?"

"It would appear that Brand wants to be acknowledged or he wouldn't have left the DNA results in Holden's mailbox, the same mailbox that also held the kidnapper's first demand," the sheriff said.

Her cheeks had reddened with anger, shock or embarrassment. He couldn't tell which, but the news had shaken her.

"I was with Holden when he read the results," Stuart said. "He hadn't known Brand was his son. But I assume you did. Or at least suspected."

"Holden knows?" Panic flickered across her face as she paled. She quickly looked away. "What do you plan to do with this information?" she asked, her voice cracking.

"Find out if Brand took Holly Jo to force his father to admit his parentage. If so, then hopefully find out where he's keeping her, get her home safely and arrest him for kidnapping."

"He didn't do it," Charlotte said firmly. Drake tried again to get her to remain silent and failed. "Not Brand. You have the wrong man. He definitely wouldn't take that little girl. He's not like…" She didn't finish, but Stuart knew she was going to say CJ, her son who was in a jail cell in Billings awaiting a criminal trial.

He looked at Drake and figured he too remembered when Charlotte had professed CJ's innocence, and look how that had turned out.

"I'm surprised Brand even left Holden the DNA results," she said. "Or that he went to the trouble to find out in the first place. He's never said anything."

Stuart watched her struggle with the DNA news before he asked, "How about you? Is there a reason you might have wanted Holden to admit the affair and acknowledge Brand?"

She stared at him before her words came as if shot from a cannon. "*Me?* You think I kidnapped the girl to force Holden to admit that Brand was his?"

Again, Drake tried to intervene, but again, Charlotte overrode his concerns.

"I never wanted him to know," she spit out. "*Never!* I never wanted *anyone* to know, especially my children." She shook her head. "I should have known once Oakley got her DNA results, the others would, too."

"You don't think Brand suspected?"

She snapped her lips shut for a moment. "I don't want you talking to Brand without my lawyer present."

Stuart nodded. "If you want to see your son—"

She shook her head and shoved the copy of the DNA results at Drake as she stood. "My attorney will handle it."

"I really think we should talk, Charlotte," Drake said as he rose as well.

"I don't need a lawyer. My son Brand does."

As they both watched her leave, the lawyer said, "I need to talk to my client alone first."

The sheriff's phone rang. "You can talk to Brand down at his cell. I'm short-staffed today with all my deputies looking for Holly Jo." As the attorney left to meet with his client, Stuart glanced at the clock on the wall. It had been hours since Holly Jo had headed for the bus stop—the last time anyone but her kidnapper had seen her. Stuart didn't want to think what could have happened to her in all that time—if she was still alive.

His phone rang again. He quickly picked up, hoping this time it would be good news.

"There is a young woman insisting that she has to talk to you," the dispatcher told him. "She says it's about Brand Stafford. Her name is Birdie Malone."

CHAPTER EIGHT

HOLLY JO FLOATED in and out of sleep. When she'd finally forced her eyes open again, she let out a sob at the sight of the small dark room. Before she'd awakened, she'd been riding Honey, her horse, the wind in her hair, the sun on her face, laughing as she did the new riding trick Pickett had taught her.

Now she looked around, not wanting to cry anymore, but afraid she would never get out of this room. She would never see her horse, or Pickett or Cooper or Elaine or even HH, again. She would never become the greatest woman trick rider in history.

Earlier, she'd drunk all of her juice. She felt so tired that she'd fallen back to sleep not long after. But she was now thirsty again. She'd hoped on waking that she would discover all of this was just a bad dream.

She began to cry again as she pulled herself up and went to the door. Her throat ached from screaming, calling for help, crying, pleading for someone to find her, to save her. When had that been? She felt confused, not sure how long she'd been here—let alone how long she'd be held here. Her hands were bruised and scraped from pounding on the door in the semidarkness of the small room. She hurt from lying on the thin blanket on the cold concrete.

Closing her eyes, she tried to sleep again, wanting to go back to her horseback-riding dream. Sleep pulled at her. She felt so weak.

When she woke again, she knew that someone had been in the room. She bolted upright and looked around, wrinkling her nose as she smelled the man's aftershave.

Her gaze shot to the corner, to the bucket and what had been put next to it. She rose slowly, crawling across the floor because she didn't think she could stand. Next to the bucket was a roll of toilet paper, another plastic bottle of juice and a couple of granola bars.

She grabbed the bottle of juice and drank down half of it. She'd never been so thirsty. Setting the bottle aside, she took one of the granola bars and hungrily devoured it, then gobbled down the second granola bar. As she moved back to her spot against the wall nearest the boarded-up window, she took the juice with her, trying not to drink it all—just as she tried not to think about what would happen if the man never came back with more juice and food.

Her body felt weightless after a few moments, and she felt herself falling back to sleep even as she tried hard to listen for the man to come back. She feared he wouldn't. All she could hear was the beat of her heart, the sound of her slowing breaths. Her eyelids dropped closed. If only this was just a bad dream and she could wake up in her room at the ranch. She promised herself that she would eat whatever Elaine cooked, that she wouldn't act like a brat, wouldn't lie. She would do anything.

A sob rose in her throat. But the memory that she'd fought so hard to push away came back in horrifying detail as sleep tried to pull her under again. The pickup and camper pulling up as she waited for the school bus. The woman behind the wheel putting down her window and calling her by name, calling her over.

Waiting for the bus? You want a ride to school?

She'd been wondering if she'd met the woman before. People knew Holly Jo because of Holden. Everyone knew HH, as she'd taken to calling him after learning his middle name was Hank. Holden Hank McKenna.

She'd looked down the road, wondering where the school bus was, when she'd heard a sound behind her. She didn't see him, just the large shape of the man, as he'd grabbed her.

He'd pressed a wet, stinky rag to her mouth as she tried to fight him off. She heard him say, *She's bigger than I thought, stronger. I'm going to have to sedate her.*

The woman had revved the truck engine. *Hurry! The bus will be coming.*

Holly Jo had felt herself being lifted off the ground and carried toward the back of the camper. She'd kicked and kicked, some of her blows landing as she screamed until he covered her mouth. After that, she'd suddenly felt sick, and everything darkened and went black.

She shoved the memory away again, wishing with all her heart that she hadn't walked over to that pickup. That the school bus had been early. That she didn't still have the nasty taste in her mouth or feel sick, her head and her stomach roiling as sleep pulled her thankfully under again.

THE SHERIFF HAD heard about Birdie Malone being in town, asking questions regarding her father's death. Before that, the PI she'd hired had been doing the same thing. Stuart was surprised this was the first time she'd come by to see him.

"Please have a seat," he said, waving her into a chair in his office. "What can I do for you?"

"You can release Brand Stafford," she said. "There's no way he knows anything about a missing person if that person went missing anytime between ten last night and noon today."

He raised an eyebrow. "How would you know that?"

"I was at a bar where he stayed until it closed at two a.m., and he went home and didn't get up until almost noon."

"You're sure he never left the ranch?"

"Positive. A friend took him home after the bar closed, and another friend followed to give the driver a ride back to town. I followed them all the way to the house where they put him to bed. He didn't emerge until, like I said, almost noon."

"You will swear to that?"

She sighed. "I would have known if he'd left."

"Let me get this straight. You followed him home, and then what?"

"I went inside the house, and we both went to bed."

"I'm assuming at some point you slept."

"I'm a light sleeper. He didn't leave the ranch."

"You and Brand Stafford?" The sheriff cocked his head at her. "What exactly is your relationship?"

"We just met this morning. I was having a look around the ranch when he finally woke up and saw me. He'd just come from the shower. Hadn't even taken the time to get dressed." She smiled. "I introduced myself, and we realized how much we had in common."

"When you followed him last night, you'd never met?"

She shook her head. "But you stayed in the house last night."

"In the bedroom next to his. It was empty." She shrugged.

"You broke in?"

"The door was open."

"You don't have a romantic relationship with him?"

"I'm trying to find evidence to prove that Charlotte Stafford killed my father. I don't plan to stop until I see her behind bars with her son CJ. I figure one of the Staffords knows something, so I'm trying to get as close to the family as I can."

Stuart leaned back, shaking his head. "I would think you wouldn't have much good to say about the Staffords. Why would you give Brand an alibi?"

"Because I know where he was during the time the person went missing." She studied him, eyes narrowing. "Why would you think Brand had anything to do with your missing person case in the first place?"

The sheriff didn't answer. "You say you followed him home. Did he make any stops?"

"You mean the friend driving him home? Just one. They stopped at the McKenna mailbox. It looked like they put something inside and left."

"Did you see anyone else around the McKenna Ranch mailbox?"

She seemed surprised by the question. The sheriff saw her start to say no, then change her mind. "I did see something. Tell me who's missing."

Stuart knew that there was no keeping a lid on this. Also, as strange as it seemed, Birdie Malone might be the key to finding Holly Jo. He had to take the chance. "Holly Jo Robinson, a thirteen-year-old ward of Holden McKenna's, was last seen headed for the county road to the bus for a half day at school. But when the bus driver got to her pickup spot, she wasn't there. We have reason to believe that she's been kidnapped. Do you know anything about that?"

Birdie sat back, clearly surprised. "You asked about the mailbox. I saw another vehicle ahead of Brand's friends. A vehicle stopped at that mailbox before Brand Stafford's pickup reached it. I'd pulled off on the top of the hill to let the two pickups get a little ahead of me. I knew where they were headed, so I didn't need to follow so closely."

"Another vehicle? Can you describe it?"

"I wouldn't have been able to, except that I saw it again later. It was a light-colored pickup, probably white, with a small, darker-colored camper on the back, maybe a burgundy red? I didn't think much about it when the driver made a quick stop at the McKenna mailbox and took off fast. Then I saw the rig as I turned in to the Stafford Ranch. The moon was full. The pickup and camper had pulled off the road in a wide spot next to the river and cottonwoods just past the Stafford Ranch turnoff."

"License plate?"

She shook her head. "Too far away. I wouldn't even have noticed it except that it was two thirty in the morning. At the time, I thought it was someone looking for a place to camp." Her keen gaze narrowed again. "I didn't even think it was strange that they stopped to put something in the mailbox. But now that I know about the kidnapping… They left the ransom note in the mailbox, didn't they? What did Brand drop off?"

"You'd have to ask him. Can you think of anything

else about the pickup and camper that might help us find it?"

"I'm sorry, but if I see it again, I think I'll recognize it."

BRAND HAD EXPECTED to see his mother, but only the family lawyer came into the cell block. "What's going on?" he demanded of Ian Drake, who shook his head and motioned him over to the bars, even though the other two cells were empty. It was just the two of them.

"Tell me about what happened at the café," Ian said.

"It was silly. I asked why I was being hauled in for questioning, and the deputy started grabbing me." He groaned. "The next thing I knew, I was in cuffs, and Deputy Dodson was telling me he was arresting me for resisting arrest and assaulting an officer of the law."

"Those charges won't hold," the lawyer said.

"So why am I still here?"

"Holly Jo Robinson, the ward of Holden McKenna, is believed to have been kidnapped. They think you might know something about it."

"What?" Brand cried. "Why would I? I don't even know her. On my mother's life, I swear I didn't do anything."

The lawyer chuckled. "That would be more convincing if I didn't know your mother." He unfolded a sheet of paper. "Your mother gave me this. Did you send this to Holden McKenna?" Drake pushed the sheet of paper between the bars.

Brand saw at once that it was a copy of the DNA results that he'd left in his father's mailbox in the wee hours of the morning. What had he hoped would happen? Certainly not this.

He rubbed a hand over his face, swearing that he was never drinking again. "What was the sheriff doing with this? And what could my DNA results have to do with this missing girl?"

"Did you send this to Holden McKenna?" the lawyer asked again.

Brand nodded even as he was grimacing inside. "I left it in his mailbox last night after the bar closed."

"Why?"

Good question, he thought. "I'm not sure. I guess I wanted Holden to admit that he was my father," Brand said and saw Ian's expression. "What?"

"You wanted him to admit the truth?"

He frowned. "Maybe. I don't know. Why? What's going on? What does it matter?"

"From what little the sheriff shared with me, Holden has received a kidnapping demand—not for money, but for him to admit the truth. The sheriff seems to think that the truth might be about Holden's relationship to you."

Brand shook his head. This wasn't happening. "No," he said, gripping the bars as he leaned back, trying to distance himself from this. "I just wanted to notify him that I knew about him and my mother. I really wish I hadn't done it. But I wouldn't kidnap some girl to make him admit it." He loosened his grip on the bars. Everything was starting to make an awful kind of sense. "The sheriff is basing his suspicion on the DNA results?" He shook his head again. "I can't tell you how much I regret all of this."

"If you took the girl—"

He saw that the lawyer didn't believe him. Shocked, he said, "I swear I didn't take her."

"She's missing, Brand, and hasn't been seen since she headed for the school bus this morning. Where were you between seven and seven thirty this morning?"

"In bed with a horrible hangover. I didn't get up until noon or so."

"Can anyone at the house verify that?" the lawyer asked.

He thought hard, remembering how empty the house had been with the housekeeper off and his brother Ryder up early and gone to work as usual. He'd never felt so helpless in his life. All he could think about was the missing girl. He'd seen Holly Jo riding her horse a couple of times and waiting for the school bus but had never even talked to her. Who would take her? What truth did they want Holden to acknowledge? It had to be something more than him fathering a bastard son.

Brand realized what he had earlier that morning. "No one was at the house. I was alone, as far as I know." As he said it, he thought of the young woman sneaking past his window. "There might be someone, but I didn't see her until I got up." Brand saw the lawyer's concern.

"So you can't prove that you never left the ranch all morning." Drake sighed. "The sheriff is going to want to talk to you." He seemed to hesitate. "But if you know where the girl is—"

"I told you I didn't take her. I don't know where she is. I'm not my brother. Or my—" He almost said *mother*.

The lawyer nodded. "I'll be back."

"Just a minute. You already knew that I was Holden McKenna's biological son, didn't you?"

"No. Why would you think I did?"

"Because you didn't seem surprised," Brand said.

"I've been your mother's lawyer for years. Little surprises me anymore."

With that, he started to leave, and would have except for the sheriff coming in to tell Brand that he was being released—at least temporarily. "Don't leave the river basin," the sheriff said.

CHAPTER NINE

HOLDEN COULDN'T STAND the waiting. It gave him too much time to think, to worry, to mull over everything that he'd done in his life to bring it to this point. His fear for Holly Jo was a physical ache in his chest, as if his ruthless heart were attacking him.

Was it possible Brand had taken her? He picked up the sheet of paper with the DNA results that had been left in his mailbox. DNA didn't lie. He knew that much. But Charlotte had. She must have known or at least suspected, and yet she'd never said a word.

More than thirty-some years ago. He'd never forgotten the times they'd made love. But had that been the last time? Or had there been another time? He tried to recall in the months after if Charlotte had tried to reach out to him.

He scoffed at the idea. She had gone back to hating him. But why wouldn't she have used the pregnancy to destroy his marriage to Margie? As vindictive as she'd been over the years, why not use the son they'd made together against him?

"Are you all right?" Elaine touched his arm.

He flinched, then shook his head. "Sorry."

"Still no word from the kidnapper?" she asked. He knew she'd been in the kitchen making food and drinks for the extra law officers monitoring the calls as well as keeping online surveillance on the mailbox at the end of the long drive.

"What is he waiting for?" Holden demanded.

Elaine shook her head. "Can I get you something to eat, to drink?"

He shook off her concern. "I'm fine." He hadn't meant to sound so terse, but she didn't seem to notice.

"I'm here if you need anything."

He nodded and smiled, and the moment she left, he began to pace his office. He let his thoughts go back to Charlotte and his son. As upsetting as it was, it was far better than thinking about what might be happening to Holly Jo at this moment.

For the life of him, he still couldn't get his head around the fact that he had another son. More than thirty-two years ago, Charlotte "Lottie" Stafford had been pregnant with a son—*his* son. He had proof, in black and white. Brand Stafford was his flesh and blood.

The truth was staring him in the face. Lottie had kept it from him. Worse, how could he not have noticed that Brand didn't even resemble his brothers and sisters? The Stafford offspring were all blond with different shapes of green eyes.

Brand was dark blond with blue eyes. Holden's own blue eyes.

He swore, wadding up the DNA results and throwing them across the room. He tried to remember when Brand might have been conceived. Clearly, they had both sneaked away and made love in secret. What had transpired after that? He couldn't recall. It had been too many years ago. One thing he did remember, though. He and Lottie had both been married to someone else. Her to Rake Stafford, a man seventeen years her senior. Him to Margie. Lottie had a son, CJ, who was a toddler. He had a son as well, Treyton, who was about the same age.

Wasn't that the time that he'd been ready to walk away from his marriage because he couldn't live without Lottie? If so, why hadn't he?

What had happened? Had he changed his mind? Or had Lottie? There'd been so many times when they'd both fought their feelings, their desires, their love, and pushed the other away. What was clear was that she'd lied to him. She'd become pregnant with his son and never told him. He frowned. Was that the time she told him that she never wanted to see him again?

His head ached as he tried to remember. She had to have known that if he had left Margie back then, he would have had to walk away from the ranch since his father was still alive and in charge of the place. He would have left destitute. His father would have disowned him. True, he and Lottie would have still had her ranch—if her husband, who'd been growing the place, didn't fight her for it in court. The scandal would have rocked the community, and there were their young sons to think about.

Holden frowned as he realized that Lottie might have found out something he himself hadn't known until later. His wife Margie was pregnant with their second son, Cooper. Was that why Lottie never told him that the child she was carrying was his?

He'd always thought that she'd never wanted to see him again because she could never forgive him for buckling under the demands of his father. Through marrying Margie Smith, Holden had been given part of the Smith Ranch, which quickly was added to the McKennas' holdings. He'd never forgiven his father for forcing him to make that choice, a choice he had regretted—but then, he wouldn't have his children.

As much as he'd loved Lottie, his marriage to Margie had been happy enough. She'd given him three sons and a daughter. She'd been a good, loving wife, even though she'd known that his heart had been elsewhere. Charlotte had gone on to have two daughters and three sons and had hated him ever since—with good reason. He'd been young and foolish. They both had, he realized now, and they'd hurt people they loved with their selfishness.

Had Charlotte planned to take this secret to her grave?

You have your own secrets, he reminded himself. Still, he couldn't help being shocked and disillusioned as well as angry.

Brand Stafford was his *son*. What was he going to do about it? How could he not confront Charlotte? He rubbed a hand over his face. He still thought of her as his Lottie, but now he wondered what other secrets she'd kept from him. Was it possible she was behind Holly Jo's kidnapping?

The sheriff had told him to sit tight, but Holden knew he had to see her. He had to hear why she never told him about Brand. He had to look into her eyes and ask her about Holly Jo. Only then would he know the truth.

CHAPTER TEN

"YOU BETTER HAVE gotten Brand released from jail," Charlotte said after opening her ranch house door to find her lawyer standing there. With a sigh, she led him into the living room. It was never any good when Ian Drake showed up at her door. "It's ludicrous that the sheriff thought he would kidnap that girl."

Drake wiped his feet and stepped into the house with his usual solemn air. He'd been the family's legal counsel for years. Tall, gray and dressed immaculately, he had an unmemorable face with an expression that seldom changed. She noticed with concern that he seemed uneasy.

"Brand's been released, yes, but he's still a suspect."

"That makes no sense. If he was released—"

"A young woman named Birdie Malone provided him with an alibi," Drake said. "The sheriff couldn't hold him."

For a moment, the name meant nothing to her since she knew no one by that name. Chest tightening, she remembered the private investigator who'd come to her house demanding information about Dixon Malone, the man she'd thought of as her ex-husband, although they'd never divorced. Dixon had disappeared years ago. She'd long since put him out of her mind. But the

PI had mentioned that Dixon's daughter had hired him. Had Charlotte even known he had a daughter?

When his body was found in the well near the ranch, the sheriff had questioned why she'd never bothered to try to find her second husband or have him declared dead after all these years—which made her look guilty of his murder. According to the coroner, Dixon had probably been at the bottom of that well since his disappearance that night so many years ago.

Vaguely, she now remembered her husband telling her that he had a daughter he wanted her to meet. Could this Birdie Malone be the daughter? "Who is this woman?" she demanded of Drake, hoping she was wrong.

"A child your second husband had out of wedlock a little over thirty-two years ago," he said.

She closed her eyes and tried to breathe. Dixon's daughter, just as she'd feared. "Why would this woman give Brand an alibi?" When Drake didn't answer, she opened her eyes to look at him.

"I have no idea. She swore that he didn't leave the ranch all morning and therefore couldn't have kidnapped Holly Jo from the bus stop."

"How could she possibly know that unless—" She felt her eyes widen. "Do not tell me that Brand is seeing this…this woman."

"I don't know how she knew that he had been in his room after closing the bar last night until almost noon today, but while the sheriff might be suspicious, he seemed to think she was telling the truth."

Pulling out her phone, she tried Brand's number. The call went straight to voicemail. He probably didn't want to talk to her. She couldn't blame him. She didn't leave a message, not sure what she would say to him.

She began to pace. "My son would not kidnap anyone. I told Stuart that." She stopped to stare at her lawyer when he didn't comment. Ian, she noted, was avoiding her gaze. "What is it you're trying so hard not to tell me? Spit it out. It can't be that…bad." Even as she said the words, though, she thought of her eldest son, CJ. She'd never in her life dreamed that he would do the things he'd done. Was it possible she was also wrong about Brand? If she was, then how could she deny that she was responsible for the way both had turned out?

"The sheriff suspects Brand because of the kidnapper's demand that Holden tell the truth." She started to open her mouth, but he rushed on before she could. "It comes back to Brand and the DNA results. You have to understand how suspicious it looks. Also, his alibi might not stand up, given who it came from. I've been your attorney for too long, Charlotte. If there is any chance you know where that girl is—"

"Of course I don't."

"Or if Brand—"

"Stop! Brand didn't take Holly Jo. He wouldn't do that." It made her furious that Drake would believe either of them was capable of doing something like that. But as he'd said, he'd been her attorney for years.

"Brand left a copy of the results for Holden McKenna the same day the kidnapper left a note demanding he tell the truth."

"I know all that. It's ridiculous. You know I already told Stuart that," she snapped, trying not to think about Holden. He knew about Brand. That alone had her chest aching with worry as to how he took the news.

"Holden can't think that my son…" His son. She told herself that she'd never known for sure Brand was his. It was a lie. She'd watched her son grow up, seeing Holden in him every day. Had Brand known or at least suspected? Was that why he'd gotten his DNA results?

Oakley, she thought with a curse. Her headstrong daughter had started this. But Brand was bound to find out eventually. Hadn't she lived with the fear for years that it would come out? Now Brand had proof, and apparently so did Holden. Worse, Holden had reason to believe their son had kidnapped his ward.

"I need to see him." She looked around for her purse, but stopped at his next words.

"Brand was released. I'm not sure where he—"

"Not Brand," she snapped. *"Holden."*

She saw her purse by the door. "I have to go." The thought made her feel physically ill. But this was a conversation she should have had more than thirty-two years ago. "I'm going to see Holden."

"I'm not sure that's a good idea. Charlotte, this would be a good time to pull the family together. You need to see Brand. If you're trying to avoid him, that will only make him look more guilty."

"Let yourself out, Ian."

"Charlotte!" he exclaimed, but she was already closing the door behind her.

As BRAND EXITED the sheriff's department through the back door, he did a double take when he saw Birdie clearly waiting for him. He looked past her, expecting to see his mother or Ian Drake. Seeing neither, his gaze returned to the young woman leaning against the side of a pale green SUV.

"Kidnapping?" She pushed off the car and walked toward him. "Really? What kind of family are you Staffords?"

He sighed. "What are you doing here?"

"Is that how you treat the person who just got you sprung from jail?" she demanded, but she was smiling as she said it.

He met her gaze. "You got me released? Why would you do that? I know how you feel about my family."

Birdie eyed him for a moment and then shook her head. "Not your entire family."

He groaned and looked around, still wondering why the only person here was Birdie Malone.

"Come on," she said. "Let's go get your pickup from in front of the café and then find someplace where we can talk."

"I can't imagine what we have to talk about."

"Really?" She cocked her head at him. "The charges have been dropped because I gave you an alibi." She tapped a spot just above her heart. "You're welcome."

Still feeling queasy from the hangover and the day he'd had, he knew he wasn't tracking well. "*You're* my alibi?"

"I know you didn't kidnap that girl," Birdie said.

"Of course I didn't, but how could you—"

"I heard one of your friends call you by name at the bar last night. I was curious about you and your family. I told you that I followed you home after you and your friends closed the bar last night. I know you didn't leave again until past noon, when you came after me. But if that girl isn't found…no one will ever believe you didn't have something to do with it." At his perplexed expression, she added, "Seriously? You really don't know what people say about your family?"

"I'm not my family," he snapped.

"So I hear. It's the talk of the sheriff's office," she said, grinning. "The question is, which side of you, the Stafford or the McKenna, are you really?"

He groaned. "It's all over the county by now?"

"I overheard one of the deputies talking about it. But Charlotte is still your mother, and even with Holden being your father…that doesn't exactly help your pedigree, does it?"

Brand hated her logic, but he couldn't argue with it. "Okay, I'm the worst kind of mutt. What is it you want from me?"

"For starters? We need to find Holly Jo."

He stared at her, frowning. "There is no way I can find Holly Jo. I'm a rancher. I'm better with horses and cows than people. I'm not a detective. I have no idea how to find a missing girl. I'm going back to what I know and letting the sheriff find her."

She laughed. "Well, lucky for you, I have all kinds of ideas."

He gave her a side-eye. "You really aren't good at listening to people, are you?"

"Just like you aren't good at accepting help, let alone saying thank you." She pointed to her SUV.

"Thank you. I appreciate that you gave me an alibi and got me out of jail, but you do realize that my truck is parked only a block away. I can walk, thank you very much." He hoped the walk would do him good.

She laughed as she opened the driver's-side door. "Get in and accept the ride. It will give us some personal time before you buy me dinner after you ruined my lunch. Anyway, you need my help, and I need yours. I know your older brother is already in jail for murder, but maybe I could talk to him. If he's the oldest, he might remember my dad."

He looked at her and shook his head. "CJ? You think *I'm* not very cooperative? Wait until you meet my brother."

"Half brother," she said as she slid behind the wheel, started the engine and reached across to open the passenger-side door. "Tell me about this missing girl, Holly Jo."

He realized that no matter how much he wanted all of this to go away, it wasn't going to happen until the girl was found. As he walked around to the open door and climbed in, he hated to think what ideas Birdie Malone might have for finding Holly Jo.

But if there was even a chance the girl could be found, Brand was willing to at least hear Birdie out. After all, she was his alibi. If he didn't realize he was in trouble earlier, he did now that he was indebted to Birdie Malone.

HOLLY JO DIDN'T know what had pulled her from the pitch blackness of her groggy sleep—just that it had her heart pounding. She pushed herself up, surprised when she looked toward the window that it was still light outside. Was this a new day? She had no idea. She leaned against the wall, feeling even weaker than before, her brain foggy.

A sound outside the room made her freeze. Someone was coming. She started to get to her feet, opened her mouth to call for help, but then she heard it. The footfalls. It wasn't someone coming to help her. It was him. She recognized the odd sound of the way he moved because of his limp. Apparently one of her kicks when he had abducted her had done some damage. Just not enough to save her. Only enough to make him swear profusely at her before everything went black.

She fell back, curling into herself tighter as she heard the key turn in the lock. She buried her face in her knees as she drew them against her.

The door slowly opened. She heard him step in, then stop. She held her breath. Why didn't he move? It was him, wasn't it? She had to look.

Peeking out, she saw him for the first time since he grabbed her and brought her here. He was large. She remembered how strong he was when she'd tried to get away from him. She hadn't seen his face then—nor would she now. He wore a mask. Black. All she could see, when she dared look into his face, was his eyes. Light-colored.

She'd heard about girls being taken to be sold to have sex with a lot of men. She'd also heard that some were taken to use as unpaid labor. She stared at the hulking masked figure, terrified that was why she'd been brought here. She didn't want to have sex at all, especially with a lot of men. Not even one man. Not even a boy. Not even Gus, her only friend at school.

She'd heard what some of the girls at school did with boys. Yuck. She hadn't even kissed a boy and didn't really want to do that either. At least, not with any boy she knew.

If he'd taken her to make her work, she didn't know what kind of work it would be. Since most everyone found fault with the way she made her bed, cleaned her room and tried to help with the dishes, she really didn't think she would be good at very many jobs.

"I brought you food." His voice was deep, raspy behind the mask. He put down a paper bag and looked in the empty bucket. "You know what to use the bucket for, right?" She didn't answer, doubted she could find her voice as badly as her throat hurt. "I'm leaving you more juice, but if you drink it all, you'll go thirsty before I come back." He stood there just looking at her as if he didn't know what more to say.

"I want to go home." The words sounded scratchy, her voice too high. She was trying hard not to cry. "Please, just let me go home."

"That's not happening yet. Be good and you'll get to go home soon."

With that, he turned and quickly left, locking the door behind him. The smell of the food made her stomach growl. She'd always been a picky eater. She especially hated meat, beef in particular. HH had made her at least try McKenna beef, reminding her that she lived on a cattle ranch. She still didn't like it very much, but had learned to keep that to herself.

She waited, listening to make sure he'd really gone before she crawled over to the bag. No matter what it was, she knew she would eat it.

CHAPTER ELEVEN

THE CLOSER CHARLOTTE got to the turnoff to the Mc-Kenna Ranch, the more she began to question what she was doing. Did she dare just show up at Holden's door? With Holly Jo missing, there would be law enforcement officers there. She hadn't thought of that. He was waiting for word on the girl. She would be the last person he wanted to see.

She desperately wanted to talk to him, to explain. Maybe if she called and asked him to meet her at the creek… Immediately she rejected that idea. That place was too intimate, and after what had happened last time—not to mention what had happened there thirty-two years ago when they'd both been married to someone else—she didn't dare.

This had been a fool's errand. Holden had more important things on his mind than her or their son. Holly Jo was missing, believed kidnapped. What had she been thinking? Her timing couldn't have been worse. This wasn't the time to talk about the past—and Brand.

She had no idea what his reaction would be when he finally saw her. All the sheriff had said was that Holden had been surprised. He hadn't known. He apparently hadn't even suspected. Would he believe that she hadn't known?

Charlotte slowed on the county road, looking for a

wide spot to turn around. Eventually she would have to talk to Holden about Brand, but now wasn't the right time to bring up old history, let alone old wounds.

And yet if he thought their son was the one who'd taken Holly Jo, didn't she need to assure him that it wasn't true?

Why would he believe her? She shook her head at her own foolishness. Ian was right. This had been a bad decision made by emotion instead of common sense.

She started to do a U-turn, but saw that she would have to wait for a pickup coming too fast up the county road. The truck was almost to her when she noticed that it was a McKenna Ranch truck, the logo on the side. Her heart jumped, her breath catching as the driver suddenly hit his brakes and swung in where she'd stopped.

Dust boiled up in a cloud as the pickup came to a stop, blocking her SUV from going anywhere. The cloud of dirt hadn't had time to settle before the driver threw open his door, leaped out and stalked toward her.

Heart in her throat, she watched Holden McKenna storm in her direction. One look at his expression and she felt sick. She'd never seen him this angry in all the years she'd known him. Hurt, disappointed, heartbroken, happy, sated and hopeful, but never looking like this. Nor did she have any doubt who had caused his fury.

A wiser woman might have locked her door. Or called the sheriff. She'd never been wise, she thought as she opened her door and stepped out, standing firm as he closed the distance between them. He came to an abrupt stop within feet of her as if worried what he would do if he got any closer.

"Charlotte." He said only the one word, but it conveyed everything. Not *Lottie*, the name he'd called her since they were kids. Just *Charlotte* in a tone that told her exactly how he felt even if she hadn't noticed his big hands balled into fists at his sides, his face a mask of pain and rage. "Where is Holly Jo? If I find out you—"

"No," she cried, meeting his gaze. What she saw made her flinch. Contempt, yes, but *hatred*? "Of course I didn't take the girl. You can't believe that I would."

He didn't look convinced, but the blazing look in his eyes dimmed a little. "Why should I believe anything you say?"

She knew that they were now talking about their son's conception. "I didn't know. Not at first, and even when I suspected…I never did a paternity test." Because she'd known in her heart. She could admit that at least to herself now.

"But you knew that Brand had."

"No. I was shocked when I heard. He hadn't said a word to me. Still hasn't." Holden McKenna was a gentle, loving man who couldn't carry a grudge long, especially against her, she told herself. She felt some of his anger dissipate. "You remember what it was like back then." She said it like a plea. He unfisted one hand to reach up to rub the back of his neck.

She couldn't bear the pain she saw replace some of his anger. She took a step toward him as if her love for him outweighed everything else right now. "Holden—"

He stepped back, holding up his hands, warding her off.

She felt the pain of his rejection as if he'd slapped her. With a wave of shame, she knew how he'd felt all these years when she'd repeatedly pushed him away, unforgiving, angry and hurt. Vengeful.

He shook his head, his expression now one of sorrow. "Charlotte."

Their gazes locked again. She found herself desperately searching for his love for her, terrified she'd finally killed it with her bitterness.

He dragged his gaze away as he retreated another step from her, avoiding even looking in her direction. "I have to find Holly Jo."

"I'm so sorry. If there is anything I can do…"

He looked out at the river for a moment. "You should have told me."

"I know."

He turned to meet her eyes again. "If I'd thought that baby was mine—"

Charlotte had to swallow the lump that formed in her throat. Would he have walked away from Margie and his marriage? Could they have been together all these years?

The doctor had her go on the pill for a while after she'd had CJ. She'd only quit taking it a week or so before she'd run into Holden that day at the creek more than thirty-two years ago. She'd told him it was safe, not that in the state they'd been in that day either of them would have cared. They'd wanted each other so badly, needed each other so badly.

"If Brand has Holly Jo—"

"He doesn't," she said quickly. "He wouldn't do anything like that. He's…he's your son, Holden. He took after you more than me."

His face crumpled, his eyes shiny. He took another step back as if needing to get away from her. "I can't do this now. I'm not sure I'll ever…" He couldn't seem to finish as he turned and stalked away without looking back.

She felt the loss of him like a death as he climbed behind the wheel and drove away without a glance.

LULABELLE BRADEN DIDN'T seem surprised to see Sheriff Stuart Layton standing on her doorstep and said as much. "Someone in Powder Crossing farts and you seem to think I know about it," she said with a laugh.

After Holden's first wife, Margie, had died, he'd remarried quickly, apparently thinking his children needed a mother. Lulabelle Braden McKenna had put him through hell for over a year before he'd ended the marriage. Apparently he'd promised himself he wouldn't make that mistake again, because he hadn't remarried.

"You here to get your palm read, Sheriff?" Lulabelle asked.

"That's right—you know all about these things," he said, unable to keep the sarcasm out of his tone. He didn't know why he was even here. Lulabelle seemed like a long shot, but what did he know? Holden had put her name down on his list, right under Charlotte's name.

She sighed. "Come on in."

"If you know so much, how about telling me where Holly Jo is?" he asked as he crossed the threshold and stopped.

She frowned as she turned to him. "That little girl Holden brought back pretending she was just someone he used to know's kid?" She shook her head. "He misplaced her?"

"You really haven't heard?" He actually thought maybe she hadn't.

"Why would I have? Holden McKenna and I are ancient history. He has boots he's had longer than he had me for a wife. How long's it been?"

"Not quite thirty years ago, and yet when his ward went missing, your name came up as someone he thought might have taken her."

She huffed. "That is so like Holden. He must feel guilty as hell about the way he treated me. Sorry, Sheriff, I haven't given Holden a second thought since I left the McKenna Ranch." That wasn't true, and they both knew it. "Even if I did have some residual feelings about the man and our marriage, I wouldn't take a child to get back at him. Not when I could make a voodoo doll and cause him all kinds of pain." She laughed, but he wasn't sure she was joking.

"I thought maybe you could use your sixth sense to tell me where she is."

"You really don't know anything about having a sixth sense, do you, Sheriff?"

"I wish I did," he said. "I thought maybe one of the people from down our way who come to you for your... help might have heard something about Holly Jo. I need to find her before it's too late." He feared it was already too late. The girl had been missing for more than ten hours. He could feel her slipping away, and he was no closer to finding her.

"You know I can't talk about what people tell me."

He raised a brow. "You're not a doctor or a lawyer or a priest."

"No, I'm much more than that. It's why people tell me things they don't tell their doctors or their lawyers—especially not their priests."

He could see that he wasn't getting anywhere with

her. "Just thought maybe you could help." He started to turn back toward the door.

She grabbed his hand and closed her eyes. "You have nightmares about her."

He scoffed and pulled his hand free. "You don't have to be psychic to suspect that. My scars are still visible." He motioned to his arms and the pale white lines where Abigail Creed's knife blade had sliced open his skin as she'd attacked him. Normally, he kept his arms covered, but it had been warm enough this morning that he'd worn a short-sleeve uniform shirt and left his jacket in the patrol SUV. Now he regretted it, since he didn't need the reminder from well-meaning people of the horror he'd been through not long ago. She was right. He did still have nightmares about it sometimes.

"The nightmares must be terrifying," Lulabelle said sympathetically. "To see her standing over you holding a knife."

He corrected her. Abigail Creed hadn't been standing over him. She'd been in the driver's seat of her SUV when she'd drawn the knife from the pocket in the door and, screaming, begun stabbing him.

"I wasn't talking about Abigail Creed," Lulabelle said. "The dreams start out that way, but it isn't her face you see." He watched her eyes fill with tears. "What terrifies you is that it's your mother holding the knife."

Charlotte leaned against the side of the SUV as she watched Holden drive away with a finality that left her feeling pathetic and broken. For so many years, she'd never questioned his love. No matter how awful she'd been, he hadn't given up on her. Until now?

The thought filled her eyes with tears that quickly ran down her cheeks. She'd done this. She had only herself to blame. She'd kept Brand from him. She'd kept the truth from him. What if he never forgave her? After all these years of pushing him away, what if this was the end?

When he'd married Margie Smith instead of her, Charlotte had been devastated. She'd thought she would die from the pain. She felt that way again now as his pickup disappeared from view.

Opening the door, she crawled behind the wheel. Her hands were shaking. She put the SUV in gear, but didn't know where to go. Not home. Not back to that empty house. She'd pushed away everyone who loved her—even her own children. Tilly was now married to Cooper McKenna. She'd heard that he was building them a house on the McKenna Ranch. She'd also heard that Tilly might be pregnant.

Charlotte shook her head. Even if she was going to be a grandmother, it would be in name only after the way she'd treated her daughter and Cooper. CJ, the son most like her, would soon be going to trial and probably on to prison. Oakley... She shook her head again. Oakley was the daughter most like her, fiery and stubborn and so independent that she'd never needed her mother and certainly didn't now that she was married to Pickett Hanson.

All Charlotte had left were Brand and Ryder. The two of them never gave her any trouble, staying clear of her on the ranch, doing what needed to be done and having minimal contact with the rest of the family. That too was her fault.

And now this. How could Brand ever forgive her?

He hadn't come to her after finding out the truth. Instead, he'd reached out to his father.

Realizing just how alone she was and how she'd brought it all on herself, Charlotte couldn't seem to move. She could drive into town, but there was no one there either. She'd alienated the community as well as her family—and especially Holden and his family—for years.

She'd once had a best friend. But then Margie Smith had betrayed her by marrying Holden. Charlotte knew intellectually that Margie was young. Her father and Holden's father put her in a position where she had little choice but to marry Holden. Still, Charlotte had never been able to forgive her for stealing her life—even when she'd learned years later that Margie was dying.

And here she was, just as Elaine had predicted, completely alone.

She reached for her cell phone. For a moment, she'd forgotten that she had one friend left in the world, the friendship no one knew about, but someone she could count on and vice versa. The line rang and was immediately picked up.

"Elaine," she said and burst into tears.

STUART SWORE AS he left Miles City and headed back to Powder Crossing. He cursed himself for letting Lulabelle get to him. She'd enjoyed his shock and discomfort. Psychic powers. Who knew where she got that crap? He tried to forget it, hating that his reaction had been so telling. The whole incident had left him feeling vulnerable.

His father used to say no one could keep a secret in Powder Crossing. That, at least, Stuart believed. Lulabelle dealt with the bottom-feeders, people who enjoyed digging into other people's trash. Had Lulabelle heard something from one of them? Or had she just been fishing with what she'd said about his mother?

He knew he should put it behind him, but he couldn't help being upset. Did she pull these same stunts with other people who came to her looking for answers?

Or did she know more than he thought? Either way, he was still shaken, because she'd hit his most vulnerable sore spot. His mother.

His cell phone rang, dragging him out of his black mood at even the mention of his mother. It was Treyton McKenna, Holden's eldest son. "I need to talk to you," the sheriff said. Treyton was the next name on Holden's list. "Where are you?"

He got the surly answer he would expect from Treyton McKenna. "Why?"

"Have you talked to your father?"

"I've been busy. I don't live on the ranch anymore. I bought a place of my own. So I don't see the old man."

"A place of your own? I can come to you. What's the address?" Stuart heard the hesitation in Treyton's silence.

"I'm on my way into town."

He would have liked to see Treyton's place for a number of reasons. He had been suspicious of the man for some time now, especially after there'd been a meth lab in the area. Whoever was running it had burned down the place, destroying the evidence, before Stuart could bust it. CJ Stafford had definitely been involved, but although they were rivals because of their families, the sheriff suspected Treyton might have been involved. It was just a gut feeling since the lab had actually been in an abandoned ranch building on the McKenna Ranch.

Disappointed, he said, "Fine, my office. Twenty minutes?" He'd pay Treyton a visit sometime in the future and check out his new digs.

"Why don't you just tell me what this is about?"

"When I see you," Stuart said and disconnected as he turned on his siren and lights and raced toward Powder Crossing.

"CHARLOTTE? CHARLOTTE! Is it Holly Jo?"

The fear Charlotte heard in Elaine's voice made her choke off her sobs. "No. I'm sorry. I don't know anything about Holly Jo. I just saw Holden." Silence. "Oh, please, you aren't going to turn against me too, are you?"

"Of course not," Elaine said. "You just scared me. I was trying to catch my breath. I was so afraid... I heard about Brand being picked up by the law. I thought maybe you might know something."

"I'm sorry. I shouldn't have called so upset. You all must be worried sick about Holly Jo."

"It's all right, Charlotte. You're sure Brand didn't take her?"

"Yes, I'm sure." She couldn't help but sound indignant. "They let him go. He had an alibi. He wouldn't do anything like that anyway." But she'd never thought he'd have his DNA tested and send Holden the results either. "Is there anything I can do?" She already knew the answer.

"No, but thank you for asking." Elaine had always been nicer to her than she deserved. Her friend was a better person than she was. Charlotte thought that Elaine should have gotten together with Holden years ago. They would have made a nice couple. Instead, Elaine had spent those years trying to get Charlotte to forgive, Margie first, then Holden.

"Let me know if you hear anything," Charlotte said. Elaine promised that she would, and they disconnected.

Feeling even worse for thinking only of herself when a child was missing, Charlotte shifted the SUV into gear and went home. She hoped Brand would be there. She wasn't sure what she would say to him when she did see him, though. There weren't really any words to explain the poor decisions she'd made in her fifty-three years.

Nor was she looking forward to the reactions of her other adult children when they heard the news. The way gossip traveled in the Powder River Basin, they had probably already heard. So as she walked in through the door of her house, she wasn't surprised to get a collect call from her son CJ, who was incarcerated in a cell in Billings.

She didn't take the call, already too aware of what he would have to say. Deserved or not, she couldn't take any more berating right now. She was sure she'd get enough of that from Brand once he decided to confront her.

Standing in the middle of her living room, the silence thick as fog around her, she knew that she could wallow in her pain like she usually did, or she could do something to help.

TREYTON MCKENNA WAS slouched in a chair in Stuart's office when the sheriff walked in. He had Holden's dark hair and blue eyes in a face that could have been considered handsome if not for his bad-tempered disposition.

He wore his usual sullen look as Stuart closed the office door, stepped past Treyton's extended legs and sat down behind his desk.

"When was the last time you saw Holly Jo?" he asked without preamble. He didn't like Treyton, never had, and wanted to spend as little time as possible in his company.

The question seemed to take the rancher's son by surprise. "Why?" Stuart waited, and Treyton finally frowned, seemed to think, then said, "A couple of weeks ago. I can't remember. Like I said, I don't live there anymore."

He knew that Treyton had moved out of the ranch house before his friend Cooper had returned from his honeymoon with Tilly Stafford, now McKenna. They were now both living at the house until theirs was finished on the ranch. Treyton's dislike for the Staffords was legendary.

A little surprised that Treyton hadn't heard that Holly Jo had been kidnapped, he knew it wouldn't be long before someone in town told him.

"Holly Jo's been kidnapped." He watched Treyton's face. It stayed sullen. Nothing registered in his blue eyes other than impatience.

"What does that have to do with me?"

"Did you kidnap her?"

Treyton blinked and sat up. "*What? Why would I do that?"

"You're at odds with your father."

"That's nothing new."

The sheriff leaned forward, holding Treyton's gaze. "If you know where she is—"

The rancher's son was on his feet. "If my father really thinks I took that brat, then he is more senile than I thought."

He shook his head. "I don't have time for this." He started for the door.

"I'm going to need the address of your new place," Stuart said.

"Better bring a warrant," Treyton said over his shoulder on the way out of the office.

"I'll let the Feds know to bring one," he called after him. They both knew he didn't have enough evidence to get a warrant. As he watched Treyton storm out, he couldn't shake the feeling that this wasn't Holden's eldest son's doing, and he needed to move on to the next name on the list.

CHAPTER TWELVE

CHARLOTTE FELT GUILTY at how relieved she'd been when she'd returned to the ranch and Brand wasn't there. She knew she was avoiding the inevitable. She'd never thought of herself as a coward, but at this moment, she didn't feel strong enough to face all her sins. She had no idea what she would say to him anyway. That she was embarrassed surprised her. Facing her grown son and admitting the lie she'd let them all—especially Brand and his father—believe and live with seemed an unforgivable betrayal. Holden definitely thought so.

For years, she'd hated Holden for what he'd done to her, betraying her the way he had. Not just once, but over again. And now she'd done something despicable to her own son and his father. She'd lied, not just to them, but to herself. She'd thought better of herself, always having taken the moral high ground. Until she'd seen the way Holden had looked at her today. She hated to imagine the look her son would give her.

As badly as she wanted to wallow in her grief, her regret, her self-disgust, she refused to allow it. She reached for her phone. The plan had come to her after talking to Elaine. Back at the ranch, she'd seen herself as if staring into a mirror. She'd only been thinking of herself, her pain. She hadn't even a thought of anyone else, including Holden's ward, Holly Jo.

Shame heated her cheeks, burned at her soul. A child was missing. She called her ranch manager and asked him to come up to the house.

Boyle Wilson had sounded both surprised and pleased at her request. Most of the time, if she had anything to say to him, she did it out at the stables.

Answering his knock, she opened the door. He pulled off his Western straw hat, wiped his boots on the mat and stepped in. His head under his hat revealed pale scalp beneath his receding hairline in sharp contrast to the deep tan of his face. Farmer's tan, Oakley called it.

Boyle wasn't bad to look at, but there was something in his eyes that had warned her years ago as a girl that he wasn't to be trusted. She would have sacked him when she took over the ranch after her first husband died, but unfortunately, Boyle knew too much, as if he'd been listening outside their doors his whole life. Maybe he didn't know where all the bodies were buried, so to speak, but he knew enough. Still, there were days when she'd fantasized about sending him down the road and letting him do his worst.

"You need me?" he said, a smirk teasing up one side of his mouth.

Charlotte quickly divested him of any thought that this was personal. "I want you to have everyone search every building on the property for a missing girl. Her name is Holly Jo. She's about twelve, thirteen."

Boyle's expression flashed disappointment, then anger. "I'm a ranch manager, not a babysitter for Holden McKenna's kid he says isn't his. Why would you think she's on our property?" he demanded. "You wouldn't be behind this, would you?" He gave her a wink that turned her stomach.

He'd never made it a secret that he had designs on her, which only proved how delusional he was about their relationship. He really did seem to think he knew enough about her and the family that he had job security for life—if not next husband material. She thought how shocked he'd be if he ever tried out that theory in the form of open blackmail.

"I want you to go with our men and make sure that every building is thoroughly searched," she said, as if he hadn't spoken, let alone accused her of kidnapping the child. "I'm depending on you, Boyle." Her last words made him stand up a little taller. "Which means I'm also holding you responsible should you miss one building that happens to have the child in it. I'm going to get other ranchers to do the same. If that girl is still in the Powder River Basin, she would be hidden somewhere away from people. I want her found."

Boyle smirked. "So, I was right. This is about you trying to get in good with Holden McKenna."

She wanted to slap that smirk off his face. "Maybe you didn't hear. Brand was taken into custody as a suspect in the girl's disappearance. I want to make sure no one hid that child on my property." Charlotte met his gaze, daring him to say anything more about Holden, let alone Brand. "That girl is out there somewhere. Only a monster wouldn't want to find her."

He had the good sense to look chastised. If he didn't know that Brand was Holden's son, he would soon enough. It would be the talk of the bar Boyle patronized in town. He stuffed his hat back on his head. "I should get on it, then."

"I'll be offering a reward for the person who finds her alive," Charlotte said as the idea came to her. "Ten thousand dollars." His eyes widened with surprise and a flash of greed. "Get the word out."

As HOLDEN HAD driven away from Lottie, his heart breaking, a memory nudged him hard. Him and Lottie, the two of them at their favorite spot at the creek.

Earlier he couldn't remember, but now he saw it all. It had been a couple of years before he'd married Margie. He and Lottie had been young lovers, both assuming they would marry. But his father had other ideas. Holden had been given an impossible choice. Either marry Margie Smith, the daughter of another neighboring rancher with some property his father wanted, or walk away from the ranch without a penny.

"Without a ranch or any money, we'll see if Charlotte still wants you," his father had said.

Holden had feared his father was right. He'd buckled under the pressure and married Margie. He never told Lottie why. Not that it would have made a difference. She'd never forgiven him—just as he'd never forgiven himself.

But he hadn't been able to get over her. Nor had he been able to stay away from her. With only a creek between their properties, it was too easy to see her. Like the day they must have conceived Brand. After making love, he had left Lottie feeling guilty and ashamed, and yet he couldn't stay with her any more than he could stay away from her. He'd told himself on the way back to the ranch that he couldn't do this any longer. He was going to tell Margie the truth.

That day at the creek, Lottie had wanted him as desperately as he had her. They'd made love, madly and passionately in the grass at the edge of the water—just as they had as teenagers. Afterward... He recalled what he'd told her, because like a lot of his mistakes in life, after seeing her today, he now remembered it only too well. He'd said to her that he was going back to the ranch and telling Margie that he was leaving her.

Lottie had cried, promising to tell her husband, and they'd held each other. They were finally going to be together, come hell or high water. Neither considered the consequences of such a decision. All they could think about was being together.

He remembered how happy Lottie had been. They planned to meet back at the creek the next day. Holden groaned now at the memory. He'd returned to the ranch to tell Margie. She was busy with Treyton, the son they'd had right away. Treyton had never been an easy child, colicky as an infant, irritable and difficult as a toddler.

Charlotte had married Rake Stafford, a man seventeen years her senior, soon after he and Margie had wed. Like Holden and Margie, Charlotte and Rake had also produced a son, Chisum Jase, CJ. Both boys were going through the terrible twos.

Holden remembered feeling guilty about leaving Margie to raise Treyton alone. He swore he'd do what he could to help her, but he had to be with Lottie.

Unfortunately, when he'd reached home that day, she had her own news. She was pregnant. Her father and his own were at the house, everyone celebrating. Margie's father was in such a celebratory mood that he was giving them more of the Smith Ranch. Holden's father couldn't have been happier to hear that.

Holden hadn't been able to tell Margie he was leaving because he'd known then that he couldn't. He felt trapped. The next day, he didn't show up at the creek to meet Lottie as he'd promised. He was too ashamed because he couldn't go through with leaving Margie.

She had been so excited about the baby. None of this had been Margie's fault, he'd told himself. Worse, he'd been a coward. No wonder Lottie hadn't told him that Brand was his when she realized that she was pregnant. *No wonder she's never been able to forgive me.* What he'd done to her and Margie had been unforgivable.

No wonder he'd thought Charlotte might be behind the kidnapping, even as he'd felt guilty for thinking it.

AFTER TALKING WITH TREYTON, Stuart stopped by the McKenna house to see Holden. He'd been upset when his deputy had called to say that the rancher had left the house and had only just returned.

"What if the kidnapper had called?" Stuart demanded once he and Holden were alone in the man's office.

"Elaine would have handled it," the rancher said. "She would probably have done a better job anyway."

Stuart could only shake his head. "Holden, what could have been more important than talking to the kidnapper and finding Holly Jo?"

"I had something I needed to take care of" was all he said.

Stuart could well imagine. The rancher had gone to see Charlotte about Brand. He let it go, still riled up about Lulabelle and why she'd said what she had about his mother. Talking to Treyton had left him even more keyed up.

He studied Holden for a moment, finally seeing how much worse the man looked. Holly Jo's kidnapping and the shock of Brand's parentage were taking a hard toll on the man. Stuart couldn't help feeling sympathetic.

He'd made his own share of mistakes. Some had come back to haunt him. One had almost killed him. He had no right to judge.

"Do you know where Treyton is living?" he asked, reminding himself what was at stake. A young girl's life. "I thought I heard he'd bought some property?"

"He did." Holden's eyes widened. "You think he has Holly Jo?"

Did he? "I don't know." He thought about a raid on the place if Holly Jo wasn't found soon, but his suspicions lacked evidence of wrongdoing. He didn't like Treyton, he didn't trust him, and he figured the eldest McKenna was up to no good, but he couldn't see him taking the girl, could he?

The truth was that he didn't feel any closer to finding Holly Jo. He'd interviewed everyone on Holden's list and had come up with nothing. Holly Jo had been missing for almost twelve long hours. He feared the kidnapper wasn't going to contact them again. The ransom note hadn't said anything about not involving the local law, which surprised him. But he worried his involvement might be what was holding things up.

Or the kidnapper could have changed his mind, had second thoughts, regretted what he'd done. Which meant he would release Holly Jo. Or kill her.

The FBI tech had already warned them that the call might be hard to trace. A call coming from a landline could be traced immediately with the new technology, the tech had explained to Holden. Even a cell phone. "What about the new burner or drop phones, the kind used only once?" Stuart had asked.

"That becomes more difficult to trace. When the number isn't associated with the person we're looking for, we have to triangulate their position off of cell phone towers," he said. "Unfortunately, Montana does not have good cell reception. Roughly sixty-seven thousand square miles have limited access to cellular data. The state has less than three hundred cell towers—but even fewer in your part of the state because of the sparse population of Eastern Montana."

When the call came through on the ranch landline twenty minutes later, Stuart realized they'd all given up hope. No wonder they were startled when the phone finally rang and it was the kidnapper. "We need to clear everyone out of the room except Holden." The sheriff had already given the rancher a script to follow, telling him exactly what to say with the help of the FBI.

The landline rang again. Stuart informed the technician. Holden took the call. The voice on the other end was obviously disguised, making it impossible to tell whether it was a man or a woman. Without preamble, the kidnapper began to read from his own script.

"You will notify news media and hold the announcement at the ranch. It will be televised as well as announced on the radio. You will admit what you did. You have twenty-four hours. If you don't do this, you will never see the girl again."

Stuart nodded to Holden to say what he'd been instructed.

"I'm going to need proof that you have Holly Jo and that she is okay."

"What do you want? A toe? Or maybe a finger?"

"I wouldn't suggest that," Holden said, going off script. "Not if you want to keep breathing." The sheriff shook his head fiercely at him.

"You would dare threaten me?" The fury in the

kidnapper's voice turned Stuart's blood to ice. He motioned to Holden to fix this.

"I need to know that Holly Jo is all right," the rancher said. "She's just a child." This time his voice cracked with emotion, although he appeared to be gritting his teeth. The sheriff worried that Holden couldn't take much more without alienating the kidnapper. The rancher's free hand was fisted at his side.

Stuart pointed to the script he'd given him. Holden said, "I need a photo of her with today's paper to prove that she is all right."

The laugh was eerie and frightening. "And where would I get a newspaper?"

"I'll give you my cell phone number." He read it off. "You can send me a photo from your phone that shows today's date."

Silence, then finally, "If you don't go public within the twenty-four hours after you get the photo, you know what happens." The kidnapper was gone.

"Did you get him?" Stuart asked when he contacted the technician.

"Tried to triangulate, didn't have much luck. All I can tell you is that he or she is still in the Powder River Basin. Used a burner phone. But should be able to send a photo on it that will show the date." Stuart hung up.

"I'm sorry," Holden said to him, clearly still furious. "That bastard has Holly Jo and is putting us all through hell. That son of a bitch is going to pay."

"I can see how hard this is," the sheriff said. "But the object is to get Holly Jo back, and then we'll deal with the kidnapper."

"The kidnapper's right. Where would he get a newspaper if he has Holly Jo somewhere around here?" Elaine said. "Printed newspapers are scarcer than hen's teeth nowadays. With luck, he might be able to find a *Billings Gazette*, but wouldn't be able to buy a recent one in Powder Crossing."

"Which is the good news," Stuart said. "It could mean that the kidnapper has Holly Jo somewhere close—and he knows the area."

The sheriff told himself that if Holly Jo was all right, they should be getting a photo of her soon. Otherwise... He refused to think of otherwise.

CHAPTER THIRTEEN

BAILEY CAME INTO the McKenna Ranch house and looked around as if surprised to see the sheriff in her father's office. "What's going on?" she asked, looking from Stuart to her father and back. Her long dark, wavy hair was pulled back, making her blue eyes seem larger, more luminous. Beautiful but wild, Holden's nearly thirty-year-old daughter seemed to be a mystery to everyone who knew her—maybe especially to the sheriff.

"Didn't you get my message?" Holden demanded.

"I haven't checked my phone." She sounded testy.

Stuart wondered why she still lived on the ranch in the home she'd grown up in. He knew from her brother Cooper that she came and went at all hours. She spent so little time here, her brother had wondered if she was living somewhere else, with someone else.

The sheriff had long wondered what kept her in the Powder River Basin. At one point, he'd thought it might be him, but lately she hadn't been coming around after months of showing up at his house unexpectedly.

She'd always just seemed to want a cold one and to talk as if curious about all manner of things—as if she was just killing time. She would curl up on his couch, drink a beer, ask him what he thought about a wide range of subjects from extraterrestrial beings and marriage to politics and local gossip. Then she would leave.

He'd thought she was lonely and just needed someone to talk to. He hadn't complained about her unannounced appearances because he'd enjoyed her visits, had gotten to the point that he looked forward to them. Then they'd stopped as abruptly as they'd started, and he'd feared that she'd finally packed up and left not just the area, but the state.

She'd never taken to ranching or Powder Crossing. Stuart remembered the girl she'd been, quiet, her face always in a book. But he'd gotten the impression that she was more aware of what was going on around her than people knew. Why she'd come back after graduating from college was a mystery, although he had a theory. He knew the look of a broken heart mixed with disillusion and disappointment. He'd been there, so he'd recognized it in the young woman who'd returned to Powder Crossing. He'd figured she'd come home to heal and then would be gone. But she was still here. Kind of.

"Holly Jo's been kidnapped," Holden said, emotion making his voice rough. "We're trying to find her and get her back."

"Kidnapped?" Bailey chuckled nervously. *"Why?"*

"What do you mean, why?" her father demanded.

"Why would anyone want to kidnap *her*?"

It was an odd question, Stuart thought, since it seemed obvious to him. Holly Jo was Holden McKenna's ward, Holden was wealthy, and Holly Jo was a child, easier to keep and control. "You think they should have taken you instead?" Stuart asked.

Bailey shifted those blue eyes to him. He caught the flash of amusement in them. "Why not? I'm McKenna blood, Holden's only daughter, the light of his life."

He heard the raw exposed sarcasm as she tried to

mask hurt. Stuart figured her father must have heard it as well. Bailey hadn't been happy about her father bringing home a then-twelve-year-old without any explanation as to why he had or what Holly Jo meant to him, according to Cooper.

"Do you know anything about Holly Jo's kidnapping?" the sheriff had to ask her.

She shot him a look as lethal as the business end of a shotgun. "Of course not. I've been so busy, I've barely seen the girl." Her look dared him to disagree. She hadn't been busy with him, not for some time now. He had to wonder what Bailey *had* been doing. No one seemed to know, especially her family.

"Is there any reason you'd want to see her gone?" he asked.

Bailey's lips formed a hard, thin line, eyes darkening. "I didn't kidnap her. Why would I?" She shook her head. "Sorry, wasn't me, but…" She shot her father a look. "I will be interested to find out who *did* kidnap her and why. If there is nothing else…" She was looking at Stuart again, a promise in her gaze stirring a need inside him that he'd been ignoring for months. The memory of another woman trying to kill him had made him gun-shy. He could see that Bailey enjoyed stirring up his libido and watching him squirm—enjoyed it much more than he did.

She'd been playing some game with him for a while now. He wondered how it ended. He figured there was no way he wouldn't come out the loser. It was the way his history with women always ended. Except Bailey was different, he told himself. She wanted something more from him. He just didn't know what it was yet.

"I'll never understand that girl," Holden said as Bailey went to her room.

"She's not a girl anymore," Stuart said, also watching her leave.

"That's what makes her even more dangerous."

The sheriff heard the warning in the rancher's voice even before the rancher voiced it.

"You don't want to get involved with that one," Holden said. "I don't know what makes her so angry, but she's a man-eater."

Stuart agreed with Holden about her being dangerous. She was the kind of woman a man would have to be a fool to fall in love with. If he thought he'd had his heart ripped out of his chest before, he hated to think what Bailey McKenna would do if he let her get to him.

IT DIDN'T TAKE long for word to spread. Charlotte had called area ranchers, asking for their help and telling them that Holly Jo had been kidnapped. She was offering a reward for anyone who found her.

She knew the sheriff would be furious with her for not checking with him before doing this, but by now, she suspected everyone had already heard the news about the kidnapping anyway. Not surprisingly, the first call she got was from Stuart. "I'm not sure a reward is a good idea—let alone telling everyone in the county that Holly Jo has been kidnapped."

"Isn't this the fastest way to find her if she is still in this river basin?"

The sheriff sighed. "The kidnapper is bound to hear about this. If he panics, he might do something we will all regret. He might also demand money now. Before, he said he just wanted Holden to admit to something he's done."

"I'm sure your list of suspects is very long."

"Your name was at the top."

"Stuart, you don't believe I kidnapped that girl. Everyone knows what Holden did to me. Anyway, he has already admitted it many times."

"Brand might not feel the same. Have you talked to him?"

"Not yet, but I know my son. He would never kidnap anyone, especially some young girl. I thought he had an alibi, anyway. You're looking in the wrong place."

"Where would you suggest I look?"

"Did Holden tell you how he came to be Holly Jo's guardian?" Silence. She chuckled. "That's what I thought. Seems you already know where to look."

After Charlotte hung up with the sheriff, her eldest daughter called. Even six months ago, that wouldn't have been a surprise. But since Cooper McKenna returned to town after being gone for two years and stole Tilly's heart, the two had gotten married. Charlotte had tried to stop it from happening by disowning her daughter, taking the one thing Tilly loved maybe as much as Cooper away from her—the Stafford Ranch.

But not even that could get her daughter to change her mind, so Charlotte had lost her. They hadn't spoken, not even at the wedding, which Charlotte had attended but quickly left after Tilly and Cooper were wed.

"I just heard what you did," Tilly said without preamble.

"That covers a lot of ground," Charlotte said, unable to tell by her daughter's tone how this call would go.

"I suppose it does," Tilly said and cleared her throat.

"The reward and getting ranchers to search for Holly Jo. Thank you for doing that."

"I needed to do something. I only hope the girl is found safe and quickly." Silence. Charlotte could feel her daughter wanting to hang up, maybe even regretting this call. She desperately wished she could take back the hateful things she'd said the last time she spoke to Tilly. "Your wedding was beautiful."

"Thank you. I'm glad you were there."

"You invited me."

"But I wasn't sure you would come."

More silence.

"How are you?" Charlotte asked, not wanting the call to end.

"Good. Cooper and I are building our house. I'm sure you've heard."

"You must be excited." She hoped that if Tilly was pregnant, she might mention it.

"I should go. Cooper and I are helping with the search."

"I'm glad you called." She wasn't sure Tilly was still there. "I...I love you." Silence. Her daughter had hung up.

Charlotte disconnected, surprised at the emotion she felt. She hadn't realized how much she'd missed Tilly, how much she'd missed hearing her voice. She swallowed the lump that had formed in her throat as her phone rang yet again. This time it was another rancher, calling to say they'd searched all their buildings. No Holly Jo.

Soon it would be too dark to search any longer. Charlotte still held out hope that the girl would be found before tonight. She couldn't imagine who had her, and she worried the girl wasn't safe. She hated to think that Holly Jo would have to spend a night away from her family with God only knew who.

"WE HAVE TO quit meeting like this," Birdie said as she and Brand attracted attention the moment they walked into the café. "People are going to start talking."

"Too late for that, no thanks to you." Brand wasn't sure if people were staring at them because they'd heard that he'd been arrested here earlier today, dragged out of the café in handcuffs, and that he'd been with Birdie Malone, the daughter of the deceased husband of Brand's mother, who was also his suspected killer.

But everyone in the café could be staring at him because they now knew that he was the result of Holden McKenna and Charlotte Stafford's affair over thirty years ago. Then again, there were those who had to be wondering if he'd kidnapped Holly Jo.

He tried not to groan. "I may have to leave the country."

Birdie laughed. "Chin up. Let them speculate. Enjoy the attention."

"I've never enjoyed attention. I like flying under the radar," he said.

Why had he agreed to meet her here? Because he still wasn't ready to see his mother. He wasn't sure he ever would be. He'd heard what she'd done, offering a reward and getting area ranchers to search the buildings on their property for Holly Jo. Had she done that because of him? He had no idea what motivated his mother and didn't even want to speculate.

His brothers had called, CJ collect from the jail, Ryder from the ranch. He hadn't taken either of their calls, just as he hadn't taken Tilly's. Fortunately, Oakley was on an extended honeymoon with her husband and McKenna ranch hand, Pickett Hanson. The two had eloped—Oakley's idea, he would bet—and taken a long honeymoon. He wondered if they would ever come back. He knew he wouldn't if he was them.

Birdie picked up her menu. "It will blow over. Trust me, I've gone through worse than this with my mother."

He looked at her in surprise. "I'm sorry."

"Don't be. Adversity only makes you stronger." She disappeared behind her menu. "I'm thinking I'll have the chicken-fried steak, mashed potatoes with gravy and green beans special," she said, attempting to change the subject as she put down her menu. It only made him wonder what her life had been like. "Don't give me that poor-you look. You've been coddled your whole life. Obviously, you haven't had enough adversity. But look at the bright side. Now you're related to Holden McKenna. People actually like *him*."

Brand shook his head, unable not to smile. The waitress came over, and as they ordered, he found himself studying Birdie Malone. "You do have an unusual take on most things," he said after the waitress left. "I would think you'd be bitter."

She laughed. "Who says I'm not? Don't forget why I'm in town."

"Right. To see my mother behind bars."

"And to find the accomplice who helped her. So tell me about Holden McKenna," Birdie said, leaping to the next subject.

Brand shook his head. He figured that along with her quest, she was trying to keep his mind off everything, especially Holly Jo's disappearance. They'd brainstormed ideas on how to find the girl—none of them viable since neither of them knew Holly Jo or who had taken her, let alone where someone might hide her.

"How would I know anything about Holden Mc-Kenna?" he said, not unkindly. "Our families have been at war for years. I just found out that he's my father."

"I thought your sister Tilly married a McKenna."

"Yeah, Cooper." He was reminded of the DNA sample he'd borrowed from his now half brother's comb. "But that's a new occurrence, and we're still feeling the repercussions of the marriage, even though our mother did show up at the wedding but quickly left once the official part was over."

"Ah yes, your mother. This all started with her, right? Your father dumped her. Now she hates his guts and has sworn to make his life miserable until she dies. Or goes to prison for killing my father."

"Seriously, the way you put things," he said, eyeing her. "Are you always this blunt?"

"I try to be," she admitted.

He studied her openly. Her dark hair was pulled up into a messy knot on the side of her head. Her gray eyes fascinated him the way they changed color with her moods. Right now they were a light, mischievous pale gray. Her face, all button nose and high cheekbones, was pretty, but he could see her growing into a real beauty with age. "I've never met anyone like you."

"Sounds like that's a good thing."

He chuckled. "You might be right." Their meals came, and they dug in.

"There's still no word on Holly Jo?" She switched topics so quickly it gave him whiplash.

"Not that I've heard," he said.

"If you didn't kidnap her, then who?" she asked between bites.

"I have no idea. I've never even met her. But while the sheriff let me go, I got the distinct impression that he's suspicious of my…" He held her gaze. *"Alibi."*

"You mean he's suspicious of me."

He cocked his head. "I suspect he thinks you have a crush on me."

"A crush? How junior high."

"What would you call the fact that you can't seem to stay away from me?"

She rolled her eyes at him. "Let's see—could I be using you to get to your mother?"

"That does sound more likely."

"Doesn't it, though." She leaned toward him. "Look, the way I see it, the only way you're going to prove your innocence is for me to help you find Holly Jo."

"We already decided we haven't a clue how to do that."

"We go visit your former stepmother, the psychic one."

"Lulabelle?" He mugged a face. "I think you mean psychotic."

"I've heard people say that she's quite good as a seer."

He shook his head. "You can't be serious."

"What do you have to lose? The sooner that girl is found, the sooner we can get back to what I came to Powder Crossing for."

"You seem to think I'm going to help you find your father's killer."

She smiled. "Oh, I've already found her. But I want her accomplice, too. And how can you not help me after I've sprung you from the jail? Anyway, you can't pretend you have no idea who murdered him and dumped him in a well near your ranch."

"I'm so glad you're keeping an open mind," he shot back.

"Like you about Lulabelle?"

The waitress appeared to take their empty plates and ask if they wanted dessert. Brand had no doubt that she'd overheard at least the last part of the conversation. "Penny," he said to her as she picked up their dishes. "I didn't kidnap anyone, okay?"

"I never thought you did. You do look like your father, though. I wonder how I never noticed that before." With that, she turned and left.

Birdie laughed. "See, not everyone thinks you're a kidnapper. Probably half the people in this café are only wondering which side of your family you took after, Holden's or your mother's."

"Thanks," he said. "That makes me feel so much better." He sobered, afraid she was right. Until Holly Jo was found, people would be looking at him thinking he just might have taken after his mother.

"You must have some idea who'd want to get back at your father. Who has a grudge against him, besides your mother?"

He pulled out his wallet to pay for their meals. "I told you. I have no idea."

"Who feels he owes them? What about his second wife?"

"Not Lulabelle again." He handed the bills to Penny as she returned before answering Birdie. "The marriage apparently lasted about a year, decades ago. So that begs the question—why wait all this time to get back at him?"

"That's a good question," Birdie said, frowning. "Maybe whatever the kidnapper wants your dad to admit happened more recently."

He shook his head, no idea. He had too much on his mind, with Holly Jo at the top of that list. He was still reeling from finding out that Holden was his father. Not to mention the prospect of eventually confronting his mother. And he was suspected of kidnapping and could still be in jail if it hadn't been for Birdie. All this time with her was crowding his thoughts.

"We need to go see Lulabelle." He started to argue the point when she cut him off. "But first we need an item of clothing or something that belonged to Holly Jo. Which means we have to find the sheriff. I heard they used some of her clothing with search dogs near the ranch."

"Lulabelle supports herself as a fortune teller. That's not the same as being able to see…things."

"I had a friend who went to her booth at the fair," Birdie said. "Lulabelle told her that she was going to meet someone who would change her life." Brand groaned. "The next day, just like that, she met a man who gave her the job of her dreams." Birdie looked up, a twinkle in her eye. "Thought this was going to be a love story, didn't you."

Brand shook his head again as they rose to leave the café.

"Seriously, maybe Lulabelle can help."

"Don't you think the sheriff has already talked to her since she and Holden were married and it ended badly? I would think she would be a prime suspect."

"I think it is more likely that you're the prime suspect even with my alibi. So right now you need to take my advice." She grinned as she took his arm. "Why else would you be hanging out with me?"

She had a point, he thought as he pushed open the café door and stepped out into the warm summer night. Montana was at its best this time of year. It was when people fell in love with it. Also when people fell in love, period.

Why was he spending so much time with this woman? She wasn't his type, if he had a type. But tonight, the idea of going to Miles City, an hour away, to visit Lulabelle had its appeal since it would get them out of town. He could avoid seeing his mother a little longer. He figured she felt the same way since she hadn't called or made an attempt to see him.

He still felt angry with himself, going back and forth between wishing he'd found out sooner about his parentage and wishing he'd never found his biological father. Given the way he was feeling, leaving Powder Crossing for a while seemed like a really good idea, especially if there was even a chance it could help Holly Jo. He was worried about the girl as darkness settled into the Powder River Basin.

HOLLY JO LAY drifting as if weightless in the darkness. She wasn't sure what had awakened her. She couldn't hear anything. She could see through the cracks in the boards on the window that it was nighttime. Her first night here? She couldn't be sure. She felt as if she'd been here for days.

Sitting up, she felt sick to her stomach. She had awakened with a heart-pounding fear whenever she opened her eyes that this wasn't just a bad dream, that this was real and that she would never be found.

Why was she here? What did the man want? When was this going to be over? She tried to calm the frightening thoughts, reminding herself that so far, she hadn't been asked to do anything. He'd brought her food. Chicken nuggets, fries, coleslaw and juice.

He'd left the paper plate and the plastic spoon she'd used. No forks. Not even a plastic knife. Too dangerous? But everything had been gone when she opened her eyes again—except for another bottle of juice.

She worried that he might be fattening her up like they did the pigs on the ranch. She knew what happened when they were fat enough. She couldn't imagine that she would taste good. Probably tough, so chewy that he'd have to spit her back out.

What bothered her was that the man seemed to be waiting for something.

The last time he'd come back, she had braced herself for the worst, but he'd only returned to bring her a mat to sleep on and a couple of old blankets—and, as always, another juice. She couldn't remember when that was. She'd been grateful for the extra blankets, but at the same time, she worried that it meant she would be staying here even longer.

"Thought you might like this." He put down a paper plate with a piece of chocolate cake on it. "She made it for you."

Holly Jo figured he was talking about the woman from the pickup, the one who'd called her over so he could grab her. It was hard to feel touched by her kindness. Still, she said, "Thank you," remembering how her mother had taught her, before her mother had gotten so sick that she barely spoke.

Holly Jo had waited until he left again before she'd devoured the cake. It wasn't as good as the cakes Elaine baked. But still, she ate every bite and drank most of her juice.

Later, she wished she hadn't, because she started to feel strange and had to lie down on the mat and cover herself up to keep from shivering.

Now she lay feeling groggy as she wondered again what had pulled her out of the deep darkness of her sleep. Listening hard, she finally heard it. The murmur of voices. Moving to the door, she pressed her ear against the narrow gap between door and wall. Had someone found her?

Her heart began to pound with hope. But as she listened, she realized it was a man and a woman speaking. She couldn't make out what was being said, but she recognized the man's voice. One thing was clear. They were arguing.

She was surprised the man hadn't come alone like he usually did. Even when she was half asleep, she would hear him walk up to the door and stand there as if listening. Then she would hear the key in the lock, and the door would swing open. He would stay behind the door as if afraid of her. He always seemed surprised to see her, especially when she was awake, as if he expected to find her dead.

They were arguing louder now, the man's voice low, the woman's growing shrill. "We need money! How will we live without it?" the woman cried.

Money? Then Holly Jo heard the words *ransom demand*.

That was the first time she'd realized that she might have been kidnapped for money. She and her mother had always been poor. Maybe not poor exactly, but broke. HH was rich.

Had these two taken her to demand money from him? Holly Jo instantly felt panicky. Would Holden pay? She thought of all the trouble she'd given him from the first day he'd brought her to the ranch. What if he didn't give them what they asked for?

She felt tears burn her eyes. But even if Holden didn't want to pay, she told herself that Cooper and Pickett would make him. Except Pickett was on his honeymoon with Oakley. For sure, Elaine would make HH pay the ransom, she told herself. Not Treyton, though. He would argue that the kidnappers should keep her. But Duffy wouldn't let his father do that. The pain in her chest began to ease. HH would pay to get her back, even as bad as she'd been.

She promised herself that if she got to go back to McKenna Ranch, she'd be good. She wouldn't cause trouble. She'd eat beef for the rest of her life if she could just go home.

CHAPTER FOURTEEN

THE SHERIFF SHOULDN'T have been surprised when Birdie Malone and Brand Stafford tracked him down. He'd been working the kidnapping case without food or rest and wasn't in the mood for whatever these two were up to.

"We need something of Holly Jo's," Birdie told him. "We're going to take it to Lulabelle to see if she can help."

He groaned. "I don't have time for this." He started to walk away.

"I know you used some clothing items of hers with the dogs at the school bus stop." He didn't need to be reminded that nothing had come of that. "Surely we could have one item of hers—"

"You need to let law enforcement do its job and stay out of this. Anyway, I already talked to Lulabelle. She wasn't any help."

"Did you give her something of Holly Jo's?" His expression must have given him away. "That's what I thought," Birdie said. "Please. Isn't finding the girl what we all want?"

He'd sworn under his breath and started to tell her that he didn't have anything handy, when he remembered the small stuffed duck he'd picked up in Holly Jo's room, bagged and put into his pocket.

With a sigh, he reached into his coat, pulled the bagged duck free and held it out to her. "Anything else, Ms. Malone?" As tired, worried and scared as he was about this case, it wouldn't have taken much for him to go off on Birdie Malone.

"No, this will do."

He reminded himself that she had given him the one and only lead they had in the case. "Now leave me alone." Let her take the duck to Lulabelle. It would get her out of his hair.

As he watched her walk back to her SUV, he saw that Brand was sitting in the passenger seat. What was it with these two? He'd been shocked when Birdie had offered Stafford an alibi. The alibi became even more suspect seeing the two of them together again. Hadn't Deputy Dodson said they were together at the café when he'd picked up Brand? He shook his head, reminding himself that the only thing that mattered was finding Holly Jo.

"I'll bring it back," Birdie called as she climbed behind the wheel of the SUV.

He started to call back, "Let me know if Lulabelle—" but stopped himself. He didn't think the woman knew any more about the kidnapping than he did at this point. Which was nothing that could save Holly Jo.

BIRDIE LIKED THE idea of surprising Lulabelle even at this late hour. She liked catching people unaware. She thought it made them more honest, although she had no proof that was true. She just remembered how her mother acted when she answered the door to an unexpected social worker or bill collector.

While she'd heard about Lulabelle, she'd never seen

her up close until the woman opened her door. Her mass of bottle-red hair appeared to have been caught in a cyclone. Her blue eyes were half-closed. A crease was left in one cheek from having fallen asleep on something wrinkled. She wore hot-pink sweats and a large tie-dyed T-shirt. Her feet, toes painted a variety of bright colors, were bare.

Lulabelle blinked, her gaze going from Birdie to Brand and back again. Her deep, raspy voice boomed when she spoke. "Wrong time of year for Girl Scout cookies."

"I'm Brand McKenna," he said. "This is Birdie Malone. Her father was—"

"Murdered and dumped in a well." Eyes now wide-open, Lulabelle let out a donkey laugh. "Wow. To what do I owe this honor so late at night?"

"It's only ten twenty," Birdie said.

Lulabelle chuckled. "Spoken like the young thing you are." Stepping back, she said, "You'd better come in."

"Aren't you going to ask us why we're here?" While Brand had asked the question, it was Birdie the older woman looked at. She winked and grinned.

"You need my help," Lulabelle said and waved them into her house. The decor was much like the woman, loud, colorful and over-the-top. Birdie liked it, but she could tell that Brand was taken aback, reminding her how different their environments and situations had been growing up.

The woman motioned them to two overstuffed colorful chairs. The room was full of almost a dozen of them, all different colors and shapes scattered around the large living room. No couch or end tables or much floor space—just chairs.

"You have a lot of friends?" Birdie asked as she picked a club chair in purple, yellow and black stripes. Brand, she noticed, had taken a brown-and-white animal-print one.

Lulabelle dropped into a lime-green high-back chair, tucking her bare feet under her. "I just like chairs. I see one I like…" She shrugged. "But you didn't come here to talk about my decor."

Birdie couldn't help but like the woman and her idiosyncrasies because, in Lulabelle's case, they weren't for show. "We need your help in finding Holly Jo Robinson," she said, since Brand was busy glancing around as if questioning why she'd thought coming here was a good idea.

"Robinson? That's the name she goes by? Huh. The sheriff didn't mention that when he stopped here," Lulabelle said and shook her head. "I can't believe Holden thought I had taken the child. He should know I'm more direct than that. If I wanted something from him, I'd tell him to his face." She laughed. "I've done it enough times."

Birdie reached into her purse and took out the bag with the small stuffed duck inside. "This is Holly Jo's."

Lulabelle took the bag as if it contained something rare and fragile. She looked at Birdie, then at Brand, before she slowly unzipped the bag. She bent, took a whiff and closed her eyes. Birdie watched her.

She didn't know if this woman was clairvoyant or not. But she firmly believed that everyone had at least a little sixth sense. Most people didn't recognize it. She thought about her father and their connection. She'd felt that connection snap all those years ago. She'd only been a child, but she had been able to feel his presence even apart. Until that one night.

Lulabelle was still breathing in the duck, eyes closed. Brand looked ready to leave as he slid forward a little in his chair. Birdie wasn't finished yet. "Do you have any idea where she might be or who might have taken her?"

"She's alive," Lulabelle said, opening her eyes. "I can't tell you where she is… It's dark." She seemed to hesitate before she took another deep breath and closed her eyes again. She sat perfectly still. "She's still in the Powder Crossing area. Near the mountains. The building… I can't… It seems to be abandoned, but not for very long… I smell sour milk." She opened her eyes. "A milking barn?"

Lulabelle looked down at the toy, then up at them. She must have seen their disappointment since her description fit a lot of the ranches and farms in the basin area and in all of rural Montana.

"She's safe," the seer said. Her unspoken words seemed to hang in the air. *For now.* Her expression was grim as she met Birdie's gaze. "She's afraid. She thinks he plans to kill her. And she might be right."

Birdie felt a chill. The message was clear. Holly Jo had to be found—and soon.

On the way back from Miles City, Brand knew he'd put it off as long as he could. It was time to go home to the ranch. "I have to see my mother," he told Birdie as she dropped him off at his pickup after their visit to Lulabelle. He stood in the open door of her SUV, finding it hard to know what to say. They'd already been through a lot together, and yet they didn't really know each other.

Fate had thrown them together, but he had no idea

why. He found himself fighting his attraction to her. She intrigued him, but at the same time, she was trouble he didn't need. That he'd never met anyone like Birdie was putting it mildly. He never knew what she would do next.

He'd spent his life keeping his head down, avoiding drama, staying in his lane. Birdie was just the opposite. She was a wrecking ball, and she'd come to town to destroy his family.

"You aren't going to get into any kind of trouble, are you?" he asked.

She laughed. "Like come sneaking around your ranch again?"

He wouldn't have put it past her. Something told him she didn't have a plan, instead tended to wing it as the mood struck her. How could he be attracted to someone so not like him? Not to mention the fact that his mother had been married to her father—not that it made them related exactly. He couldn't let himself forget why she was in Powder Crossing. Or what she planned to do before she left.

"You look worried," she said, studying him openly. "Something bothering you?"

He let out a bark of a laugh. "Just thinking what an unlikely pair we are."

She grinned. "We must look pretty good together, because everyone seems to be staring at us."

Glancing around, he saw at least that part was true. There were several couples outside the bar smoking. They all looked in his and Birdie's direction with interest before talking among themselves. He hated to think what the locals were saying, and he doubted they knew the half of it.

"We should exchange cell phone numbers, don't you think?" she said.

He hesitated, but told himself he'd rather know what she was up to than be surprised. He handed over his phone. She entered her number, texted herself from his phone, then handed it back. "Call me," she said. "And good luck with your mom."

"Right." He let out a sigh.

"I'll only be a phone call away," she said, then added, "Or closer."

He chuckled and shut the passenger door of her SUV. *Birdie Malone*, he thought and shook his head, but he was smiling as he climbed into his pickup and drove out to the ranch.

As Brand pulled up to the ranch house, he saw his mother's SUV parked out front and lights still on in the house. He'd never wanted to have this conversation and still didn't know what he was going to say. What was there to say? He was the son of Holden, the man his mother had reputedly hated for years.

He and his siblings had grown up under the dark cloud of her bitterness toward Holden and his family. Brand couldn't blame everything on his mother. After his trial, CJ would probably be on his way to prison. But life certainly would have been more pleasant without the Stafford-McKenna rivalry since they were neighbors, with only a creek between their two ranches.

But all of that was ancient history, Brand told himself. Just like his conception. It had happened. The question was, where did they go now?

He opened the front door, feeling almost as if he should have knocked. But he was still living here, still welcome here. At least, he thought so. Then again, except for Ryder, the rest of his siblings had already left—either because their mother had thrown them out or they'd gone to jail or they'd escaped through marriage. Brand wondered how much longer he could live here.

The moment he stepped in, he saw her. Charlotte Stafford, tall and willowy like the empress overseeing her realm. Her long blond hair was reined into a braid that fell more than halfway down her back. He saw more gray threaded through it than he had noticed before.

She turned as he entered the house, looking as if she'd been waiting for him, wearing her ready-for-battle expression.

"Mother," he said, surprised at the bubble of anger that welled up at the sight of her. Maybe he should have waited longer before confronting her.

Something flickered in her emerald green eyes. Fear? It was gone in an instant. She would have prepared herself for this, built up her defenses. Hell, she probably had practiced what she was going to say. He was no match for her, never had been.

He started for his end of the wing and his room when she said, "We aren't even going to talk about it?"

Brand stopped and turned back to her. "There really isn't anything to say, is there?"

She opened her mouth, but then closed it for a moment before she said, "I'm sorry you had to find out this way."

He nodded.

"I'm sure you were shocked."

"I'm not sure how I feel about it. No, that's not true. I've always wondered why I was so different from the rest of you in this family. I even suspected when I got older that my real father was Holden. If anything, what was shocking was having it confirmed and then doing the math. How am I supposed to feel about my father being a man you have openly despised and disparaged all my life? But I think it's the hypocrisy that is the hardest to take."

"I don't know what to say."

He shook his head and turned to walk away, but not before he heard her last words.

"I love your father. I always have. I love *you*." The last three words ended in what sounded like a sob. Except that he'd never seen his mother cry. And wondered if he'd imagined it.

CHAPTER FIFTEEN

STUART HAD BEEN hoping for a break in the case. There had still been no word from the kidnapper since the earlier call and Stuart's demand for proof of life. Nor had he heard back on Holly Jo's father's death from the Billings police force. Area ranchers were still searching old buildings on their property. Still no sign of Holly Jo. With every passing minute, they were losing valuable time as well as losing hope of finding Holly Jo alive.

Was Holly Jo already dead? He had a BOLO out for a white pickup with a red camper that had been seen in the area the night before the kidnapping. So far nothing but dead ends.

He hadn't slept well, the nightmares worse than usual. Even in daylight, he felt the weight of them, making the waiting for some kind of news unbearable. He felt angry, out of sorts, scared, knowing that he needed to keep his mind on the kidnapping case—not sort through the rubbish of his childhood. Lulabelle had hit a nerve, and she'd known it. Trying to prove to him that she had some gift?

He'd been digging through Holden McKenna's past looking for dirt. He hadn't found anything worth kidnapping an innocent girl over and he'd already worked his way through the list Holden had given him. He couldn't shake the feeling that the rancher hadn't been straight with him.

At the McKenna Ranch, he found Holden in his office. "Tell me you aren't holding back on me."

Holden shot to his feet, his face twisted in anger. He didn't look as if he'd gotten much sleep either. "Do you really think I would do something like that? If I knew who was behind this, no matter how bad it was for me, I would have told you the moment I saw those ransom notes. I don't know who has her, let alone what he wants."

Stuart could tell that the waiting was getting to the rancher as well. "If you really don't know, then how are you going to make an announcement?"

Holden wagged his head. "It has to be about Holly Jo's father. You've tried to find out if Bobby had any relatives?"

"I haven't found any. But, Holden, I'm depending on you to keep your cool no matter what we find out."

"All I care about is finding Holly Jo and getting her home safely."

"What about the person who took her?"

The sheriff saw the change in the rancher's expression. "I'll let you handle that."

It was a lie and they both knew it, but Stuart didn't call him on it. They would find Holly Jo, then deal with the kidnapper.

In the meantime, they were all on pins and needles waiting for the proof-of-life photo. Then the clock would start running on Holden making the announcement. Stuart feared the reason the kidnapper hadn't sent it yet was that Holly Jo was no longer alive.

He fought the fear, but if they didn't get the photo soon...

Stuart's cell rang, startling him. He shook his head at Holden's questioning look. Not the kidnapper. Instead, it was the call he'd been waiting for from the Billings Police Department. Stepping outside for privacy, he quickly picked up.

"You inquired about Robert Robinson?" the cop asked. He rattled off Robinson's date of birth—and death.

"He fell from The Rims, right?" the sheriff asked.

"Died on impact when his head struck a boulder, according to the coroner's report. His death was ruled an accident since apparently he'd been alone at the time and his blood alcohol concentration was over the legal limit. At least, he appeared to have been alone, since no one came forward after the accident."

"What about next of kin?" Stuart asked and listened to the man tapping on his computer keys.

"The body was identified by his wife," the cop said. She was apparently pregnant at the time with Holly Jo, according to Holden.

"What about an obit? I couldn't find one."

"Sorry. I don't believe there was one."

Stuart considered that. No obit, no funeral? Odd since he did have a wife and child. "Where was the body taken?"

"Sanderson Funeral Home here in Billings."

HOLLY JO WOKE, her mouth dry, her eyes caked shut. She rubbed at them. She'd been sleeping so much, too much. Her head hurt, and she felt funny. Realization came slowly. They must be putting something in her food or maybe the juice they brought her. With a start, she realized that the juice had always been opened when she got it.

The knowledge made her angry at her kidnappers, but even more angry at herself. Everyone said she was smart.

Her mother, her teachers, Holden, Cooper, Pickett and Elaine. Even Duffy had said she was smart, although he seemed surprised that she might be smart.

Well, if she was so smart, how had she not noticed that she was being drugged? Ahh, *ding*, she thought—because she'd been drugged since the moment her kidnapper had grabbed her. Guiltily she realized that she hadn't minded falling asleep after she drank the juice. What else did she have to do? Staying awake, all she did was worry, fearing that she would never be found or that the man would kill her or worse.

Now she knew that she'd been kidnapped for money.

But even if HH did pay, the man might not let her go. She'd seen the woman. She would recognize her if she ever saw her again. How could he let her go?

She'd lost track of her original thought and had to wind her brain back to the juice and whatever must have been put in it. She wouldn't drink it again. Even when it didn't put her to sleep, it still made her feel weak, her brain foggy, and it was hard to move. She would dump it down the drain in the floor. She hated to do that, though. The juice was the one thing she looked forward to since he brought it with every meal.

But if she wasn't knocked out all the time, she reasoned, maybe she could find a way to escape. She wished Gus was here. He would help her. He thought she was smart. He also said that she was creative and clever and talented.

Maybe Duffy was right. Maybe Gus did have a crush on her. Would Gus miss her now that school was out for the summer? She wondered if she would ever see him again. If she would ever see anyone she knew. She didn't even know how long she'd been in this room.

She'd seen a movie where the abducted man had made marks on the wall so he knew how many days he'd been trapped. When the man brought her food again, she would try to use the plastic spoon to make a mark on the wall. Or dig herself out of this room. She was thinking that neither plan seemed very smart when she heard the man and woman arguing again. Their voices sounded louder than before.

She listened, afraid HH hadn't paid the ransom, afraid of what the man planned to do now.

Then she heard the footfalls. It sounded as if the man and woman were both coming down the hall toward her. Before she could scramble away from the door, she heard the woman cry, "Why do *I* have to do it? Please. Don't make me hurt her."

CHAPTER SIXTEEN

STUART WENT BACK inside the McKenna Ranch house. He hated to leave Holden to his own devices, but his instincts told him that Holly Jo's deceased father was a lead he had to follow.

As he came back into the house, he looked up to see Bailey coming down the stairway dressed as if heading out on a date. The sundress bared her shoulders and most of her long legs. She smiled, aware that she had caught his attention and clearly enjoying it. The sweet scent of citrus beat her down the stairs.

Holden came out of his office as she started past, headed for the front door. Stuart moved to the side to let her by. She didn't ask about Holly Jo, but then again, anyone could see that the girl hadn't been found yet.

She slowed to pass him. Holden seemed to think Bailey was angry. She sure appeared that way. Defiant as well. But she was also in pain, the sheriff thought as he glimpsed something raw flash in her eyes. She met his gaze, held it for a split second. Then, dragging it away, her jaw tightening, she walked out.

He watched her go, more curious and intrigued by her as he followed the sexy swing of her hips with his eyes, unable not to. In the time they'd spent together during her middle-of-the-night visits, they never talked about themselves. As the night got late, she could withdraw as if afraid of getting too close.

Bailey was hiding something and not just from him, he told himself. Nothing to do with Holly Jo, though. No, it was something else, something she'd been hiding for months, maybe even years.

Why was it that the women he'd been most interested in were the ones who lied to him? Or kept secrets from him, some deep and dark, some downright dangerous. He wasn't necessarily drawn to these women, he told himself. They were the ones who came after him. Was it because he was the law? Was that the attraction? Or did some women love getting close to the flame, but bailed before it engulfed them?

He, on the other hand, kept getting burned.

Dragging his gaze away, he told himself that he wasn't going to let Bailey draw him into anything that risked his life or his heart. He'd already risked both and almost lost both. He wondered about Bailey's relationships with men. Had she ever been romantically involved with anyone? Not that he knew of.

"Where's she going?" Holden asked as he joined Stuart to watch his daughter drive off.

The sheriff shook his head. He didn't have a clue. He'd been suspicious of Bailey's secretive behavior for some time now, but since it didn't appear to be illegal, he hadn't pursued it.

"She's been acting so distant lately," the rancher said, more to himself than Stuart. "I don't know about her."

Neither did he. The worst part was that the more Bailey kept him in the dark, the more he wanted to drag both her and her secrets into the light. He realized that could be a fatal flaw of his when it came to women.

"I need to check out something," Stuart said. "You know what to do if you hear from the kidnapper." He started to warn Holden about keeping his temper, but knew it was a waste of breath. Holden McKenna did what he wanted despite the consequences, he feared— which could explain Holly Jo's kidnapping. "Call me," he said and headed for Billings and the Sanderson Funeral Home.

HOLDEN HAD NEVER been good at waiting. After the sheriff left, as he paced, he grew angrier. He hated feeling so helpless, and he swore what he'd do when he got his hands on the kidnapper. At the same time, he prayed that Holly Jo was safe and that he'd get her back.

Praying didn't come naturally since he'd never done it before. His father hadn't held with religion. "Bunch of thieves, telling you what a sinner you are while they take your money," his father used to say. Margie had believed, though. He remembered her on her knees each night, thanking the good Lord.

He'd envied her faith. He had wanted to believe and wanted it now more than ever. He prayed, feeling as if he was covering his bets even as he suspected being such a hypocrite would eventually send him straight to hell. But he would do whatever he had to if Holly Jo got to come home. He'd done enough wrong in his life that he figured he was headed to hell anyway.

At the sound of the front door opening, he turned quickly to see his eldest son enter. Alone. Treyton stopped in the doorway as if not sure he wanted to come inside.

"Treyton." He motioned him into his office. "Close

the door." He saw his son bristle and tried to moderate his tone. "Holly Jo's missing."

"I heard." Treyton sneered and looked as if he was trying not to laugh.

"There is nothing funny about any of this." That his son found humor in it both infuriated him and disappointed him deeply. How could Treyton be Margie's son? No one was kinder than the boy's mother. But Margie had died, leaving Holden to raise the kids pretty much by himself. He had no one to blame but himself for the way his eldest had turned out.

"What did you expect?" Treyton said, going on the defensive. "Who is she, anyway? And don't give me that malarkey about you doing some friend a favor."

Holden bit his tongue. Every time he tried to reach his eldest son, it turned into an argument. He wasn't up to one today. "I just wanted you to know what was going on. If you hear anything…"

Treyton shook his head. "Why would I hear anything?"

"If you should see her…"

"Trust me, I'm not going to see her." He turned and opened the door but stopped as if not finished.

Holden's cell phone rang, saving him from whatever hurtful thing his son was about to say—and the argument that was bound to follow. "Close the door on your way out."

His hope that the call might be something about Holly Jo vanished the moment he heard the neighboring rancher's voice. He listened to the man say how sorry he was and finally cut him off with a thank-you and, "We need to keep this line open."

He disconnected, trying to remember a time when

he'd felt this miserable, this scared, this hopeless. He heard his father's voice as clearly as if he were standing in this room. "Looks like your chickens have come home to roost."

THE ORIGINAL OWNER of the Sanderson Funeral Home, Lloyd Sanderson, was long deceased. The person who greeted Sheriff Stuart Layton was John Banner, manager. Banner led him into his nicely appointed office and offered him a chair.

Stuart introduced himself and told him that he was inquiring about Robert Robinson, who died after a fall off The Rims. He gave him the date the officer had provided for Robinson's death and waited as the man searched his files.

"Yes, I have it here," Banner said. "He was cremated. There was no service."

Stuart had been afraid of that. "I need to know about next of kin."

"There's his wife—"

"What about siblings, parents, aunts, uncles, anyone?"

"I wasn't employed here at the time, but according to the records, his wife came in, requested a cremation. There was no viewing. *This* is odd, though."

Stuart waited. "What's odd?"

"No one picked up the ashes. It looks like the bill was paid, but…" Banner looked up and frowned. "I think we still have his ashes."

Minutes later, Banner came out with a cardboard box with Robert Robinson's name and a date on it.

"I need to borrow these as part of an ongoing investigation," the sheriff said and signed a form saying he would be responsible for the ashes.

Once out in his SUV, he swung by the crime lab and left the ashes. He needed to know why a man's wife hadn't cared enough to retrieve her husband's remains. All his instincts told him the answer would be in the DNA results.

HOLLY JO FRANTICALLY looked around the room for something to fight off the two people as she heard their footfalls growing closer. But there was nothing even if she had felt strong enough. Earlier, the man had taken her plastic spoon and the paper plate, leaving her with only the bottle of juice. She spotted the small plastic bucket and her empty juice container on the floor in the corner, her heart sinking as she heard the key in the lock.

As the door swung open, she knew there was nowhere to run, no place to hide. For the first time, they both came into the room, making her terror rise after what she'd heard the woman say outside the door. The man had his mask on. The woman didn't wear one. Her face was pale in the dim light, and she looked as scared as Holly Jo felt.

But it was what she held in her hand that had Holly Jo too terrified to cry or speak. The woman carried a large pair of scissors.

Holly Jo frantically looked around the room again for something to use to defend herself. There was nothing. There was no one to save her, and even if she hadn't felt so weak and tired, she knew she couldn't fight them both off.

"Let's just get this over with," the man snapped, shoving the woman toward Holly Jo and closing the door.

She pressed herself against the wall as they approached and heard herself begin to whimper. Her body felt so sluggish from the juice drug that when the man rushed her, she could hardly lift her arms to fight him off. He forced her down on the floor.

She tried to curl up in a ball, but he jerked her head up by her hair.

"I'll hold her. You do the cutting," he snapped at the woman, who had stopped in the middle of the room. "Come on. Do this."

The woman took a step closer, then another. She was shaking her head and looked close to tears. "You said I wasn't going to have to do anything."

"Oh, for crying out loud. You want the money? Then get over here and do it."

The word *money* made the woman look up. "But you said—"

"I've changed my mind. You're right. After everything we've had to go through, I should be reimbursed. But I want a whole lot more than some ten-thousand-dollar reward. Now do it." He pinned down Holly Jo's arms and forced her into a sitting position.

The woman came over and knelt beside them. "Once we do this, we get the money, let her go and leave, right?"

"Just do it," he ordered.

Holly Jo tried to pull away, but the man snapped, "You want her to cut your throat? Hold still or you're going to bleed." She stopped fighting, closed her eyes and held her breath, not knowing what the woman planned to do with the scissors. Her heart raced. The man's grip was painful, and he was sweaty and gross.

When the woman took hold of her hair, Holly Jo opened her eyes. She heard the snip and saw a lock of her hair flutter downward. That was all they had planned to do? Take a little of her hair? She felt so relieved that her eyes burned with tears. She took a shaky breath, her chest aching.

"What is wrong with you?" the man demanded. "You aren't giving her a trim. I said cut off a chunk. A big chunk, right in front. I want it for the photo."

The woman grabbed hold of her hair again as the man held her too tightly. She watched the woman grab a handful of hair at the front and begin sawing through it only inches from her scalp.

"No!" she cried as she thought of all the nights her mother used to brush her hair, saying how beautiful it was. Then her mother had gotten sick and died. Heartbroken, Holly Jo had chopped her hair off one day in her grief. In all the months she'd been at the ranch, it had finally grown out. It had become beautiful again, the memory of her mother brushing it no longer breaking her heart. "No!"

"There," the woman said, holding out the thick hunk of hair to him as he let go of his grip on her. Holly Jo struck out at him and tried to kick the woman.

"Stop it!" he ordered her, grabbing her hair and hauling her up to shove her against the wall. "We aren't finished. You have to help," he said to the woman.

The woman took hold of Holly Jo like he had, pressing her against the wall and at the same time trying to stand back as much as she could. All Holly Jo could do was glare at the phone as the man took photos of her. She swore that she would never drink the juice again no matter how thirsty she got. She would find a way to escape. After she got away, HH would find these two. Then they would be sorry for what they'd done.

CHAPTER SEVENTEEN

THE DISPATCHER PUT the call through to the sheriff's cell phone. "It's Penny, the waitress at the café. I found an envelope on a table here after the evening rush with a note that says, *Give this to Holden McKenna.*"

"Did you see who left it?"

"No, but the cook said he thought it was a woman. Didn't see her, but he said she didn't seem familiar. Probably not from around here."

"Don't let anyone else touch the envelope, please," Stuart said. "I'll be right there."

Five minutes later, he was bagging the envelope with a large chunk of dark hair inside. He didn't need to wait for the DNA report to know it was Holly Jo's or question why it had been left at the café. He was only thankful that it hadn't been a finger or a toe. The fact that it was a thick chunk of her hair made his stomach roil. He feared what might come next. He swore he would find this kidnapper if it was the last thing he ever did.

Once they had proof of life—the hair didn't prove that Holly Jo was still alive. He needed a photo. As he left the café, he got the call from Holden that a photograph had been received. The FBI lab already had it.

He would make arrangements to send the hair on to the lab so it could be matched with the hair from Holly

Jo's brush. He saw no reason to show it to Holden, who was already furious over the photo and what had been done to the girl's hair.

Stuart was anxious to hear about the cardboard box of Robert "Bobby" Robinson's ashes from the funeral home that were also now at the FBI lab and asked that a DNA sample be compared to Holly Jo's DNA. He knew he was spitballing as he drove out to the McKenna Ranch. It was late. He'd grabbed a sandwich and ate it as he drive.

His mind whirred. What wife didn't pick up her husband's ashes? She'd paid the bill but hadn't wanted an urn. The ashes had never been picked up? Maybe she'd been too angry at him for dying—especially since alcohol had been involved after the rodeo. Or maybe, his gut told him, something was wrong.

Stuart was anxious to talk to Holden about what he'd found out. He was positive now that the rancher knew a whole lot more than he was telling him—starting with Holly Jo's father.

BIRDIE WAS OUTSIDE the Wild Horse Bar, visiting with some locals who had known her father, when she saw the pickup. The men, mostly ones who were regulars at the bar, had been confirming what she already knew. Her father and Charlotte had not gotten along. One of them was saying that if he had to bet on who'd killed Dixon, he'd put all his money on the matriarch of Stafford Ranch.

Nothing new there. It was how to prove it. Something had made Birdie look up as a white pickup slowly passed the bar, catching her eye. The driver, though, was a woman—not a man. That made her hesitate—until she saw that the truck was missing its tailgate. The tailgate would have had to be removed to slide a camper shell on and off. It was enough to make her apologize for running off as she quickly left. She still wasn't sure it was the right truck. But then she noticed the back license plate. It was covered with mud as if someone had purposely tried to make the identifying numbers and letters unreadable.

Decision made, she quickly climbed behind the wheel of her SUV and went after the pickup. The woman had been driving slowly through town, obeying the speed limit, but once she hit the edge of town, she sped up and headed northeast toward Broadus instead of taking the road toward Miles City.

Birdie had thought about calling the sheriff but wanted to make sure this was the right pickup first. She hurriedly called Brand, who said he was in town at the general store picking up supplies.

"Do not go after the truck by yourself," he said.

"You're right. I'll come get you. She's headed on the road toward Broadus. We're going to follow her."

"What?"

"Wait outside the store. I'll be right there. We can't lose her."

He was standing on the curb as she roared up. She saw him hesitate, but only for a moment, before he opened the passenger door of her SUV and climbed in. "Why are you following this woman on your own?"

"I'm not on my own. I have you."

Brand groaned. "And now you're following the truck? Birdie, don't you realize how dangerous this could be? You need to call the sheriff."

"I want to make sure it's not a false alarm first," she argued.

"Birdie, I'm calling the sheriff," he said as he pulled out his phone. By then, they were racing out of town after the woman and the pickup.

AT THE MCKENNA RANCH, the sheriff was on the phone with the FBI technician, who was going over the proof-of-life photo, looking for clues to where the girl was being held as well as who might have taken her. Still, it didn't feel like enough. Stuart felt no closer to finding her.

"Did you see what they did to her?" Holden demanded.

Stuart had seen. He'd known the moment he looked in the envelope left at the café that a large chunk of Holly Jo's hair had been cut away. He just hadn't known it was in the front, close to her face. It would grow back in time.

He studied the photo the kidnapper had sent. The look on Holly Jo's face made his blood boil. She was a tough kid, smart, fairly mature for her age, he'd been told. She looked defiant as she glared at the person taking the photo, but it was easy to see the fear behind the expression. Stuart tried not to think about how she was holding up or what was being done to her.

"We know that he isn't working alone," the sheriff said. As badly as he wanted to nail this son of a bitch, he couldn't let emotion take over. *Just do your job*, he kept telling himself. *You're going to bring her home.*

Stuart pointed to the hand in the photo. A woman's left hand. Polish had been applied to the fake fingernails, a shimmery pale blue. But it was the ring on her finger that drew his attention. What appeared to be a large diamond wedding ring. She was married? To the kidnapper?

"This is good news," the sheriff said to Holden, who seemed to grow angrier with each passing hour. Stuart knew he was scared. They all were. "Holly Jo is alive. Judging from the look on her face, she's holding her own. On top of that, she should be safer with a woman in the picture, literally." He had no idea what the statistics were, but he took it as a good sign since women were often kinder than men. Just not always, he reminded himself, thinking of his mother.

"The bastard is asking for money now," Holden said. "Two million dollars, along with me admitting what I did and apologizing for it. How can I do that when I don't know what I did?"

Stuart wasn't that surprised money was now part of the ransom demand. He hoped that Charlotte Stafford's offer of a reward hadn't caused the change. He did wonder if the woman with the kidnapper had anything to do with asking for money or what part she was playing in all this. The pickup and camper Birdie Malone had described hadn't sounded like a newer model. He suspected the "diamond" on the woman's hand wasn't real.

Who were these people, and what exactly did they want? Was it possible that their first demand had been bogus, that they didn't even know Holden, didn't want acknowledgment at all, that it had always been about money? He shook his head, wondering, if true, why. There was so much he didn't know—just as he couldn't shake the feeling that Holden was keeping a whole lot from him.

He motioned for the rancher to join him back in the

man's office. Once inside, he closed the door. Holden seemed to brace himself. "Holly Jo's mother never picked up Robert Robinson's ashes at the funeral home," Stuart said. He watched the other man's face. Not shock. Not even mild surprise. "Don't you think that's strange?"

Holden shrugged. "It doesn't matter. It doesn't help us find Holly Jo."

"Maybe not. But it certainly brings up more questions. Why wouldn't his wife pick up his ashes?"

The rancher moved to the window, his movements impatient, irritated. "They weren't getting along. She wanted him to settle down and quit rodeoing. 'Grow up,' that's what she told him." Turning toward Stuart, he added, "It sounded to me like she was planning to leave him."

This was news, but the sheriff had to question whether it was important to Holly Jo's kidnapping. "The crime lab took a DNA sample from the ashes." True surprise this time from Holden.

"They can get DNA even after a cremation?"

"They can. I had the DNA checked against Holly Jo's." The DNA results weren't back yet, but Holden didn't know that. Shock registered before all the color bled from the rancher's face. Stuart went with his instincts. "You knew Bobby wasn't Holly Jo's father, didn't you?"

Holden said nothing. Stuart tried to check his anger but couldn't. "You didn't think that was important? Holly Jo's biological father could be behind the kidnapping. I need the truth and I need it now," Stuart said. "If Robert Robinson wasn't Holly Jo's father, then who was?"

The landline rang, making them both jump. The kidnapper was calling.

The sheriff swore. "We aren't finished."

Holden's jaw was set as the landline rang again. He stepped to the desk, took a breath, let it out and, without looking at Stuart, reached for the handset.

"Do exactly what I told you to do," the sheriff warned him, afraid the rancher had gone rogue long before now. "Hello?"

HOLLY JO KEPT touching the place where her hair had been chopped off. It felt bristly and made her cry. Cutting it like this had been mean. The man had just wanted to make her look ugly in the photo he took. Did he send it to HH?

She'd cried for a while after they left her alone, but now her tears were angry ones. She was mad and determined to get back at them. She realized that she'd been waiting for someone to save her. Now she knew she would have to save herself. She couldn't trust either the man or the woman to let her go once they got what they wanted. She'd seen the woman's face when the man hadn't said what would happen once they got the money. Did she realize that Holly Jo could tell the cops what she looked like and they could find her? Had the man already figured that out?

Walking around the room, she felt stronger. She hadn't drunk the last three bottles of juice he'd brought. She was thirsty but had made herself pour some in the bucket and the rest down the drain. Her head felt better, too. She didn't feel as fuzzy. She didn't want to sleep as much.

What she wanted to do was escape. She thought of ways she could get loose. The next time the man came, she could rush him, knock him down and then run. But even as she thought it, she knew that if she succeeded, she had no idea where she was. If he came after her, he would probably be able to catch her.

She moved to the window and saw it had a rusty latch on it. She tried to turn it, but it wouldn't budge. She could break the window and push on the boards covering the space, but if she couldn't get out, the man would notice the broken glass on the floor.

In her mind, she saw the shards of glass on the floor. She could use one as a weapon. The thought of gripping a piece of sharp glass in her hand made her sick to her stomach. Even if she didn't cut off her hand, could she really stab someone? Or would she freeze? Would the man take the glass from her and cut her throat?

She shook her head. Getting the window open would be better. She heard him coming and quickly lay down on the mat, pulling the blanket over her and squeezing her eyes shut. She had to pretend she was still drinking the juice, still tired and confused.

The door opened. She kept her eyes closed, but she could hear him standing there. "I brought you more juice," he said. She didn't respond. With fear, she heard him walk across the concrete floor toward her and stop. "I said I brought you juice." He nudged her leg with his toe, and when she sat up and rubbed her eyes as if dragged from a deep sleep, he took a step back before he held out the juice bottle. "You should drink it. You must be thirsty with all that crying."

So he hadn't left earlier. He'd listened outside the door. Or the woman had.

She didn't reach for the juice. "I'm not thirsty right now."

"I need you to drink it."

Holly Jo could see his light-colored eyes behind the mask. He wanted to watch her drink it. Would he force her if she refused? "I have to pee. I can't drink it until I pee." She glanced at the bucket, then at him, and didn't move.

He sighed and put down the juice on the concrete floor. "I'll check on you later to make sure you drank it. You want to stay alive, don't you? So you can go home?"

She nodded and squirmed as if she would wet herself if she didn't pee soon.

She got up, picking up the juice bottle as she moved to the bucket. She hadn't heard him leave. If he was waiting outside the door, he was waiting to hear her pee. She opened the juice as quietly as possible and began to pour a little of it into the bucket. Then she listened until she heard him limp away before she walked over to the drain and poured out the juice, her mouth watering as she did.

Then, taking the plastic bottle, she went back over to the window and began to scrub the rust off the window latch. The plastic at the mouth of the bottle wasn't quite sharp enough, but if she scraped long enough...

CHAPTER EIGHTEEN

STUART HADN'T BEEN surprised that the kidnapper wanted two million dollars. He'd listened to the recording. "I'll call back to let you know where to bring it. Come alone. Or the girl dies."

After that, Holden had erupted, going off script, but it hadn't mattered. The caller had hung up.

The sheriff had hoped to question the rancher further about Holly Jo's father, but Holden had been so upset that he'd stormed off toward the stables.

Stuart watched him go before Brand Stafford called. "Brand, if this is—"

"Birdie thinks she saw the pickup from the night before the kidnapping. We're following it, even though the camper wasn't on the back and the driver was a woman, but the tailgate is missing. We're headed northeast on the road to Broadus."

Stuart groaned. "Neither of you have any idea what you're doing," the sheriff argued. "Where are you now?" Brand told him. "Do not, I repeat, do not approach this person." He groaned as he headed for his patrol SUV. Arguing with these two was a waste of breath. He just hoped they didn't get themselves killed, and Holly Jo as well.

But Birdie was the only one who'd seen the pickup and camper the night before Holly Jo was taken. She

just might be on to something. It was a chance he had
to take. Also, what neither Brand nor Birdie knew was
that the kidnapper had an accomplice—a woman.

The missing tailgate also sounded like this might be
the pickup. The kidnapper and accomplice must have
taken off the camper and were staying in it, possibly
somewhere near where they were keeping Holly Jo.

He thought about pulling off a deputy for backup but
couldn't spare one. Brand said the woman had been alone
in the pickup. That meant the kidnapper was still out
there somewhere, maybe stranded back wherever they
were keeping Holly Jo. Or they could have a second vehicle, but then why go to the trouble of removing the
camper to drive into town? Of course, there could be
more people involved in this than he knew. Not to mention Birdie and Brand could be following some woman
who had nothing at all to do with Holly Jo's kidnapping—
and now Stuart was also following them.

Either way, he knew he couldn't pass up a possible
lead. There was little traffic this time of day on the highway. He passed a farm truck full of hay, then a car, all the
time looking ahead for Birdie's pale green SUV.

As he came around a corner, he saw a road off to his
right that turned down by the river. He was hit with a
shitstorm of blood-drenched memories. That was the
road Abigail Creed had pulled down minutes before
she'd started stabbing him. He realized he hadn't been
up this way since *the incident*, as it was being called.
He'd been such a fool. He hadn't known why she'd
pulled off the road. He'd thought she'd done it to talk—
until she pulled the knife—but he should have known.

He whizzed past the road and didn't look back, but

he was sweating and had to turn up the air conditioner. He kept telling the psychiatrist he was required to see that he was fine. But right now, he was anything but.

Brand called. "The woman just turned off on Cache Creek Road."

"Keep the pickup in sight, but don't approach. Wait for me." Stuart was a good ten miles away. He pushed the patrol SUV up to over a hundred, afraid of what kind of trouble Birdie Malone was driving into and taking Brand Stafford with her.

BIRDIE HAD DRIVEN fast until she sighted the pickup. She had backed way off, afraid that the woman would realize she was tailing her. From a good distance, she'd seen the pickup turn onto Cache Creek Road. Then she'd taken her time reaching the turnoff.

"The sheriff said not to approach her," Brand repeated. "Birdie? This is not the time to do anything impulsive. If you're right, this woman is dangerous."

She seldom had doubts about the seemingly impetuous things she did—even though she was aware that she should more often consider her actions before leaping in. "The thing is, if I hadn't skulked around the Stafford Ranch the night before the kidnapping, I wouldn't have been able to provide you with an alibi. You could still be locked up in jail."

"If only," he said under his breath.

"Also, I wouldn't have seen the pickup and camper near the McKenna Ranch that night and later down the road from your ranch," she continued, as if she hadn't heard him. "So it must be fate, wouldn't you say? Fate that we met and are now following the possible kidnapper."

"Fate?" he demanded as she made the turn onto Cache Creek Road. "It wasn't fate that you followed me home from the bar that night."

"We can't lose sight of her," Birdie argued. "I'll just go up the road a little way until we find out where she's going."

She couldn't see the truck ahead and sped up, determined not to lose her. She was mentally kicking herself for dropping back so far, thinking she'd already lost her, when she came up over a rise in the road and saw that the driver of the white pickup had stopped in the middle of the road.

Birdie hit her brakes and skidded to a stop as the driver's-side door opened and the woman climbed out and headed back toward them. She heard Brand let out a curse.

At a glance, the woman looked to be in her late forties or early fifties. Her bleached-blond hair was pulled up into a ponytail, and she wore jeans, a blouse, boots and a leather jacket. She didn't look like a kidnapper. Then again, Birdie had no idea what one looked like.

"I don't like this," Brand said under his breath as the woman approached the SUV. "I think we should get out of here *now*."

Birdie couldn't help noticing the rock on the woman's ring finger. If it was real, it must have cost a bunch. The woman's other hand was buried deep in her jacket pocket. She tapped on the window with her free hand, the ring catching the light, her nails appearing to have been professionally done recently, except that one of the blue-painted nails had been broken.

Birdie hesitated, caught between throwing her SUV

into Reverse and needing to hear what this possible kidnapper was going to say.

"I'm lost," the woman said the moment Birdie whirred down her window. "On top of that, I'm running late. I'm supposed to be there by now. They'll be sending out a search party. Do you know the Mullenses?" She glanced from Birdie to Brand and back.

Birdie shook her head, surprised and worried that she'd been wrong about everything, including this woman she'd followed.

"I think I should have turned left instead of right back at the main road." She looked pointedly at Birdie. "I have to turn around and go back. Can't wait for all the blond jokes when I tell him what I did." She swung her ponytail and let out a laugh as fake as her nails.

Birdie looked toward the pickup. She couldn't swear it was the same one. She feared everyone would be making fun of her for going off half-cocked. Her mother used to warn her about that.

"Birdie, sometimes you need to take a breath and think things out before acting."

So maybe she'd always been this way. "Sorry I can't be of more help. I also need to turn around. I didn't realize how late it was."

"Oh, I thought maybe you were lost, too." The woman looked at her suspiciously as she shoved both hands into her leather jacket pockets and looked back up the road in the direction they had come. She seemed anxious to get moving, as if afraid of who else might show up.

Birdie realized the sheriff could show up at any moment. The woman was making her nervous, given how deep her hands were in her leather jacket pockets on this warm summer day.

"If you were following me, you were really following the wrong person," the woman said. "I never get directions right. Unless you're going to the Mullens ranch, too."

Birdie shook her head. "Just driving around on our way to Broadus. Realized we'd never been down Cache Creek. Do you know where this road comes out?"

"Not a clue," the woman said. "Clearly, I'm not from around here."

Birdie glanced at the pickup's license plate. This close, she could see that it was a Wyoming plate. She could even make out the numbers and letters under the smear of dried mud. The woman's hands were still in her jacket pockets. She was glancing back down the road again, visibly nervous now as if she heard someone coming.

"Good luck finding the Mullenses. I better get going. I'll back up so you can," Birdie said and put her window up. The woman started to reach out as if to stop her from raising the window. Her fingers pressed against the glass for an instant. Birdie saw the clear print in the dust, and so did the woman, her eyes widening.

Birdie threw the SUV into Reverse and hit the gas, forcing the woman to step back and keeping her from wiping the print off the glass. As she hurriedly backed down the road, she saw the woman rush to her pickup. For a weapon? Or had she been fingering a gun in her jacket pocket while they were talking?

Would she chase after them? No. The woman had climbed behind the wheel and was now taking off down the road, leaving only dust behind.

For just a split second, Birdie thought about going after her again. She kept telling herself that she hadn't been wrong about the pickup or the woman, even as doubt tried to shoulder its way in. *Can't wait for all the blond jokes when I tell him what I did.* Before that, the woman had said *they*, as in the Mullenses. Just a slip of the tongue?

Birdie found a place to turn around, but didn't get the chance before the sheriff came flying up on them. She knew before she saw his face that he wasn't happy. She looked over at Brand. He was shaking his head as he reached for his door handle as if he couldn't get away from her fast enough.

STUART COULDN'T HIDE his fury. He knew part of his mood wasn't Birdie's fault. She wouldn't know what seeing the place where he'd almost lost his life would do to him. He hadn't either. He'd thought he was working past it, but now realized it was still too fresh—just like when he looked in the mirror and saw all his visible scars. Abigail Creed had taken him by surprise and in a frenzy had stabbed him repeatedly as he'd tried to fight her off until he'd finally pulled his gun and killed her. By then, he was bleeding to death. If he hadn't made the 911 call and help hadn't been close by...

"It isn't just that you risked your life," he said to her after he'd gone down the road looking for the pickup and the woman Birdie had followed. He'd driven all over back in there, but had found no sign of the pickup or the woman. She was gone—just as he'd suspected. "It's that you may have made things worse."

Both Birdie and Brand were waiting when he returned from his search of the area for the possible kidnapper. Now he wrote down everything she remembered about the woman, including her Wyoming license plate number and that she suspected the woman had lied about where she was headed. He wasn't surprised by any of it, except for the fact that Birdie hadn't gotten herself and Brand killed.

Back in his patrol SUV, he ran the pickup's plate. The pickup was owned by Jason Thomas of Laramie, Wyoming. Stuart had been unable to reach him and had asked Laramie law enforcement for their help. Laramie law enforcement called him back after contacting Jason at work.

He'd told the officer that his sister, Melanie Baker, borrowed his pickup and camper a week ago, confirming that Birdie's instincts had been right. Given everything Stuart now knew, Birdie had followed one of the kidnappers. Like in the photo with Holly Jo, the woman wore a diamond ring that Stuart suspected would be a match, given Birdie's description. The woman's fingers had been buried in Holly Jo's hair in the proof-of-life photo, so he probably wouldn't be able to tell if she'd had a recent manicure or if one of the nails was chipped, as Birdie had said. But her nails had been painted blue.

As much as Stuart wanted to throttle her, Birdie had given them a definite lead. But if the woman was Melanie Baker and involved with the kidnapping, she had probably realized Birdie was following her and seen through Birdie's guise. Ultimately that could get Holly Jo hurt—or killed.

"If she thinks you suspected her, she might talk her partner into moving Holly Jo. We've been waiting for the kidnapper to call with details on the ransom drop. You might have scared them off. You should have waited for me."

Birdie shook her head. "I would have lost her. I wouldn't have gotten a description of her and the pickup or the license plate number. You wouldn't know who she is." She looked toward the road she'd taken before encountering the woman. He could see that she still believed the woman hadn't gone far.

"Do you know how many secondary two-tracks are off this one? She knew you were following her. I wouldn't be surprised if she turned down this road only because she was afraid of leading you to where they were really holding Holly Jo."

Birdie looked unconvinced.

"Birdie, I went all the way up the road to the mountains. There was no sign of her and no sign of any place where they could have been holding Holly Jo—let alone any sight of the camper that was on the pickup when you first saw it. She led you down a rabbit hole, and you took the bait. You're lucky she didn't pull a gun on you and shoot you and Brand."

He saw Birdie shudder as if she'd realized that—before she'd gotten away from the woman. "The problem is, now she knows what you drive, what you look like. It won't take much to find out who you are, Birdie."

"If you're trying to scare me—"

"I'm trying to make you see that you have no business taking things into your own hands," the sheriff said. "I'm waiting for the kidnapper to contact me with a drop site," he explained patiently. "He might panic now and not call."

She shook her head stubbornly. "They want Holden McKenna to confess, but what they really want is money.

They have asked for money, right?" Birdie said and nodded as if she could read the answer on his face. "They aren't going to jeopardize that. Anyway, now you have the woman's fingerprint. The moment she touched my driver's-side window, I saw that she regretted it, but she couldn't wipe it off because I pulled away too quickly."

"Stop playing detective," the sheriff snapped. He blamed all the crime shows on television and the rise of amateur sleuths. "I know my job." He had taken a copy of the print she'd photographed and sent it, hoping as clear as it was on the glass, they could get a match to see if the woman had a rap sheet. None. "Her fingerprint isn't in the system, and the pickup and camper were borrowed, not stolen. What we have so far is circumstantial at best." He pocketed his phone. "I need you to go back to Powder Crossing. Stop trying to do my job for me. That goes for you too, Brand."

Brand hadn't said a word. In fact, the sheriff was pretty sure that the two had argued while he'd been gone in search of the pickup and the woman.

"I'm not planning to do anything, trust me," Brand said. He looked at Birdie and shook his head. "You could have been killed."

She rolled her eyes. "You've forgotten. I can take care of myself."

Stuart was thinking that Birdie and Brand couldn't have been a more unlikely couple. If that was what they were. Brand Stafford had always been quiet, had never been in trouble, seldom even came into town to the bar. Birdie…well, she was a loose cannon. Anyone could see that. While the two had been thrown together because of Birdie's quest to find her father's killer, the sheriff couldn't see whatever this was between them going much further.

He shook his head as his cell phone rang. He saw it was the McKenna Ranch. Expecting it would be Holden, he was surprised when the voice on the other end of the call was Elaine's.

"The kidnapper called with the location of the ransom drop tonight at midnight," she said.

That was quick. Because the kidnapper was worried after his accomplice returned to tell him that she'd been followed? "Where is Holden?"

"He's on the phone with his banker. He's planning on making the drop by himself."

Of course he was. Stuart swore under his breath. "I'm on my way." Disconnecting, he looked at Birdie. "I have to go. Get back to Powder Crossing. Stay out of trouble. Please." Neither she nor Brand said anything as he climbed into his patrol SUV and, hitting his siren and lights, headed back to the McKenna Ranch, hoping to get there before Holden did something that could get him killed.

As the sheriff drove away, Birdie said, "You know what we have to do."

Brand looked over at her from where he'd been leaning against the passenger side of her SUV. He'd seen this look in her eyes before. What was it about this woman that he couldn't seem to help himself when it came to her? He knew she was trouble and yet...

"Did you not hear anything the sheriff said?" He could see that it hadn't mattered. "Whatever it is, I want nothing to do with it. I'm doing what the sheriff said. Keeping my head down and staying out of it."

She laughed. "Brand Stafford, I suspect you've been keeping your head down all of your life. Aren't you tired of it yet?"

He started to argue, but it was true. He and his younger brother, Ryder, both escaped their older brother CJ's brutality by keeping their distance from him. They spent their days away from the house, leaving as quickly as possible in the morning and not returning until long after dark. Brand had told himself that they were busy running the ranch. Which was true. But they had also been avoiding their treacherous brother and their mother and the Stafford Ranch drama.

"You don't know anything about me," he argued, even though she seemed to know him better than he knew himself—and she'd just met him. Worse, given the grin on her face right now, she knew that he was attracted to her—against his will. Why else had he agreed to come with her today?

"What are you so afraid of, Brand?" she teased as she began to close the distance between them.

"You," he said, holding up both hands to ward her off. "You scare me. You're too impulsive. Like today. You didn't give a thought to what you were doing. You risked your life and mine!" She kept coming toward him until she was within inches of him. He dropped his voice as he looked into her gray eyes, fighting that pull he'd been battling since he'd laid eyes on her. "I can't do this."

"Do what?" she whispered. "Throw caution to the wind? Let yourself go? Take a chance? Or do this?" She leaned into him, stealing his breath and his determination to keep her at arm's length as she brushed her lips over his, teasing, taunting, daring him to act on his feelings.

Oh, he felt all right. Birdie made his body come alive, all of it aware of this woman in a way he'd never felt before with any other woman. She was everything he'd spent his life avoiding. Trouble wrapped in temptation. Kissing her was like diving out of an airplane with a parachute—but having no idea how to pull the cord. Her kiss was a promise of something he'd told himself he didn't want or need even as he knew he wanted it more than his next breath.

He drew back to look at her. She had no idea what she'd stirred up in him, and while it scared the hell out of him, she was right. He was tired of playing it safe. "Birdie." Her name came out on a ragged breath.

She chuckled and started to turn away.

He grabbed her arm, spinning her around and into him. He moved quickly, remembering how fast she'd put him on the ground yesterday. He turned her to press her against the side of her SUV in the same spot he'd been only moments before.

"My turn," he said, his voice rough with emotion and need. He didn't sound like himself, nor did he feel like himself as he kissed her. He didn't tease or taunt. He kissed her like he'd been fighting doing since he'd met her. Her lips parted to him, and her arms encircled his neck. He deepened the kiss as he molded his body to hers, pinning her against the side of the SUV.

Desire burned like hot syrup through his veins, sweet but more powerful than he'd ever felt. If a car hadn't gone by and honked on the highway some distance away, he thought he might have taken her right there.

"Wow," she said, seeming at a loss for words as they drew apart. She grinned, her gaze meeting his. "I knew you had it in you, Brand Stafford. I've just been waiting for it to come out." Her grin broadened. "Wow."

He shook his head. He'd succumbed to this impulsive, maddening woman and now felt as if there was no turning back. He wanted her in every way he could imagine, even as a less testosterone-fueled voice inside him warned that she was going to get him killed.

"You still scare me, Birdie," he said as he brushed a lock of her hair back from her face.

"I'm not what scares you," she said with a laugh. "It's how we make each other feel that scares you." Her gaze burned into his, daring him to say differently. He feared she was right, but he wasn't about to admit it to her.

"But right now we have to think about Holly Jo," she said, getting down to business. He felt both relief and disappointment. "I know the sheriff said that Melanie Baker probably only turned up this road to throw me off because she spotted me tailing her. The thing is, he doesn't have the manpower to search this entire area." She frowned. "I just have a feeling Holly Jo is somewhere near here. I'm going to have to check it out. You don't have to come with me. I'll take you back to town and come back alone."

He groaned. "Birdie, that's a bad idea."

She shrugged and walked around to the driver's side of the SUV. "Well, I have to try."

"You're determined to go looking for Melanie Baker, a probable kidnapper, to give her another chance to kill you?" he asked from the other side.

"I'm going looking for Holly Jo," she said over the top of the SUV. "I can give you a ride back to town. Or if you're that afraid of me, you could hitchhike back to Powder Crossing. Or you could come with me and save us both the trip." She grinned.

He looked back up the road toward the highway, then at Birdie. All his instincts told him to stick out his thumb and start walking away. But he couldn't.

CHAPTER NINETEEN

AT THE McKENNA RANCH, the sheriff listened to the recording of the call between the kidnapper and Holden with instructions for the ransom drop. Midnight tonight, just as Elaine had said. "Suicide Pass. Come alone. I see anyone but you up there and the girl is dead."

"You will have Holly Jo with you," Holden had said, not a question. "We'll make the trade then. If you don't have her, all you'll get is a bullet."

The kidnapper laughed in a spooky computerized voice. "Fair enough. You try anything and I kill her right before your eyes. And you'd better have the money."

"Midnight," the rancher had said, and the call ended.

Stuart looked up at Holden sitting behind his big desk, his expression set in a hard line of determination.

"The kidnapper chose one of the worst places in the area for the drop," the sheriff told him, even though the rancher had to know that. "From the top of that pass, he will be able to see anyone coming or going. There won't be any way to have deputies up there waiting for him. Whoever the kidnapper is, he knows the area, might even be a neighboring rancher or someone who worked for one. Don't you think it's time you told me who the person is?"

"Don't worry about it. I'm taking the money," Holden said stubbornly. "I'm going alone."

The sheriff shook his head, ready to argue, but Holden didn't give him a chance. The rancher rose and walked out of the room, headed outside—just as he had earlier.

Trying to find both patience and diplomacy, Stuart followed Holden. "There's only one reason you're determined to do this alone. You know who you're meeting." When the rancher didn't answer, he said, "You've been lying to me from the beginning, haven't you?"

Holden had stopped a few yards from the house and was now staring out toward the river. "I know what I'm doing. I need you to just stay out of my way." His voice broke with emotion. "I'm trying to save my family."

"Or cover up the truth?"

The rancher shook his head, his gaze shifting to Stuart for a moment before returning to the river. "I've already spoken to my banker. He's gotten the money together. I'll make the drop tonight by myself."

"Even if it gets Holly Jo killed?" Stuart saw the slight slump of the man's shoulders.

"I have no choice."

He didn't ask what would happen if the kidnapper showed up without Holly Jo. He already knew the answer. Holden had already said he would kill the man.

"What's to keep the kidnapper from shooting you and taking the money? You'll have no backup. At least let me hide in the back of your SUV."

"Not happening." The rancher looked over at him. "Don't try to stop me. Once we get Holly Jo back, I'll tell you everything. But right now, there is nothing more you can do. He wants me. He'll be able to see me coming—and if he sees anyone else…"

"I just hope that by then it won't be too late," Stuart said as a vehicle came racing up the road. "At least tell me the kidnapper's name." Even as he said it, he didn't expect an answer.

"His name is Darius Reed. I honestly didn't know until he said the ransom drop would be Suicide Pass. But his name won't help you. There is only one way to stop him."

"Why would this man take Holly Jo?"

"Too long a story to tell." The rancher stepped off the porch to head toward the SUV as it came to a dust-boiling stop in front of the house.

Stuart watched as a man handed out two large brief-cases to Holden from an open window before driving away. Then he pulled out his phone. Darius Reed had a rap sheet longer than the sheriff's arm. He'd been given a temporary release to attend his sister Constance's funeral a few weeks ago. After the funeral, he'd assaulted an officer and gotten away. There was a BOLO already out on him.

HOLLY JO COULDN'T believe how long she'd been scratching the rust off the window latch. Her arms ached. Her fingers were numb from gripping the plastic juice bottle. Worse, she didn't feel as if she was getting anywhere and was ready to quit in tears, when she tried the latch again.

To her shock and joy, the latch turned just a little. She wanted to shout, she was so happy. She could already see herself prying off the boards nailed over the window and getting away. She hurriedly dropped the empty juice bottle and used both hands. The latch opened. Feeling jubilant, she lifted the window.

To her despair, it would only move a few inches— not nearly wide enough for her to escape. Her joy and

excitement fell like a punctured balloon. She wanted
to sit down and cry. Refusing to give up, she pushed
harder on the window. The result was the same, though.
It was stuck. She wasn't getting out.

Fighting tears of frustration, she thought about what
Pickett would do. Cooper and Duffy always said that
the ranch hand could fix anything. Pickett had figured
things out in unusual ways that actually worked. He once
fixed a water pump when Cooper and Duffy had been
ready to buy a new one. She remembered Pickett's grin
when he said, "Told you I could fix it." The memory
brought tears to her eyes. She might not see him again.

She brushed the tears away as she considered what
she could do to get the window to open high enough
that she could get out. Wouldn't make any difference if
she couldn't get the boards over the window off, she reminded herself. She reached in the opening she'd made
and pushed on one of the boards. It didn't budge. She
pushed again as hard as she could on the lowest board
and was about to give up when the board moved just a
fraction of an inch.

She laughed and suddenly had an idea. They'd studied levers in school. If she could get the board off, she
could pry the window open higher. She could escape.

At a sound beyond the room, she froze. Someone
was coming! Hurriedly, she tried to push the window
closed as quietly as she could. But it wouldn't go all the
way down. She tried again. It wouldn't move no matter how hard she pushed. She heard the key in the lock.
Any moment the door would open. Would he notice?

Having no choice but to leave the window like it was,
she snatched up her ruined juice bottle and rushed to her
mat. She'd just sat down when the door swung open. It

wasn't until that moment that she realized the footfalls she'd heard hadn't been the man's distinct limp.

The woman hesitated at the door for a moment as if listening before she came a little farther into the room. She looked nervous, scared. Had she come back to cut off more of Holly Jo's hair?

"Do you think you can walk?"

It was an odd question until Holly Jo remembered that the woman probably thought she was drugged from the juice. Since they'd come in to cut her hair and take her photo, the man had brought by two more juices. She'd dumped one down the drain and poured the other in the bucket so it looked like she'd peed.

She would have loved a drink of water, but she could see that the woman hadn't brought anything. "I think I can walk," she said, wondering what was going on.

"We're going to have to hurry before he comes back."

Holly Jo rose, pretending to be a little unsteady on her feet. Was the woman helping her get away? Or was this a trick? If it meant getting out of this room, she didn't care. She moved toward the door, realizing she didn't know what was beyond it since she had no idea where she was.

The woman led the way out of the room and down a hallway. It appeared to be a narrow barn. Holly Jo wrinkled her nose as she caught the scent of sour milk. A milking barn?

She squinted as the woman pushed open a door. Twilight poured in, half blinding her for a moment. She breathed in the fresh air as she saw a pickup camper— but no pickup attached to it. Nor did she see any other buildings other than the one they'd just exited. "Where are we going?"

"He took the truck, so we have to walk. We have to hurry. Can you do that? I don't know how quickly he's coming back."

Hearing the woman's fear as they headed down a narrow dirt road, Holly Jo nodded. She walked fast to keep up. As she did, she looked around for something familiar about the landscape. She didn't recognize anything. As they topped a rise, she could see nothing for a long way but river bottom, the tops of the cottonwoods and the rough outline of the mountains dotted with scrub brush and rocky outcroppings.

What stilled her heart and stole her breath was the sound of a vehicle engine revving up and heading their way.

WHAT IS IT about this woman? Birdie just didn't give up. She was determined that Holly Jo was out here. To Brand, it felt like looking for a needle in a haystack. Too much country, too many roads that didn't go far. What was he doing here with her?

He caught his reflection in the side mirror and didn't even recognize himself. The old Brand, the one who kept his head down, never caused trouble, followed all the rules and didn't complain, that cowboy would never have climbed into a rig with this woman. The old Brand wouldn't be riding shotgun with this impulsive, reckless, impetuous, brash, stubbornly determined woman.

One impulsive action, sending away his DNA sample for the results, and look what had happened. He was now throwing caution to the wind, risking not just his heart but his life. And the scary part? As he looked over at Birdie, he had to smile. He'd never felt more alive, more like his true self, whoever that was.

Birdie slowed to turn down another dirt road. It had been hours since they'd followed Melanie Baker. "I just have a feeling," she said now. It was the same thing she'd been saying for hours.

He'd already made the argument that it was too easy to disappear back in the rocky terrain and scrub brush of what felt like endless country.

"Okay, maybe she did realize she was being followed and turned off Cache Creek Road as a decoy," Birdie conceded. "But I think she was headed to the place where she was keeping Holly Jo. Haven't you ever just gotten a feeling that was so strong you had to run it down?"

"Yeah, recently, actually, when I decided to have my DNA tested, and look how that turned out."

"Point taken," she said. "Is that the first impulsive thing you've ever done?"

"But not the last, apparently," he said, looking over at her.

She grinned. "I knew you had it in you. I guess you just needed me to come along and draw more of that spontaneity out of you."

He chuckled and looked at the twisting, narrow, rocky road ahead. "Even if it kills me," he said under his breath. They hadn't gone far when Birdie slowed. He recognized the expression on her face and shook his head. "Here we go," he said as she followed an obvious hunch and turned.

The road narrowed as it wound back toward the mountains until it was almost a Jeep trail. But it didn't deter her. They bumped along with him wondering how long it would take before she admitted she might be wrong—if ever. Ahead, he could see that the road only got worse as it led back into the rugged foothills and probably petered out shortly after that.

"Did you want me along as the voice of reason? Or just someone to fix the flat after one of these rocks punctures a tire?" he finally asked.

"All right," she said with a sigh. "I'll look for a place to turn around."

AT THE SOUND of the vehicle coming, the woman cried, "Quick!" Even in the dimming light, Holly Jo could see that she looked terrified. It ratcheted up her own growing terror. Her heart pounded so hard, it felt as if it would break free of her chest. "Down this way."

The woman barreled off the road and through the scrub brush and rocks, nearly falling. Breathing hard, Holly Jo did the same, sliding down the slope as the sound of the vehicle grew louder and closer. She could see another road below them.

"Duck!" the woman cried, turning to wave her to the ground as she lay down. Holly Jo dropped to the dirt, rolling over on her stomach to look back up the hillside. On the road above them, a white pickup roared past, sending up a cloud of dust. Before it could settle, the woman was on her feet again.

"Hurry. We have to go," she whispered hoarsely. She started down the steep slope again, sending rocks cascading after her, and Holly Jo followed, scared that the man might have seen them or that he could hear them. It wasn't until they were almost to the road that she realized it wouldn't be long before the man discovered them both gone. All he had to do was look in the room where she'd been held. They'd left the door standing open.

Just yards from the road, the woman fell and let out

a cry as she reached for her ankle. She'd apparently twisted it on a rock. She was bent over it, crying softly.

Holly Jo slid down to her. She'd been worrying where they were going, how far it would be before they reached a county road or a ranch house. From what she'd seen, there were none around. The man would come looking for them. Holly Jo knew it and suspected the woman did as well.

Above them, they both started at the sound of the man's bellow. *"What the hell, Melanie! What have you done!"*

As the woman tried to get to her feet, she let out another cry and fell back. "I can't put any weight on my ankle." She looked at Holly Jo with tears in her eyes. "You have to go on alone." She looked terrified. They could both hear the man swearing and throwing things. "Go! Run. You can't let him catch you! Go!"

Holly Jo scrambled on down to the road, then took off running. She could hear the man yelling back up on the hill. She was afraid he would see her and come after her in the pickup. As she reached a curve in the road, she finally dared glance back. She saw the woman lying where she'd left her. Above her, the man was silhouetted against the sun high on the slope they'd slid down.

The man hollered down to the woman he'd called Melanie. "I'm going to kill you!"

BIRDIE SLOWED THE SUV as the road got worse and sighed. She hadn't even noticed it getting so dark. In the headlights, she could see more of the same rough country. There just seemed to be an endless supply of badlands, brush and scrub broken only by narrow roads that were choked with weeds as they wound back to old mines or abandoned homesteads.

The sheriff had said there were endless old mining roads back in here, and he'd been right. Birdie felt as if she'd driven down them all. Most petered out at a rock pile or just ended for no apparent reason.

She hated to admit defeat. It went against her nature. She hoped there was enough gas left to get back to Powder Crossing. To Brand's credit, he had helped her search for Holly Jo without complaint. Even now, he looked at her almost with sympathy, as if he knew how hard it was for her to quit.

"You were right to search," he said. "There was the chance we would find her."

She couldn't work up even a thank-you smile, feeling instead close to tears. She'd been so sure they would find her.

"By now, Stuart has a BOLO out on the pickup and Melanie Baker, all because of you," Brand said. "Tomorrow is another day."

She nodded, biting her lower lip as she looked out through the glow of the headlights at this desolate-looking country now filled with deep shadows as darkness descended. Clearly it took a certain breed to stay, fighting the weather, the land, even the river, to make a living ranching here. She had to admire that kind of toughness.

It made her think of Brand and his family. Of his mother, who'd put up that fight alone for years. The woman Birdie had come here hoping to send to jail. Now she thought about what would happen to the ranch, to Brand and the rest of his family, if she succeeded.

"Want me to drive?" he asked.

She nodded and stopped to let him slide behind the wheel. "I think we have enough gas to get back to town."

He chuckled as he shifted into gear. "Only if this rig runs on fumes." Birdie leaned back in the seat and looked at Brand, his strong hands on the wheel, his gaze on the road ahead as he headed off the mountainside. *Don't fall for this cowboy rancher.* The voice sounded a lot like her nana's.

Give him a chance, she said silently to her grandmother. *I really like him.*

She looked out the windshield, the headlights piercing the darkness for at least a few yards ahead, and felt bereft. She'd been so sure Holly Jo was out here. Just as she was so sure Charlotte Stafford had killed her father?

Birdie closed her eyes, told herself that once she finished her business in the Powder River Basin, she would leave, but not yet. She didn't want to leave Brand Stafford. She felt a pull that worried her. Maybe she was more like her mother than she'd wanted to admit, because this cowboy rancher was awfully tempting.

Her eyes flew open as she heard Brand curse and hit the brakes. Flat tire.

HOLLY JO COULD hear the man yelling behind her. When she dared glance back, she could see him still silhouetted against the last of daylight etched against the mountains to the west.

She'd expected him to go down the hillside to where the woman was crying, saying she was hurt, saying she was sorry.

But he hadn't moved. He was yelling down at her, "Where is the little brat? What did you do with her?

So help me, Melanie, you fool…" Then she heard the gunshot and the woman's scream.

Holly Jo stumbled and almost fell as the boom of more gunshots rang in her ears. She realized that she could no longer hear the woman crying. Her legs ached from running, and yet she pushed harder, tears blinding her. She raced down the road as hard and fast as she could. Her side ached, and her legs trembled with the exertion after all the hours of drugged sleep.

All the while, her thoughts whirled in a terrifying tornado. The man had killed the woman. He could kill her too if he caught her. She was sure of it. The thought had her heart pounding. She couldn't let him catch her.

Her ragged breaths came out in gasps as she pushed harder, legs pumping as her feet pounded the ground. The road was little more than a trail. She knew there had to be another road, a more main one that went to where there had to be people.

Ahead there was nothing but more of the same scrub brush and rocky terrain appearing out of the growing darkness. The landscape looked endless. No lights blinked from houses or vehicles on the road ahead. She wasn't even sure she was running in the right direction.

At the sound of the pickup's revving engine, she knew she had to get off the road. Frantically she looked around for a place to hide, seeing none. All she could do was bail off the narrow road and down through the rocks and bushes in hopes of finding cover. The loose ground moved under her feet. She began to slide as the sound of the pickup's engine grew louder.

Her left foot hit a large rock. She felt herself go airborne, off balance, headfirst down the hillside. The ground came up fast and hard. She hit and rolled, tumbling crazily downward from one switchback to land on the road below. She felt searing pain, but it was nothing compared to her terror as she heard the roar of the pickup growing louder and louder.

As she tried to get up, in pain and bleeding, she was caught in the blinding headlights of the pickup. It came directly at her.

CHAPTER TWENTY

"HERE, WIPE YOUR FACE," the kidnapper snapped and tossed her a dirty rag he'd picked up off the floorboard of the truck. "You're a mess."

Only minutes ago, he'd jumped out of the pickup, leaving it running, and rushed toward her through the golden haze of the headlights. Holly Jo had tried to get up and run, but she'd known it was useless. There was nowhere she could go to get away from him. The woman was dead. She feared that if she fought him, he'd kill her, too.

He'd grabbed her, half dragging her to the truck and shoving her into the passenger seat. "Move and so help me…" He'd slammed the door.

She could feel blood running down her leg. Her clothes were filthy, but also torn and bloody. Her arms were scraped, and the top she wore was torn like her jeans. Her leg hurt bad, but that wasn't why she hadn't been able to stop crying when he'd caught her. She'd almost gotten away. Maybe if she hadn't fallen…

The real pain made her chest ache. What if she never got another chance to escape before he killed her, too?

As he drove through the darkness, she took the smelly rag and wiped at the snot from crying from her face. Then she dabbed at her bleeding leg. He didn't seem to notice as he gripped the wheel, mumbling to himself.

She could feel the tension coming off him in waves. Her fear heightened with each dark mile they traveled. In the side mirror, she saw that her forehead was also bleeding. She wiped at it with the disgusting rag.

"Spit on the rag," he ordered her. "You're missing this whole side of your face. Use the side mirror."

She reached over and rolled down the window. Earlier when he'd gone around to slide behind the wheel, she'd tried to open the door, but she shouldn't have been surprised to find the door handle missing. The sweet scent of summer night air rushed in as she put the window all the way down, spit on the rag and began to wash her face, trying hard not to gag.

As she finished, she noticed that the lower part of her shirtsleeve was torn, splattered with blood and dirt, and now barely hanging by a thread. It was her favorite shirt, white with little pink horses on it. She'd put it on that morning because she and Elaine were going to Billings to shop for her room redecoration. She'd been so excited because HH had said she could do whatever she wanted. Now she might never see her room again.

She didn't even know how long she'd been gone or if anyone was looking for her. It seemed forever since she'd headed down to the bus stop. She'd argued with Elaine that morning, saying, "Why even go to school? It's the last day before summer break, only for a half day. We could leave now."

But Elaine had held firm. "No missing school. You'll want to say goodbye to your teachers for the summer. I'll pick you up in a few hours. It will pass quickly." Did she now wish she'd never made her go to school?

If only she hadn't, Holly Jo thought as she ripped the lower part of her favorite shirt's sleeve the rest of the way off, held it out the window and let the wind suck it out to disappear behind them.

"Don't be throwing nothing out the window," he yelled at her. "Put it back up. Let's see your face. Better," he said, shooting her glances as he drove the narrow dirt road. "At least you're cleaned up a little."

"Are you taking me home?" she asked, her voice betraying her with its pitiful ring of hope.

"Soon," he said without looking at her. "Depends on Holden. If he comes through tonight…" His voice trailed off, and she felt her heart drop. She was never going home. She could feel it. Tears burned her eyes, but she didn't dare let them fall.

In the headlights, she looked out at the landscape for anything familiar, seeing nothing. Weak and bleeding, she closed her eyes, hoping that whatever he did to her would be quick and not hurt. She just needed this to end.

"YOU'RE MAKING A MISTAKE," Stuart said as Holden loaded the two briefcases, a shotgun and a box of shells into his SUV. The rancher was already wearing a loaded six-shooter at his hip.

"Not a mistake as big as the one you'll make if you try to stop me—or interfere," Holden said.

The sheriff shook his head. "You're going to get yourself killed."

The rancher's smile was grim. "I'll be taking the kidnapper with me to hell, then." He stepped past Stuart to head toward his vehicle parked out front but stopped to turn back. "Your daddy, when he was sheriff, was in the same place you're standing right now. I hope you're half as smart as he was and leave it alone. Don't fol-

low me. Whatever happens is on me. I started this—
I'll finish it."

With that, Holden climbed behind the wheel. Stuart
moved so he could close the door, then watched him
start the engine and pull out of the drive. Was it true?
Had his father backed down because of Holden? Had the
former sheriff let the rancher take the law into his own
hands? He tried to imagine the man he knew standing
by and letting that happen.

Well, he thought as he watched the SUV disappear
down the road, he wasn't his father.

"You aren't going to let him do this alone, are you?"
Elaine asked as she joined him just outside the front
door.

"No. I can't stop him, and he sure as hell won't let
me go with him, but maybe I can keep him from getting
himself and Holly Jo killed." He wasn't even sure about
that as he stepped out to his patrol SUV and swore.
Turning back to Elaine, he said, "I'm going to have to
borrow one of the ranch pickups. Seems I have two flat
tires." Holden had known he wasn't like his father and
hadn't been taking any chances.

"You can take my car," she said.

He shook his head. "A pickup would be better." He
was headed up Suicide Pass. He knew the area and had
realized immediately why the kidnapper had chosen it.
The road wound like a rattler into the mountains with
dangerous drop-offs. No way to box the kidnapper in.
No way to get out quickly if there was trouble.

Once back in there, the kidnapper would be able to
see anyone who came up the road and would be waiting. Holden was walking into a trap. He seemed to think
he knew who had Holly Jo. If it was Darius Reed, then

Holden was meeting a career criminal with nothing to lose. Stuart feared that the rancher knew it and was still determined to do this as if having accepted the outcome.

"The keys should be in that pickup over there," Elaine said, pointing to one of the newer ranch trucks. She grabbed the sheriff's arm. "Good luck."

STARING INTO THE dark road ahead, Holden gripped the steering wheel until his hands ached. He'd spent every minute since Holly Jo had been kidnapped trying to figure out who hated him enough to jeopardize the life of a child to get back at him.

The list shouldn't have been as long as it was. He honestly hadn't known. Not until Darius Reed had chosen Suicide Pass for the ransom drop.

Holden knew exactly who he was meeting tonight on that lonely, dangerous road in the middle of nowhere. It had been chosen because there was no way for the sheriff to get deputies set up in there for an ambush. But also, from the single narrow road that climbed the mountain, a person would see anyone approaching for miles.

There was no place to hide. If Holden had let the sheriff send men in earlier, it wouldn't have worked. They would have been spotted. The drop would have been negated and Holly Jo's life put in even more jeopardy.

No, Holden had to do this himself. What bothered him was that he hadn't figured out sooner who had taken her. The name Melanie Baker had meant nothing to him—just as he was sure that the woman meant nothing to the man he was meeting tonight.

He'd put himself through hell, digging up old grievances, old slights, old betrayals. What little sleep he'd gotten had been filled with ghosts from his past reminding him of the kind of man he was. One flawed to his very soul. A man who had only recently been trying to make amends for his past, worried about the legacy he was leaving his children and grandchildren. He should have known his past would catch up to him.

Ahead, he saw the turnoff to Suicide Pass and slowed. He knew the spot where he'd find the kidnapper waiting. He remembered it too well. It had been the beginning of his lies and regrets, his first true introduction to gut-roiling guilt. Little did his sixteen-year-old self know that he would have a lifetime of regret ahead of him.

Holden made the turn onto the narrow dirt road, then stopped and pulled his weapon from his holster to lay it on the console next to him. That he was going to kill the man who'd taken Holly Jo had always been a foregone conclusion. If only he could kill the rest of the past that haunted him as easily.

He gave the SUV gas and started up the road, his headlights cutting a swath of pale gold into the darkness. He couldn't see the future, but the past was with him, riding shotgun. He was sixteen again and about to make the worst decision of his life.

Then again, Holden thought as he drove, maybe he was about to make a far worse decision tonight.

CHAPTER TWENTY-ONE

THE SHERIFF KNEW better than to try to follow Holden. He'd studied a map and found an old mine road that connected to Suicide Pass Road. Holden had left early with the money, giving himself plenty of time.

That also gave Stuart plenty of time. He'd thought about taking deputies with him, but they were all too green for something this sensitive. If the kidnapper showed up with Holly Jo, her safety had to come first. He hated to think what Deputy Dodson might do in a standoff. The man had a hair-trigger temper and a chip on his shoulder. Look how badly he'd handled bringing in Brand Stafford for questioning.

Which was why Stuart was driving up into the mountains alone tonight in a borrowed pickup. He'd brought plenty of firepower but hoped he wouldn't have to use it. If he could depend on Holden to just make the trade and not try to stop the kidnapper...

He knew that wasn't in the cards. Holden McKenna was determined to make the kidnapper pay with his life—even if it meant risking his own, not to mention Holly Jo's. Stuart hated the thought that Holden was meeting Darius Reed. He told himself the rancher could be wrong about who was waiting for him. Hopefully it would be someone not as criminally cutthroat as Reed.

The sheriff took a breath and let it out slowly. He needed to be the calm, levelheaded one with the single purpose of getting Holly Jo back safely with as little bloodshed as possible.

He took a road to the west a few miles from the turnoff to Suicide Pass. The last thing he wanted was for Holden to know what he was up to. He hadn't gone far when he saw the old mine road. It looked like a Jeep trail. He turned onto it and started back into the mountains. Suicide Pass was above him like a dark, ominous shadow hanging over him. He knew how dangerous this was. If his presence tonight fouled the ransom drop or, worse, got Holly Jo killed, Holden would shoot him. That was if the kidnapper didn't.

But it was another reason he hadn't brought a deputy or two. If this didn't work, he had only himself to blame. He didn't want to get his men killed as well.

There was no moon tonight, the stars feeling distant because of the low cloud cover. He looked up toward the rough outline of the mountain against the slightly less dark sky. He saw no lights. Holden should be making his way up the mountain, though his headlights were not visible from below.

He knew he couldn't go much farther up the mine road without his headlights being seen. After parking, he grabbed his shotgun. He already had his sidearm loaded in his holster. He shoved a couple more shotgun shells into his jacket pocket and set off on foot—just as he'd known he would have to.

The climb was long and rugged. Normally he kept in good shape, but his near-death experience and time in the hospital months ago had left him feeling weak and out of shape. As he scaled the rough terrain of the mountainside, he thought about all the things that could go wrong. What if he miscalculated the spot where the kidnapper would be waiting for Holden? Or got there too late?

He pushed himself and was breathing hard when he heard the labored sound of a vehicle engine. Holden's SUV. He couldn't see any headlights since he was still below the road, but he could hear the SUV's approach. He angled up the mountainside, trying to get ahead of the rancher.

Even over his labored breathing, Stuart heard the SUV halt, the motor idling. He'd been right. Holden had stopped just short of the top. The kidnapper must be waiting a dozen yards ahead of him. Stuart scrambled toward the road above him, telling himself that the kidnapper would have parked near the wide spot.

The sheriff planned to climb up on the road on the backside of the kidnapper's vehicle. Holden's SUV would be a little farther down the road. With luck, neither man would see him.

HOLDEN'S HEADLIGHTS ILLUMINATED the man standing in the middle of the road. Darius Reed was smaller than he remembered. He'd aged, just as the rest of them had, but he looked older than his years. He also looked more dangerous with a gun dangling at his side.

Behind him was an older-model white pickup parked against the side of the mountain away from the dropoff. It was the spot he and Constance had parked that night. He hadn't been up here since.

He fought the urge to hit the gas, run Darius down and take the chance that the man couldn't get a lethal shot off before his body met the SUV's bumper. But from this distance, he feared the man might be able to dive out of the way before he could hit him. Same with firing his weapon. Worse, it might risk Holly Jo's life further.

Holden whirred down his window and yelled out, "Where's Holly Jo?"

"Where's the money?" Darius called back.

He reached over and picked up one of the briefcases from the passenger-side floorboard. He held it out the open window and dropped it on the ground next to the SUV. The metal briefcase nearly went over the edge of the road to careen down the mountainside.

"Bring it to me."

Holden had to bite his tongue to keep from saying what he was thinking. "Not until I see the girl," he yelled back. "The next briefcase full of money I will throw over the side of this mountain if I don't see Holly Jo. Now!"

The man hesitated. "She's in the truck. Once I see the money and you admit what you did and apologize to my face, we can make the trade."

Sure, that was going to happen. Was Holly Jo waiting in the man's truck? Holden wouldn't bet his life on it. "We both know what I did. What's the point of me apologizing to you?"

"Are you serious? After what you did to my sister? Constance deserved better. You ruined her life that night on this mountain, and you know it. She was never the same after she lost your son—the one you refused to claim. Worse, you insulted her, throwing your daddy's money at her."

Weeks after his night together with Constance on this mountain, when she and her brother had contacted the ranch to tell him she was pregnant, she'd made the mistake of going to his father for help. Of course his old man's answer was always to either throw money at the problem or use force if necessary to make it go away.

"You're not marrying that Reed girl, so don't even think about it," his father had told him after sending Darius running for his life from a few ranch hands and paying off Constance. "I won't let one mistake ruin your life. It's taken care of. They won't be back. Just make sure this doesn't happen again."

It hadn't been the first time he hadn't stood up to his domineering father, nor would it be the last. That he might be anything like his father made him sick to his stomach.

Holden now recalled seeing Constance's obit in the *Billings Gazette* only weeks ago. Her brother had always been a hothead. In the obit, it had said that Constance was only survived by her brother Darius of Rawlins, Wyoming. What it didn't say was that Darius was doing twenty to life for second-degree homicide at the state penitentiary in Rawlins.

"You want this money or not?" Holden called back. "Harming Holly Jo won't bring back your sister or her son."

"*Her* son?" Darius let out a bark of a laugh. "See, that's the problem. You never took responsibility. Danny was *your* son. Things could have been different if you had done the honorable thing and married her—or at least claimed your child. Now you're not the only one who's going to have to pay for your sins. Bring me the money or you won't see Holly Jo again."

Holden swore as he opened the SUV's door, tucked his weapon into his jacket pocket and picked up the briefcase from the dirt. He itched to pull his gun and finish this, but common sense overrode his fury, telling him to not risk it. He needed to get closer. He needed to look Darius in the eye when he pulled the trigger.

Clearly anxious, Darius shifted on his feet. Maybe he was worried that Holden planned to kill him. He should be. Within six yards of him, Holden stopped.

"Open it on the ground so I can see the money," Darius said, lifting his weapon and aiming it at him. "I'll get her as soon as I see the money. But unless it is all there, she won't be leaving this mountain."

STUART CLIMBED UP onto the road in the dark shadow of the mountain, yards from the kidnapper's pickup. He'd been listening and had hoped the two would keep talking. The noise would cover his footfalls as he hugged the mountain, and the added darkness it provided would enable him to work his way toward the white pickup.

He desperately wanted to end this before blood was shed, but he had to know if Holly Jo was in the truck. If the man Holden called Darius Reed hadn't brought her, then Stuart needed to make sure the man lived long enough to tell them where he'd left the girl.

Once he knew she was safe—

"If I don't see Holly Jo in the next few seconds, you're not getting a dime," Holden yelled. Stuart could hear him getting angrier. He doubted the rancher planned to let Darius walk away with any of the money. Not tonight. Not ever.

"I told you to open it so I can see the money," Darius said, sounding like he was losing patience. Holden was already on edge, a loose cannon. Stuart couldn't trust that he wouldn't lose his temper and kill the kidnapper before they had Holly Jo.

The sheriff reached the pickup and edged along the side. If Holly Jo was in the truck and he could make sure she was safe before—

The pickup was empty. No Holly Jo. He felt his heart drop as he pulled his weapon and started to work his way to the rear of the pickup. He would have a clear view of Darius Reed's back once he—

"You didn't bring the girl, did you, you lying son of a—"

The sound of gunfire filled the air, echoing off the side of the mountain.

HOLDEN HADN'T EXPECTED he would be the one to escalate things so quickly. He had tossed the heavy briefcase into the air at the man, pulled the gun from his pocket and begun firing. The first shot struck the briefcase. The second went wild.

He didn't realize that Darius was firing back, even though the air seemed to fill with gunshots. Just as he didn't feel the first shot that hit him in the shoulder or the next one in his side. He was emptying his gun in the direction the man had been standing. Unfortunately, most of the shots must have been going into the dirt, because when the dust settled, the man and the briefcase of money were gone.

As he fell to the ground, he heard more shots, then the roar of a truck engine that needed a good mechanic.

By then, he was looking up at the stars—and Stuart Layton's face.

"I thought I told you to stay out of this," he said to the sheriff before everything went dark.

CHAPTER TWENTY-TWO

AFTER HIS ATTEMPT to stop the kidnapper had failed, Stuart felt the rest of the night blur past, starting with a call to 911 for an ambulance to meet him at the turnoff to Suicide Pass. He'd done what he could for Holden, gotten him into his SUV and driven him down the road as the ambulance and EMTs arrived. From there, Holden was airlifted to Billings, while the sheriff made the call to the family.

"And Holly Jo?" Elaine asked after he'd informed her of Holden's injuries.

"She wasn't in the kidnapper's truck," Stuart said. "He must have stashed her somewhere. I've already sent deputies out to search for her in the ransom drop area."

"What about you? Are you all right?" she asked, no doubt hearing the despair in his voice.

He'd been determined to take Darius Reed alive, afraid otherwise they would never find Holly Jo. He'd shot to wound the man, but unfortunately, Darius had pinned him down with gunfire. He couldn't be sure that he'd wounded the man before Darius had jumped into his truck and taken off.

"As well as I can be with Holden fighting for his life and Holly Jo still missing," he said in answer to Elaine's question. "You'll let the rest of the family know?"

"Yes. I'm headed to the hospital now," Elaine said.

"Thank God you were there, Stuart. Otherwise… You saved his life."

That wasn't the way he saw it. He'd failed, and the ransom drop had gone south. He knew he had to put it behind him. He hadn't slept since Holly Jo had been taken. Getting so close and letting the kidnapper get away was devastating, but not as much as the thought that Holden McKenna might be dying.

As the sun rose, he knew the clock was still ticking. He had to find Holly Jo and the man who'd kidnapped her before it was too late. Unfortunately, Darius had gotten away with one of the briefcases full of money. He might decide that it was enough and take off, figuring to cut his losses. Where did that leave Holly Jo, if she was still alive?

CHARLOTTE HAD PROVED in her more than half century of life that she wasn't above lying to get what she wanted. She was ready to do whatever it took to get into Holden's hospital room short of taking a nurse hostage. But not even that was out of the realm of possibility.

When Elaine had called to tell her that he'd been shot twice, her heart had shuddered to a stop. All breath had rushed out. She'd had to sit down. "Is he—"

"He's still alive, but he's in critical condition," Elaine told her. "He's been airlifted to Billings. The kidnapper got away with half of the ransom money. There's been no sign of Holly Jo."

Charlotte had begun to cry. This woman who had spent years refusing to let one tear drop for Holden McKenna sat down and bawled. All she could think about was the last time she'd seen him. She couldn't bear the thought that she might never see him again. That he would die with things the way they were between them.

"He's not dead," Elaine said, quickly trying to comfort her. "You know how strong he is. If anyone can pull through this, it's Holden."

Charlotte knew it was true, but she had to see him, had to tell him how sorry she was, had to beg him to forgive her. She choked back the sobs, wiped at her tears and tried to pull herself together. "How are you?"

"I'm worried about Holden, worried about Holly Jo. Cooper's at the ranch, waiting to see if the kidnapper calls. If he still has Holly Jo, he might. If he's greedy enough, he might want to make a deal for the other briefcase full of money."

"I have to see Holden."

"He hasn't regained consciousness after the surgeries to remove the bullets," Elaine said.

"I'm coming to Billings. I will stay in the waiting room down the hall until he wakes up."

Her friend sighed, aware how single-minded the woman was. Charlotte was capable of just about anything when she wanted something badly enough. "Take your time driving to Billings. With luck, he will be conscious by the time you get here. But, Charlotte, he might not want to see you."

Those last words struck like a poison arrow to her heart. "I know. I'll take my chances."

"Call me when you get to the hospital. Also, I'll have a better chance of getting you in to see him if there isn't a scene."

"You know me so well." Charlotte felt a lightness in her chest as she disconnected. She'd never appreciated Elaine's friendship more than she did at this moment. They'd gotten close over the years, even though their face-to-face time had always been limited. It often amazed her how the friendship had started, let alone grown over the years.

"Hang on, Holden," she said as she hurried to get dressed for the trip to the hospital. "Don't you dare die." She packed an overnight bag, knowing she would stay as long as it took.

BIRDIE OPENED HER eyes and blinked at the bright sunshine coming through the passenger-side window of her SUV. She sat up, confused for a moment about why she'd just spent the night in the middle of nowhere in her car.

As she looked up the road, she spotted Brand walking toward her, carrying what appeared to be a red gas can. Realization dawned. Driving out of this rugged country last night, she'd hoped there was enough gas to get back to town after Brand had changed the tire in the dark. It appeared she'd been wrong.

She climbed out of the SUV and stretched, wondering how far he'd had to hike to the nearest ranch for gas—and why he hadn't awakened her. Smiling to herself, she walked toward him. She admired the way he moved, that lean, muscular body, those long legs, those broad shoulders and the tilt of his Stetson. She felt a hard tug at her heart again and couldn't help but remember his kiss. The man was dangerous. She didn't need her grandmother to tell her that.

Dangerous to her heart, yes, but otherwise, her hero, she thought as he grew closer. He'd supported her yesterday. She wouldn't have dragged him along if she hadn't been sure they were going to find Holly Jo. It was a feeling she hadn't been able to shake after her run-in with the woman believed to be Melanie Baker.

That she'd been wrong made her question what she was doing—not just with Brand Stafford but with this quest of hers to prove the kind of man her father had been and see that his killer and accomplice went to prison. Brand was right. She was too impulsive, jumping in before seeing how deep the water was. She'd told herself that she'd never been a risk-taker when it came to men, though—until she came to Powder Crossing. Before that, she'd done everything that her grandmother would have expected of her, gone to a good college, done well, graduated and gotten herself a good job.

The only thing she hadn't found was that good man.

Then she'd come to the Powder River Basin and had thrown caution to the wind the first time she'd laid eyes on Brand Stafford.

Birdie was almost to him when she heard something rustle in the morning breeze and glanced in the tall weeds beside the road. She'd heard stories of the size of the rattlesnakes that lived in the badlands.

But to her relief, the sound came from a torn scrap of fabric caught on the top of a weed. Her eyes widened when she saw that the fabric was white with little pink horses on it—except where the dark color of dried blood had left a stain.

CHAPTER TWENTY-THREE

As THE SHERIFF pulled in behind Birdie Malone's green SUV, he saw that she and Brand had actually listened. They were waiting in the vehicle. They got out as soon as he stopped. By the time he opened his door, they had climbed out as well.

"Down there," Brand said. "On the right side of the road in the weeds."

He looked to where the rancher pointed and saw a piece of cloth fluttering in the breeze. Even from a distance, he could see what appeared to be part of the top Holly Jo had been wearing when she was kidnapped.

Moving closer, he saw the splattered blood and swallowed hard. He'd feared there was a reason she wasn't in the kidnapper's pickup last night. Because she was already dead.

Stuart squinted up at the rugged mountains and the Jeep trail that led back into them. He felt a chill. "What made you drive back in here?" he asked Birdie. He'd known yesterday that she wasn't going to quit looking for the girl.

"Just a feeling," she said.

He nodded. "Have you two been out here all night?"

"Ran out of gas," Brand said. "After getting a flat tire."

"Then you haven't heard." Stuart cleared his throat, remembering that Brand was Holden's biological son.

He had no idea how Brand felt about that. "Holden Mc-Kenna was shot last night during the ransom drop. He's in critical condition at the hospital in Billings." He saw Brand swallow and looked away. Birdie reached over and squeezed Brand's hand before letting go. "Thought you'd want to know."

"We should get going," Brand said, looking to Birdie, who nodded. She looked as discouraged as he felt as they left.

This time the sheriff had brought two deputies to help in the search. He bagged the torn scrap of Holly Jo's shirt and ordered a search for her body and any other evidence.

Holly Jo hadn't been in the pickup last night. This road where the scrap of fabric had been found would eventually lead to Suicide Pass. Stuart had little hope that the girl was still alive. He was still waiting to hear from the kidnapper, but feared he might not.

This morning he'd called the hospital. Holden had come out of surgery but was still in critical condition. He had not regained consciousness.

The sheriff couldn't help his desolation. Everything had gone so badly last night up on the mountain, and it seemed to be getting worse as his radio barked. One of the deputies he'd brought to help search the area had found something. Near an abandoned milking barn on private property belonging to an out-of-state landowner. The body of a woman who'd been shot numerous times.

Stuart listened as his deputy described Melanie Baker.

"There's an old camper hidden in the trees behind the barn," the deputy said. "I think this is where the kidnapper was keeping Holly Jo."

"I'll be right there," the sheriff said and called the crime techs. He didn't know what they could find that would help at this point. They knew who the kidnapper was. Darius Reed. They knew why he'd taken Holly Jo. They knew that he had already killed one person and wounded another.

What they didn't know was if Holly Jo was still alive, and if so, where she was. With her kidnapper? Or buried somewhere out here in the badlands or down in the fertile soil next to the Powder River?

BRAND DROVE BACK to town to the store where he'd left his pickup yesterday. The day was beautiful, all clear blue sky and sunshine. A perfect Montana summer day. Summer was so short this far north that this day felt wasted on them because neither was going to enjoy it the way they should.

"I need to pick up the supplies and take them out to the ranch," he said to Birdie.

She hadn't said two words on the way into town. He could see how she was feeling, much like he was. He'd actually hoped that Birdie's intuition would lead them to Holly Jo. She'd been right about the girl being in the area, not that it helped under the circumstances.

"Are you going to be all right?" he asked her.

"If Holly Jo is dead, it's my fault. If I hadn't followed the woman—"

"If you hadn't, we would never have found more evidence," Brand said. "We don't know that Holly Jo is dead." But the hollow-eyed glance Birdie gave him made it clear that she no longer believed that.

She looked away.

He desperately wanted to assure her, but he had so

little to give at this point. "We can only hope that she'll be found alive and well. It's still possible."

Birdie gave him a skeptical look, but seemed to appreciate that he was trying. "Are you going to the hospital to see your father?"

"The timing doesn't seem quite right, but maybe. I haven't seen Ryder in days, and I haven't been taking his phone calls. I got a text that the supplies need to be picked up before noon. Also, I could use a shower and a change of clothes no matter what I decide to do. What about you?" He couldn't stand leaving her alone the way he knew she was feeling.

She cleared her throat. "I have a couple of leads on my father's murder that I was following up on yesterday before I saw the pickup go by. That is why I came to Powder Crossing to start with."

Brand didn't know what to say. "Maybe I'll see you later, then." It felt strange leaving her, both of them feeling down. Last night after they'd run out of gas, they'd both been tired and discouraged. They'd put their seats back and stared up at the stars through the moonroof and fallen asleep. He hadn't awakened her this morning when he left to find some gas, but even then, it was hard to leave her.

They'd been together so much over the past couple of days, he hated the thought of her alone and up to her own devices.

But it was a good reminder that she was still intent on proving his mother a killer. That emotional crevasse would be between them until Birdie found justice—or maybe even beyond that. Looking for Holly Jo had just been a short reprieve from what was bound to come. It was clear where her road led—out of Powder Crossing, once she saw her father's killer and her accomplice behind bars.

He climbed out of her SUV, leaving it running, and waited while she went around and slipped behind the wheel. He thought of their kisses yesterday as he closed her door and stepped back. He'd never become this attached so quickly. There was no denying the chemistry between them, even though they both seemed to be fighting it. *Let her go*, he told himself even as he worried about her. Who knew what kind of trouble she could get into on her own?

With a small wave, she drove away, and he headed into the store.

"TELL ME HE'S conscious and that he's going to make it," Charlotte said the moment Elaine met her at the hospital entrance. They took seats out of the way as Elaine provided what information she had.

"He's still unconscious, but his vitals are good, and the doctor is optimistic that he will pull through."

She had to fight the relief and took a moment before she said, "What happened?"

"He's Holden McKenna. He stubbornly went to make the ransom drop by himself. If the sheriff hadn't followed him against Holden's orders, he would have bled out in the middle of that mountainside road."

"And Holly Jo?"

Elaine shook her head. "No word on her."

"You think the girl is still alive?"

Elaine took a long breath and let it out. "I'm praying so. Now Stuart is waiting for the kidnapper to contact him. If he doesn't, then Holly Jo's chances aren't good."

"Oh, I'm so sorry." Charlotte could see the toll this

had taken on her friend. Elaine was the strongest woman she knew. She'd only seen her this upset one other time. Both times had involved loss. She reached over and took her hand.

"That girl is strong and smart," Elaine said, as if trying to convince herself. "She won't give up. She can't. We can't. We're going to find her."

"And Holden is going to pull through. It can't end like this."

Elaine nodded but didn't look any more convinced than Charlotte felt. She couldn't bear the thought of that girl being gone and what it would do to Holden. Nor could she bear Holden dying. Even if he never forgave her, never loved her again, she had to know that he was still with her, even if at the ranch next door.

Even if she never saw him again.

"Please, I need to see him," she said. "I promise I'll make it quick."

THE GOOD NEWS, the sheriff told himself, was that they didn't find Holly Jo's body at the abandoned milk barn or in the small old camper parked behind it or anywhere on the road on the way to Suicide Pass.

The coroner had come out and picked up Melanie Baker's body after the crime techs had finished. Stuart had taken photos, searched the premises and found the room where it appeared Holly Jo had been held.

A plastic juice container had been bagged as evidence, along with the blanket, mat and bucket. He suspected they would find her fingerprints on the juice bottle and her DNA on the blanket. As he'd looked around the dark room, he'd thought about the hours she must have spent here, terrified that she wouldn't be found, wouldn't be saved. He tried to swallow the lump that formed in his throat as his cell rang.

Unknown caller. His pulse kicked up a beat.

Stuart stepped out into the beautiful Montana summer day and took the call, his heart a thunder in his chest.

"Hello, Sheriff." The man's voice was the same one Stuart had heard last night up on Suicide Pass. "I missed you last night." The laugh was eerie, too high-pitched. "But at least I hit my target. Tell me he's dead."

"Sorry, I can't do that. He's going to pull through. Where's Holly Jo?"

"I thought I was a better shot than that. As for Holly Jo, you still owe me money since I didn't get the other million dollars."

"I'm going to need proof that she's still alive," Stuart said.

"Sure." He heard what sounded like the rustling of fabric, then "Say hello to the sheriff."

"Sheriff—" That one word came out in a rush of emotion.

Stuart felt it knock the wind out of him. "Holly Jo—" But she was gone. The kidnapper was back.

"If you want her to *stay* alive, you will do exactly what I say," Darius said.

Just hearing her voice had his heart pounding. She was alive! Scared. Still in trouble. But alive. No doubt she was wondering if she would ever be rescued. He wanted to bellow at the pain in his chest. She was alive! At least for the moment.

"Don't hurt her." The words came out between clenched teeth.

"Don't threaten me. Just listen."

Stuart took a breath and let it out slowly. "I'm listening."

Once he disconnected, he checked to see if the call had been traced.

"Nothing. Maybe he'll make another call closer to a cell tower. If he forgets to turn off his phone, we still might be able to at least get some idea where he is. That's if there are cell towers nearby," the tech told him. "We'll keep trying."

Stuart called his FBI agent contact. "The girl is still alive. He wants the rest of the money. He says he's written an obit for Holden McKenna. He wants it published."

"I thought the rancher wasn't dead."

"He's not."

"What about the exchange?"

"I'm meeting him this evening at a crossroads in the middle of nowhere. He definitely knows this area. He picks places where it's impossible to set up an ambush," the sheriff said. "This time he won't get the money unless I get the girl."

HOLLY JO HAD heard the sheriff say her name before the phone was ripped out of her hands. She'd cried out in frustration. There was so much she needed to tell him. But the kidnapper had slapped tape back over her mouth and pushed her against the passenger side of the pickup, where he tied her to the grab bar again. He'd fixed the door so she couldn't open it or roll down the window, saying he couldn't let her spoil his plans.

His plans were what she'd wanted to tell the sheriff about. The large cans of gas in the back of the pickup and what the man was saying he was going to do to the McKennas and their ranch house.

Last night, he'd left her tied up in a shed. He hadn't come back until almost daylight. He'd brought a metal briefcase that he kept opening. She saw that it was full of money. He'd counted it. So much money, and yet he didn't seem happy about it.

He'd started ranting about how he'd listened to Melanie. Trying to make her happy, he'd asked for the money, a mistake. He had just wanted the truth to come out. But now…now he wanted more. He wanted revenge.

She'd listened to him debate how to get to Holden in the hospital. After a while, he'd finally given up on that idea and pulled some old papers out of the glove box and a pen. She'd watched him scribble something onto the paper.

When he'd finished, he folded the paper and put it into his pocket. He smiled over at her. "I know just how to take Holden down," he said more to himself than to Holly Jo. "I'll destroy everything the man has built. Everything he holds dear."

The look in his eyes when they focused on her sent a chill through her. If the sheriff didn't find her soon, she was going to die.

CHAPTER TWENTY-FOUR

CHARLOTTE HATED THE hospital smell, the sounds of machines and squeak of nurses' shoes scurrying around, but worse, she hated the worried, scared looks on people's faces as they waited for news about their loved ones. She promised herself she wouldn't break down even as tears burned her eyes. She pushed open the door to Holden's room.

He had always been big and strong, like a tree that had withstood years of storms to stand tall to the very end. She knew this man's heart, had heard it pound in sync with hers. She couldn't bear the thought that it might stop beating and she might never lay her head on his chest and hear it again.

She moved to his bedside slowly, afraid that he might already have left her. Relief filled her eyes with fresh hot tears as she saw the rise and fall of his chest. She swallowed the lump that had risen in her throat, her heart breaking at the sight of him lying there so helpless.

"Holden, I'm here." Her voice broke as she looked down at his hand. It was large like his heart, strong, and yet it could be so gentle. She lifted it from the bed to hold it to her lips for a moment.

Her words came out a whisper. "I love you. I've always loved you. Will always love you. I'm so sorry." She placed his hand back on the bed and brushed her fingers over his cheek. "I understand if you can never forgive me. But don't leave me. Please don't leave me."

She heard the hospital room door open. Hurriedly she wiped her tears, then turned, knowing her time was up. Holden would survive—she had to believe that. But she feared he would never forgive her and would be lost to her forever. Taking a deep breath, she let it out as she nodded to the nurse and left, her heart shattered in a million little pieces.

IT WAS SOMETHING one of the regulars from the Wild Horse Bar in town had said that had gotten Birdie thinking— and had gotten her mind off Holly Jo and her fear for her for a little while. She found elderly retired ranch hand Elmer Franklin on his usual stool, bellied up to the bar, drinking coffee with a couple of his friends.

His face lit up when he saw her. She walked up to him. "Mind if I have a word?" She motioned to a table against the wall, away from the bar.

Elmer flushed, looked to his friends, then slid off his stool. "Get you somethin' to drink?" She shook her head, so he brought his cup of coffee with him as he followed her over to the table. As she pulled out a chair and sat down, she could see that he was nervous. It made her even more certain that he knew something.

Birdie waited as he sat down. He was about the age her father would have been now. She swallowed that thought. "You said something yesterday that got me thinking."

"Can't imagine anything I would say that would be worth mulling over." He said it into the coffee cup before taking a sip.

"You said that the last time you saw my father, he was threatening to do something crazy."

"Did I?" He chuckled and looked back in the direction of the bar.

"Elmer, I need to know what he said to you. Please."

"Not good to speak ill of the dead," he muttered. "Especially to his daughter."

"I'm looking for the truth. So don't honey-coat it." Her grandmother had told her that she might not like what she learned. At the time, she hadn't believed that it might be true. Nana had always spoken favorably of her son. Was this going to be what her grandmother had been talking about?

"What was he threatening to do?" she asked quietly, leaning toward Elmer, and waited.

He cleared his throat, licked his lips and met her gaze. "He was upset, worse than usual. I never much paid attention to anything he said when he was upset." She waited as patiently as possible as Elmer shuffled his feet under his chair and took another sip of his coffee. "He was trying his best to get along with that woman. Everyone knew what Charlotte was like." Still she waited. "He said he'd discovered something interesting that he might use against her."

"Something about…"

"Brand, her son. She'd been talking to the boy––he must have been about five, I think––but when he left to go outside, she said, 'He is so much like you. Damn you, Holden.' Dixon got out of there lickety-split, but he said he'd noticed before that the boy didn't even look like the others."

"What did he plan to do with this information?" she asked, heart in her throat as Elmer looked away and shifted in his seat. "He threatened to use it against Charlotte." That most certainly could have gotten him killed, she thought.

But Elmer was shaking his head. "He was more interested in talking to the boy's father."

"He told Holden McKenna?"

"You've got to understand," Elmer said. "He'd pretty much given up on making the marriage work. He was broke, and Charlotte had made it clear that when she kicked him out, he wouldn't be getting a dime. He thought Holden might be willing to help him out to keep the truth about Brand quiet."

"Blackmail?" Birdie didn't want to believe it. But she'd known that her father must have been desperate. "So what happened?"

Elmer shrugged. "I never saw him again. Who knows if he went to the McKenna Ranch or if he went back to Charlotte that night? No one saw him again."

HOLDEN OPENED HIS EYES. *PAIN.* For a moment he couldn't remember what had happened to him. Then it came back in a rush, accompanied by even more pain.

"Holly Jo?" The words came out a whisper, his throat so dry, his tongue felt as if it was covered in cotton. "Holly Jo?" He looked over at the person sitting in the chair next to his bed, not surprised to see Elaine.

She rose quickly to come to his bedside. He'd never seen her so upset, but she regained control and said, "Holly Jo's still alive, but we haven't been able to bring her home yet."

He looked around the room, then at Elaine. "Charlotte?"

"She was here. She's been here since she heard, but they are only allowing family in to see you."

Holden frowned. "I must have dreamed—"

"I talked them into letting her see you for just a few minutes," Elaine said. "You know how she is. She would have found a way to see you one way or another."

He nodded, struggling to keep his eyes open. "I've made such a mess of things."

"All you need to worry about is getting well and out of this hospital bed."

"I need to see the sheriff."

"Holden, I don't think—"

"Stuart. Tell him. Please." He closed his eyes and felt himself drifting. Lottie. He hadn't dreamed it. She'd been here. But had the rest been merely a hallucination? He looked down at his hand, remembering her touch. She'd said she loved him. That definitely could have been a dream.

He must have slept, because when he opened his eyes again, Sheriff Stuart Layton was sitting in the chair next to his bed. He tried to speak, his throat too tight, his mouth too dry.

Stuart got up to get him a cup of water.

He took a sip, so thirsty he wanted to down the entire cup. "Holly Jo?" he managed to say after a few sips.

"She wasn't in the pickup last night. Darius hadn't brought her with him for the trade."

He'd suspected as much.

"Still trying to find her and the kidnapper," the sheriff continued. "He wants the rest of the money. He called. I'm making the drop this evening. I'm going to get the girl back."

Holden could see the weight of all this on the sheriff. He hated that he'd only added to that burden by letting his anger get the best of him. He could have gotten them both killed up on that mountain.

"You need to know the truth," Holden said. "Should have told you sooner. You were right. He doesn't really care about the money or an apology or acknowledgment. He wants to destroy me." He grabbed the sheriff's hand. "I know now. He'll kill Holly Jo."

BIRDIE PRIED OPEN the window and swung her leg over the sill. She listened for a moment before she dropped into the room. Looking around, she saw that she'd guessed right. It was a bedroom. But was it the right one?

The room was at the back of the house. From where she stood in the dim early light of morning, the room showed no sign of being inhabited. The bed had been made to perfection as if the place was a five-star hotel. It smelled good, too.

As she rounded the bed, headed for the closed closest door, she stumbled over something that had been left on the floor. Looking down, she saw what she had tripped over. A pair of cowboy boots casually kicked off. A few feet away was a long-sleeved Western shirt. She picked up the shirt and took a sniff, smiling at the familiar male scent. This was the right room.

As her eyes adjusted to cool darkness, she followed a trail of discarded clothing from the man-size cowboy boots to the door she suspected went to the bathroom. She could hear water running as she got closer. The room had taken on a different scent, distinctly male, as she moved past socks, jeans, a T-shirt and finally a worn straw cowboy hat.

Quietly, she opened the bathroom door into the steam-filled room. She could see Brand behind the frosted glass. He'd told her that she was too impulsive. She wondered if he'd still feel that way in a few minutes as she stripped off her clothing and opened the shower door.

BRAND THOUGHT FOR a moment this amazing creature coming through the steam was only a dream. But he couldn't have dreamed this beauty before him. Water beaded on her long dark hair. Rivulets ran down over her full breasts, into the hollow of her flat stomach and straight to the V between her legs.

My God, she was extraordinary. Birdie smiled at his obvious surprise at seeing her appear in his shower as she joined him under the warm spray and closed the shower door behind her.

"No water at your hotel?" he asked as he stepped back to give her more room in the large shower.

"How did you know?" She gave him an innocent look.

"Probably no soap either?" he asked as he reached for the bath gel, poured some into his palm. Moving closer, he slowly began to lather her shoulders. She leaned into him as he massaged her neck, gently caressing her throat.

"You know where this will get you, don't you?" she asked, holding his gaze.

When he didn't respond right away, she added, "Need some time to think about it?"

He chuckled as he slid his soapy hands slowly down to her breasts. "I'm pretty happy right where I am." Her nipples were already hard and pulsing as he smoothed the gel over the rock-hard tips, cupping her breasts, thumbing the rosy tips until she let out a pleasurable sound.

Their gazes locked. "So we're finally no longer skating around this? We're really going to do this?"

She smiled. "Give the county something to really talk about, you mean?"

He nodded, unable to believe he was here with this woman. The old Brand would have run like hell from a woman like Birdie Malone. That Brand didn't take chances, especially with his heart.

But here he was, and he'd never felt more alive, more ready to put that man he'd been behind him. Loving Birdie was risky. It was scary as hell, but he was already halfway there. He drew her closer, their bodies molding together as he dropped his mouth to hers.

BIRDIE TRIED TO catch her breath as they drew apart from the kiss. His hands cupped her wet breasts before trailing down over her belly, dipping between her legs. His fingers were slick and wet. She had to lean back against the shower wall as her legs began to quiver. He leaned into her, kissing her as his fingers moved. She moaned against his mouth, gripping his shoulders as the heat inside her rose and rose, catching fire as her climax came hard and fast, making her shudder with the intensity of it. She fell into him, his arms coming around her as she caught her breath, legs wobbly. He drew her closer, kissing her tenderly, his hands cupping her buttocks.

Drawing back from a kiss, she picked up the shower gel and, after filling her palm, began to explore his body. She'd already seen his impressive naked chest, but the sight of the muscular rest of him was truly spectacular. She said as much, making him laugh.

"Haven't been with a man for a while?" he joked.

She moved her hands over his chest, his hard nipples, and went lower, avoiding his gaze.

"Birdie?" he asked and reached down to capture her hands, to still them in his. "You have been with other men, right?"

She let out a laugh. "Of course." Still she didn't meet his eyes.

"How many?"

"Seriously? You want to have that conversation now?" She raised her eyes slowly. Their gazes locked. "Not that many, okay? Don't laugh, but maybe I've been saving myself for a good man, the right man, like my grandmother told me to."

He let go of her hands. "You sure you don't want to keep looking?"

She leaned into him, kissing him as she felt his desire throbbing against her belly. "Don't count yourself short, Brand Stafford. You're a good man. The right one?" She cocked her head. "I guess only time will tell." She took him in hand, making him groan.

"You're going to be the death of me, Birdie Malone."

She laughed and pulled him close. "I'll be right there with you all the way."

The water turned cold in an instant. Ice-cold. They both yelped, then began laughing as Brand hurriedly turned off the shower and they pushed open the door, stumbling out to grab towels.

As Birdie wrapped one around her chilled body, she felt Brand's gaze on her. She swallowed as she looked up at him. *In for a penny, in for a...* Whatever. She couldn't remember all of her grandmother's sayings.

He took a step toward her, and her mouth went dry.

Maybe he wasn't the right man—at least, he didn't think so—but she wanted him, more than she'd ever wanted anything. *Sorry, Grandma.*

HE SAID HIS name was Darius Reed. As they waited in the truck back up a gully for the cover of darkness, he talked, telling Holly Jo stories about growing up in the Powder River Basin. The more he talked, the sadder he sounded, frightening her. It was as if he'd given up. He was no longer talking about starting a fire out at the McKennas' or spending all Holden's money. He talked about the past and the death of his sister, Constance.

"Why do you hate Holden?" she'd asked as he'd fallen silent for a moment. After his phone call, he'd taken the tape off her mouth, but left her tied up.

He'd looked up, tears in his eyes. "Constance was my older sister. Holden ruined her life." She listened as he told her how Holden had taken advantage of his sister, getting her pregnant up on Suicide Pass, Holden's father throwing money at her instead of making his son do the right thing. "She had a son."

"What happened to him?" Holly Jo asked quietly.

"Constance couldn't handle him when he got older. He died robbing a liquor store down in Wyoming when he was fourteen. He needed a father, his real father, not the men Constance brought into the house. She never got over Holden. She'd had a crush on him for years. Our father worked for one of the oil drilling companies way back when. She met Holden at a rodeo, thought he was somethin'."

She tried to imagine HH at sixteen and couldn't. Just a boy not that much older than her.

"The last time Constance saw Holden, he showed up with his father. Now, there was a real bastard. The old man said there was no way his son was going to marry her and shoved money at her, warning her that he never wanted to see her again. I was too young to do anything about it. Not that Constance would have let me. She had a lot of pride, blamed herself for falling for him. But I've always known that it was Holden who ruined her life. She died alone. No son. No husband. Not even me since I didn't even know she was so sick."

She heard him making excuses for not being there for his sister. "My mother died of cancer."

He looked over at her. "I think I heard that." He frowned. "Why'd Holden take you in?"

She shook her head. "He says he promised her that if anything happened to her, he would take me."

"Huh. You know there's more to that story, right?"

Holly Jo suspected so.

Darius fell silent for a few minutes before he said, "I need to get some sleep. Got work to do tonight. It all ends tonight." With that, he curled in the corner behind the steering wheel and fell into a troubled sleep.

She waited, then tried to untie herself, but the rope was too tight. It bit into her wrists. Even if she could free herself, her side of the pickup was missing the door handle. She would have had to climb over the man to get out.

Finally, she closed her eyes. Whatever he had planned tonight involved gasoline and fire and the McKenna

Ranch. Holly Jo couldn't even cry, her tears long dried
up. It would end tonight, just as he said. She no longer
held out any hope that someone was going to find her
in time.

CHAPTER TWENTY-FIVE

BIRDIE LAY IN Brand's arms, spent and smiling as the shadows in the room grew longer and darker.

"Are you all right?" he asked, snuggling closer.

She could feel his breath on her neck and shoulder, along with the stubble of a day's growth of beard. It made her think of his mouth on her, all over her, the slight roughness of his tongue, the rougher feel of his beard on her skin.

"I've never been better." She was still in that wonderful euphoric cloud, her body tingling. Brand had proved to be a generous lover. Not that she had a lot of experience in that area, she had to admit.

They'd both explored each other's bodies, finding the sexy sensitive spots, learning about each other through touch and taste.

"Glad you didn't end up in my brother Ryder's shower." They both laughed. "Seriously, Birdie, what are you really doing here?"

"Isn't it obvious?" He rolled her over to face him.

"I know you better than that," Brand said. "Not that I'm complaining. Being with you…is incredible." His gaze locked with hers. "You still scare me, though."

She smiled. "I think that's a good thing. I'd hate to become commonplace with you."

"I'd always be aware of you, intensely so, I suspect."

Her smile couldn't help itself. It broadened. "I did have something else on my mind before I climbed in your window and stepped into your shower. I certainly hadn't been expecting this kind of reception, though. But it was definitely an added bonus."

He glanced toward the window, cool fresh air blowing into the room where she'd left it open. He shook his head in amusement. "I didn't even question how you got in. You know you could have knocked and used the front door. No one's home but me. It's not like you haven't walked in before."

"I wanted to surprise you," she said.

"You certainly did that." She could feel him studying her. "You just do whatever pops into your head, don't you."

It wasn't really a question, but still, she thought about that for a moment as she ran a finger over his shoulder and down his bare chest. "I'm not afraid to take a risk. It's not such a bad thing sometimes, don't you think? When I find a naked cowboy in a warm shower…" She shrugged. "You could have thrown me out."

He chuckled. "Not a chance. Anyway, I wouldn't change a thing about you."

That made her laugh. "You're a terrible liar."

"Birdie, I still have to ask. What was your plan when you climbed in my window?"

She pushed up on one elbow to meet his gaze. "This," she said. "You and me. It's wonderful, but I still need to find out who killed my father and I'm still worried about Holly Jo. I wish we had found her."

He pulled her to him. "I know," he whispered. "I do, too."

She drew back a little. "I did find out something

about my father—and possibly yours. As much as I hate to admit it, I think it's possible that your mother is innocent. She might not have killed my father."

THE SHERIFF HAD been waiting at the crossroads for the ransom drop for twenty minutes. He'd arrived early, hoping to get this over with. Finally. He'd brought the second briefcase. He was determined to make the exchange and take Holly Jo.

His cell phone rang with a call from the FBI tech who'd been trying to track Darius Reed's phone. Because of the sketchy cell phone cover in this part of the state and the kidnapper remembering to turn off his phone after he used it, there had been little luck in locating him.

"Your kidnapper just turned his phone back on," the tech said excitedly. "I was able to triangulate his burner between cell phone towers because he was passing through Powder Crossing, headed south on the county road."

Stuart swore. "You're sure? I'm at the ransom drop. He's supposed to be here in about ten minutes."

"If he still has the phone he used to call you, he's no longer in your area."

That meant that no way was he getting to the ransom drop in ten minutes.

"He must have realized that he left his phone on. I've lost him," the tech said.

"Keep me posted," he told the tech. He disconnected and looked at the time, unsure what to do. He could see all the roads leading into the crossroads stop. There was no sign of the white pickup. No sign of Darius Reed.

Was this a test to see if Stuart followed the phone

and hung around to make the ransom exchange? Or was Darius making a run for it?

Stuart had put out a BOLO on Darius and the pickup, expecting that if the man made a run for it, he would head out of the area one of three ways—west to hit the interstate and get out of Montana, east to North Dakota and all points beyond, or north toward Canada and a lot of open prairie and few people.

He'd never expected him to take the county road south, because he would have to go right through town. Why take a chance by going anywhere near Powder Crossing? Why head south? Toward Wyoming?

Unless… He felt his pulse bump up with a jolt. Unless he was headed for the McKenna Ranch. Did Darius not know that Holden wasn't there? That the rancher was still in the hospital?

He told himself he could be wrong. But what if this ransom drop had been a ruse, as he was beginning to suspect? Then Darius was making a run for it, trying to get as far away from the Powder River Basin as possible. He already had a million dollars. Why take a chance of getting caught?

Or maybe Darius wasn't finished with Holden. Because it had never been about the money?

He felt his heart spasm at the thought. She'd been alive—at least earlier, when Darius had called. She'd sounded terrified. Stuart had been so sure he was going to get her back, he'd quickly agreed to the trade, even though it meant a long drive out here to this desolate spot.

He'd never completely trusted his instincts and feared doing so now. It was a good twenty-minute drive back to town and another fifteen to the McKenna Ranch. Did he dare act on a hunch? Did he dare not?

THE STRONG SMELL of gas made Holly Jo's eyes burn as the man who called himself Darius Reed half dragged her inside the house. Earlier he'd awakened as it was getting dark. "It's time," he'd said and had started the pickup.

He'd had a gun lying within his reach in case they came across anyone as he drove into the ranch. But no one seemed to be around. She'd seen at once that Elaine's SUV was gone. HH's was in the drive, though, and she knew there had to be some ranch hands way down at the bunkhouse.

She looked for the ranch manager to come up from the stables, but no one appeared as her kidnapper parked. They'd sat in the pickup cab, waiting for a few minutes. Nothing moved. No one came outside from the house. No one walked up from the stables or the bunkhouse. Everyone was gone or hadn't heard them. How was this possible?

"Guess they're all at the hospital, waiting to see if Holden pulls through," Darius said and laughed. "Won't they be surprised when they come back to find everything burned to the ground. Come on." He'd untied her from the grab handle above the passenger-side door, but left her hands bound as he'd gotten out and pulled her after him.

Once inside the house, he'd taken her into the dining room and tied her in a chair, attaching the chair to one of the large legs of the massive table. "So you can watch," he said before going back outside and returning with one of the large gas cans.

He'd wandered around through the empty house with the gas can. She could hear him muttering to himself as she heard the splashing sound. The gas fumes grew stronger. "Must be nice living in a place like this," he said as he passed through on the way to another part of the house. "My sister could have lived here. Terrible shame to burn it down. Ashes to ashes, you know, and karma is a bitch, isn't it, Holden McKenna."

She could hear him getting angrier before he threw down the empty gas can and went out to get another. Her eyes burned from the gas, from fresh tears. She wanted desperately to believe he would untie her. He wouldn't leave her here to burn alive.

But when she saw his expression as he returned with the second gas can, she knew that was exactly what he planned to do. He disappeared down the hallway to the kitchen wing of the house. She heard him banging around over the sound of a vehicle. She felt her breath catch, her heart pounding with hope. Someone was coming.

CHAPTER TWENTY-SIX

"WHAT WOULD YOUR father have done if mine had tried to blackmail him that night at the McKenna Ranch?" Birdie asked as she turned off the county road and drove toward the house.

Brand knew that she didn't expect him to come up with the answer. Not that she gave him a chance to even speculate.

Earlier, she'd gotten out of bed, put her clothes on and told him the plan. He would have been happy to spend the rest of the day in bed with her, but apparently that wasn't what she had in mind. "If he didn't want the truth about his affair and your parentage to come out, he would have killed him."

"That's one thought," he'd said, climbing out of the bed to get dressed. "Seems a stretch to me, but from what I've heard about Holden, I doubt he'd appreciate being blackmailed, especially by his ex-lover's new husband."

"My father was desperate for money so he could come get me," she'd said defensively.

He'd turned to look at her. "I don't think Holden McKenna killed him. According to my mother, Holden didn't know about me. If he wanted to kill anyone, I think it would have been my mother."

"Still, I think my father ran into someone over there,

and that's how he ended up in a well. I'm just wondering what they did with his pickup."

Brand had wondered about that, too. "I doubt it's still on the McKenna Ranch, if that really is where he was killed."

"I have to find out if that's where he died and who's responsible." She'd started toward the open window. "Also, there might be an older ranch manager or hand who was around back then who remembers something from that night—especially if things got as violent as I believe they did."

"Hold on. Where are you going?"

"Weren't you listening? To the McKenna Ranch. I'm betting that most everyone has gone to Billings to see your father in the hospital. I called, and no one answered at the house. This is a good time to search the place."

"How about using my front door instead of the window?"

She'd grinned at him. "You are so thoughtful." She'd moved swiftly to him, kissing him passionately but slipping away before he could put his arms around her and take the kiss to the next level. "Are you coming?"

Brand had groaned and reached for his hat. "I know I'm going to regret this," he'd said under his breath as he followed her to her SUV parked down the road.

He wasn't about to go to the McKenna house in a Stafford Ranch pickup with the logo on the side. Even some of the ranch hands at both the McKenna and the Stafford ranches were at war—because of the feud between his mother and biological father.

Birdie had no idea what she might be instigating. But he also knew that she would go alone if he didn't go with her. "I can't imagine what you're hoping to find," he said now. "A smoking gun?"

She shook her head. "As far as I can tell, the last time anyone saw my father was when he turned in to the McKenna Ranch. With Holden in the hospital and everyone away from the house, it's like they are inviting us to see what we can find over there."

"I am fascinated by the way your mind works." He'd never been in the McKenna Ranch house. He'd never stepped on the property. It had always been off-limits. Now he could admit that he was curious about the place— about his father. He told himself he was only going with Birdie to save her from herself, but he knew that wasn't all there was to it.

Under other circumstances, he might have been raised on the McKenna-Stafford Ranch with two loving parents and no range war between them. He thought about CJ, behind bars awaiting trial for what would probably be a life sentence. Would his life have turned out different if Holden and Charlotte hadn't been at each other's throats all these years? One thing was definite. Brand wouldn't have been a bastard, unsure of where he belonged in all this.

Brand pushed away the what-ifs as he got his first glimpse of the house. It wasn't until they drove closer that he saw the smoke. It billowed up from the far end of the sprawling ranch house.

LIGHTS AND SIREN ON, Stuart swept through Powder Crossing and onto the county road. As he did, he saw the smoke. It rose into the sky, ebony against the pale gray twilight. He couldn't tell exactly where it was coming from—just in the general direction of the McKenna

Ranch. At first there didn't seem to be that much smoke rising from behind the stand of cottonwoods.

He told himself it would be a bush fire, but as the plume of smoke widened and grew, he alerted the fire department, afraid he knew exactly where it was coming from. No simple brush fire, he told himself as he raced toward the McKenna Ranch—and the flames were now rising above the tops of the cottonwoods along the river. If he was right, it was coming from the main house.

His mind spun. Holden was still in the hospital in Billings. As far as he knew, Elaine was there as well. Cooper and Tilly had moved into their new house some miles from the main ranch house. Treyton had moved out. Oakley and Pickett weren't back from their extended honeymoon. Given all that, who was left at the house? The ranch hands could all be at the bar in town. Wasn't this poker party night?

He didn't have to guess who might have started the fire if his instincts were right. But where was Holly Jo?

As the McKenna Ranch house came into view, Birdie slowed and let out a gasp. "That's his pickup." She looked over at him. "That's the kidnapper's pickup parked out front."

"He's set the house on fire," he said, pointing to the far wing. "If Holly Jo is in there…" Brand was already throwing open his door and getting out even before she brought her SUV to a stop. "Call the sheriff!" he yelled and ran toward the house.

Of course, Birdie was right behind him, calling 911 as she ran. She reached him as he scaled the front steps and stopped. He grabbed her, drawing her aside. "Do you smell gasoline?"

She nodded and pointed to the splattered wet spot on the weathered wood of the porch. "The sheriff is on his way." They exchanged a look that said they both feared he wouldn't get here in time.

Brand tried the front door. It was locked. A locked door in rural Montana? He really doubted any of the McKennas had locked the door when they left. Just as he didn't believe they had doused the place with gasoline.

There was only one reason for the kidnapper to lock the front door. He'd left something in there he didn't want anyone to get to.

Holly Jo.

"You don't happen to have a weapon in your rig, do you?" he asked.

"I'm the only weapon I've needed so far."

"Right," he said. "Please stay here and wait for the sheriff."

She gave him her *you really don't expect me to do that, do you?* look.

"I'm going around back. We have to find out if Holly Jo is in there."

"It's a big house. We need to split up," she said.

"Bad idea. We don't know where the kidnapper is."

If Birdie heard him, she didn't answer as she moved to a window and tried it. This was rural Montana. No one locked their windows either. She shoved it open—just as she had his bedroom window earlier—and before he could argue, she swung a leg up and over to drop into the room and disappear from view.

Brand swore and ran for the back of the house. On

the way, he looked for something he could use as a weapon. He found a fallen limb from one of the cottonwood trees. It was a good three inches around and about two feet long. He hefted it as he kept racing toward the back door.

The moment he went around the corner of the house, he saw more smoke curling out of a broken window in the far wing. The smell of smoke and gasoline was stronger back here. Brand felt the clock ticking. He had to find Holly Jo. If the kidnapper had brought her here, then she was somewhere in the house. He had no idea where the kidnapper was but knew that the man might ignite the entire house at any moment.

At the back door, he felt the doorknob. Not hot yet. He opened the door and saw that it led into the dining room. Beyond it was the living room. And there was Holly Jo. She was tied to a chair, gagged and frantically trying to free herself.

When she saw him, her eyes widened first in alarm, then in hope. Both were heartbreaking to see in the girl as Brand rushed to her, the smell of gasoline filling his nostrils as if the kidnapper had drenched the entire house in it.

"I'm Brand Stafford. It's going to be all right," he promised her even as she shook her head as if no longer believing that. He set down the limb he'd picked up and removed her gag before hurriedly trying to untie her. She'd been bound to the large chair and tied to a metal ornament on a log coffee table.

"He's going to come back!" she cried. "He'll catch you and kill you. He has a gun!"

"It's okay," he said, realizing that there wasn't time to untie her. "I'm going to get you out of here."

She began to cry, shaking her head, then staring behind him as if she expected the kidnapper to appear at any moment. He felt the prickle on the back of his neck, worried that she was right. Her kidnapper had wound yards of rope around her, tying intricate knots as if determined that she wasn't going to be set free in time.

Brand pulled out his pocketknife, but he wasn't even sure he could free her by cutting some of the rope away. He began sawing at the thick rope binding her not just to the chair, but to the huge coffee table next to her.

As he tried to reassure Holly Jo, he worried that Birdie might have already crossed paths with the gun-toting kidnapper. He hadn't heard a gunshot, but would he have, given how noisy the fire was? Smoke rolled up the hallway and began filling the living room. He figured the flames wouldn't be far behind. If he could have freed the chair from the heavy coffee table, he would have carried it out of the house. No doubt the kidnapper had thought of that, expecting someone to try to stop him and save Holly Jo.

He'd cut through a half dozen of the ropes around her and was trying to pull one free when he saw Holly Jo's eyes go wide. She opened her mouth and screamed, "No!"

Brand still had the pocketknife in his hand as he swung around. He only caught a glimpse of the man before the butt end of a gun slapped into the side of his head. The blow stunned him. He fumbled with his free hand for the tree branch he'd dropped by Holly Jo's feet while he struck out with the knife.

At the kidnapper's cry of pain, he drove the blade deeper into the man's thigh and tried to avoid another blow. He'd knocked the man a little off balance, and yet the next blow dropped Brand to his knees.

As his vision began to darken, he spotted Birdie. He opened his mouth to warn her. Behind him he heard Holly screaming right before everything went black.

BIRDIE HAD WORKED her way through the house looking for Holly Jo. There had been so many doors to open, so many rooms to do a quick search in. She'd heard the roar of the fire growing louder, her heart pounding as time raced by. *If you don't find her soon...* The words were like a mantra keeping time with her running footfalls.

She'd searched the entire wing before coming out in the living room to a scene that threatened to stop her heart. Holly Jo tied to a chair. Brand knocked to the floor, unmoving. All she could think was that she had to get to him. Get to him and the girl.

Holly Jo screamed as she saw Birdie, her eyes wide with alarm and fear—and warning.

Birdie's first impulse was to attack. The kidnapper's back was turned. He seemed to be holding his thigh as if in pain. She lunged forward, already moving toward the man, when she saw what the kidnapper had in his hand. A gun.

She slid to a stop on the wet floor, her gaze going to Holly Jo, who seemed to be motioning with her head for Birdie to hide.

HOLLY JO FELT her throat close, the last of a scream dying on her lips as she looked from Brand Stafford lying face down on the floor to Darius standing over him. She told herself not to look in the woman's direction for fear Darius would see her. Someone had said her name was Birdie Malone. She liked the name Birdie, so she'd remembered it.

She wanted to scream again, afraid he was going to kill the man who'd come to save her. Darius stared down at Brand Stafford for a moment, then pocketed the gun. She'd seen Brand around too, though she hadn't known his name, only that he was from the Stafford Ranch and that no one over there liked the McKennas.

Her kidnapper was bleeding and whimpering as he pressed a hand over his thigh and blood rushed over his fingers. He swore and picked up the gas can he'd been carrying when he'd hit Brand with his gun.

At a sound deep in the house, he frowned. "Stay here," he said to her. As if she was going anywhere. He turned and started up the stairs, sloshing gas over the steps as he went.

Holly Jo waited until Darius disappeared upstairs before she looked in the direction where she'd last seen Birdie. She wasn't there. What if she didn't come back? The smoke from the burning wing was growing thicker. It hurt to breathe. She looked down at Brand. Was he dead? She didn't think so. She thought he was still breathing. She strained against the ropes binding her. He'd managed to cut some of them away, but not enough. She tried to nudge him with her foot. She touched his leg, but he didn't move.

Then she spotted the pocketknife. If she could reach it, drag it to her…

As she pulled harder, one of the loops of rope gave from where he'd cut it. She realized she might be able to get free. Darius had gone out of his way to tie her securely, no doubt determined that this time she wasn't getting away.

She pulled harder and was able to wiggle one hand free, then the other. She began to work frantically at getting her ankles free. Any moment Darius could come back down those stairs. Brand had cut enough of the rope that she was able to unwind most of it, but there was one piece tied to the coffee table that would not give. She was fighting it when Birdie came out of the smoke like an apparition from the hallway to the kitchen. She had what appeared to be a wet towel wrapped around her face, two more in one hand and a large butcher knife in the other. Holly Jo wasn't even sure she was real until she fell to her knees and said, "Wrap this towel around your mouth and nose to keep out the smoke."

Holly Jo watched her put the other towel over Brand's face as he began to stir on the floor. Then the woman began to cut the rope—just as Holly Jo heard Darius coming back.

He was halfway down the stairs when he looked down and saw Birdie. In his surprise, he splashed gas from the can onto his pant leg. Holly Jo saw his face tighten in fury. Birdie hadn't seemed to notice; she was too busy cutting the rope with the huge knife.

But Holly Jo saw his look. She knew what the man was capable of even as she felt the rope binding her loosen and begin to fall away.

"No!" she screamed as she saw Darius fumbling in his pocket for his gun. "No!"

He staggered a little on the stairs as he dropped the gas can, the flammable liquid splashing over his feet as he hurried to get his gun from his pocket. She saw that one of his pant legs was dark with blood and now gas. He jerked the gun out, but at the same time, he pulled out something else.

Holly Jo didn't see what it was at first, but the object caught his attention as it fell to the carpeted step he was standing on and the puddle of gasoline he'd spilled. It wasn't until she heard a whoosh that she realized what had happened. He'd accidentally dropped his lighter, flicking it on as it fell, setting the lower part of his pants on fire, then falling to the gasoline-soaked stairs.

Flames seemed to leap all around him. She heard him cry out and begin to run down the stairs, the fire chasing him like a mad dog. She saw flames lick at his heels and the hem of his jeans, climbing higher. He tumbled down the last few steps, slapping at the flames engulfing his clothing as he found his feet and ran toward the front door of the house.

The flames rippled across the floor after him like a river of fire and smoke. Fueled by the gas that had soaked into the old wood floor, the fire rushed after him as if in a race. He reached the front door and tried to open it. Holly Jo remembered that he'd locked it, saying he didn't want to be interrupted before he finished what he had to do.

She saw the flames catch him, racing up his back. Over the roar of the inferno, the last thing Holly Jo heard was Darius's screams as he unlocked the door and threw himself out past the porch and into the yard, taking fire with him.

AS THE SHERIFF raced down the county road, he could see the flames on the other side of the stand of cottonwoods. They rose high into the air as if licking at the sky darkening around them. Smoke billowed up in ebony clouds.

The McKenna Ranch house was on fire—just as Stuart had feared.

Siren screaming, lights flashing, he made the turn down the long drive, praying there was no one inside.

That was when he saw the kidnapper's pickup parked out front. To his horror, as he pulled into the yard, a figure engulfed in flames came running out of the house to fall into the grass.

The sheriff leaped out and ran to the blackened creature, seeing at once that it was too late. He rose quickly and ran toward the burning house as he heard fire trucks coming up the road behind him.

THE STAIRCASE WAS ABLAZE, the smoke getting thicker. The flames rippled down the stairs to the hardwood floor. All the time Darius had been spilling gas on the stairs, Birdie had been working frantically to cut the rope. Holly Jo felt it finally give. She was free!

"Keep the wet towel over your nose and mouth," Birdie whispered next to her ear. "Get down on your hands and knees and crawl toward the front door."

For a moment, Holly Jo didn't know which direction to go. Birdie pushed her toward the door, yelling over the sound of the flames. "I'll be right behind you."

All she could think about as she dropped to her hands and knees and began to crawl, each breath painful and making her cough, was Darius. She felt bad for him, even though she knew that he had planned to leave her in the burning house. He'd never planned to take her home. She was his revenge. Setting the house ablaze was just icing on the cake, HH would have said.

She thought of HH now, the smoke burning her throat even through the wet towel, the heat making her feel like she was on fire. Darius hadn't poured gas on the floor in the living room, but the fire moved hungrily toward her from the staircase. She realized that if she didn't reach the front door, the fire wouldn't kill her. It would be the smoke.

On the floor behind her, she heard Birdie and Brand. Coughing, she covered her mouth with the hem of her dirty, blood-splattered shirt and kept crawling, afraid she would never find the front door.

Moments later, Birdie and Brand were helping her to her feet. The three of them, arms wrapped around each other, moved through the smoke and out into the fresh air as the sheriff ran toward them.

"Is there anyone else inside?" the sheriff cried.

They all shook their heads as they stumbled away from the house, into the cottonwoods, sucking in air, coughing and finally dropping into the grass as they fought to breathe. The sound of sirens and fire trucks couldn't drown out the roar of the flames. Holly Jo could hear crashing inside the house, feel the heat even this far way.

She lay in the grass, staring up at the darkness filled with sparks and smoke. She was alive. It didn't seem possible. For so long, she'd thought for sure that no one would find her, no one would rescue her from her kidnapper, no one would ever be able to get to her in time.

"Holden," she said between coughing bouts.

"He's fine," Brand said. "Everyone from the ranch is fine."

She nodded, fighting tears. "My horse," she said, her voice a scratchy whisper.

"The horses are fine," Brand assured her. "The flames are far enough away from the stable."

She closed her eyes and began to cry in huge body-shaking sobs. As she did, Birdie put her arms around her and pulled her close. "You're safe now. You're safe."

When the EMTs insisted on taking all three of them to the hospital, it was Brand who said, "Holly Jo needs to see her horse first." The EMT started to argue.

"You have no idea what this girl has been through. She sees her horse first."

Holly Jo saw Birdie smile at him and Brand reach over to squeeze her hand.

"You'll come with me," Holly Jo said, not wanting to let either of them out of her sight. They'd saved her life. She still couldn't believe it as she looked toward the house engulfed in flames even as the firefighters pumped water over it.

If it hadn't been for them, she would have still been inside there—on fire.

CHAPTER TWENTY-SEVEN

ELAINE WAS WITH HOLDEN, along with his doctor, when the sheriff walked into the room. He saw Holden's anxious face and was immediately waved forward.

"Tell me everything," the rancher demanded.

Stuart didn't know where to start since he was sure that Elaine had filled the rancher in on the high points. "Darius Reed burned down your house. It couldn't be saved."

"I don't give a damn about the house. How is Holly Jo? I want to see her."

"She is being held for observation here at the hospital." He raised his hands quickly and hurried on. "For smoke inhalation. She's fine. The doctor also wanted to check her over, given what she's been through."

"I need to see her," Holden repeated and started to get out of the bed.

"You aren't going anywhere yet," the doctor said. "We'll bring her to you just as soon as we can."

The rancher growled at the doctor but lay back on the bed. Turning to the sheriff, he said, "Tell me about Darius Reed."

"He's dead." Stuart thought about the figure he'd seen running out of the house in flames. "He was caught in the fire." He cleared his throat and continued. "The ransom money was found in his pickup. I didn't count it, but I suspect most of it is still in the briefcase."

Holden waved that away. "He never wanted the money. He just wanted to destroy me."

The sheriff hated to point out the obvious. "He almost killed you."

"But he didn't. So he burned down my house." Holden waved that away, too. "I can build another house. I'm just worried about Holly Jo, what she's been through because of me."

"I'm sure she was traumatized, but from what I can see, she's tough, like you," Elaine said.

Stuart nodded. "Brand Stafford and Birdie Malone saved her life. If they hadn't gotten to her when they did…"

The rancher frowned. "I need to see my son, too."

"He's also here at the hospital," the sheriff said. "Darius hit him pretty hard when Brand was trying to free Holly Jo. She was tied up in the house. Brand has a concussion and smoke inhalation, but his doctor said he should be fine."

Holden shook his head, his eyes suddenly filling with tears. He wiped hastily at them, clearly angry with himself for even that sign of weakness. "This is my fault. Every bit of it."

"We've all made mistakes in our lives," Elaine said.

He scoffed. "Not like me."

"You might be surprised," she said and rose from the chair where she'd been sitting beside his bed. "I'm going to see if Holly Jo is ready to come up and see you." He nodded, his eyes filling again.

"I'll leave you to get some rest," Stuart said and left the room with Elaine. "Are you all right?"

She nodded. "I will be. This almost killed him."

He looked over at her, realizing she wasn't talking about the bullet wounds that had put him in the hospital.

HOLDEN COULDN'T WAIT to get out of this hospital bed. He had so much to repair and rebuild, the house the least of it. When his hospital room door opened, he wasn't sure who would come through it. He thought he remembered Charlotte in his room, but even if it had been her, she hadn't come back that he knew of.

Right now, he just wanted to see Holly Jo. He couldn't rest until he saw the girl, saw with his own eyes that she was all right.

He couldn't imagine what she'd been through. Elaine had suggested that she might benefit from some counseling. Whatever she needed, he would get it for her. He'd never forgive himself for putting her through this.

But the person who came through the door was Brand Stafford, his son. He swallowed the lump that rose in his throat. He'd never felt so much emotion since this nightmare had begun. He felt weak with it. He needed to be strong now more than ever.

As he looked at Brand, he was filled with his own recriminations. How could he not have known? he thought as he took in the young man. How could he not have seen himself in that build, in those eyes, even in the expression on that face?

His throat went dry as Brand moved toward his bed. He searched for words and found none even as his heart constricted in pain. He didn't think about the lost years or Charlotte's deception. None of that mattered.

This was his son.

There was so much he wanted to say, needed to say.

He promised himself that there would be time for that as he extended his hand, his eyes brimming with tears. "Brand. My son."

BRAND HAD PLANNED to wait to see Holden until the rancher was out of the hospital. But after waking up in the same hospital this morning, he knew he couldn't put it off. The nurse assured him that Holden was on the mend and could have a visitor, especially when told about Brand's relationship to him. "He's my father."

But even as he pushed open the hospital room door, he hadn't known how this was going to go. He had no idea what he was going to say. He wasn't even sure still how he felt. He just knew it was time. He had to get this over with.

Seeing Holden lying in bed, his face as pale as the sheets, he'd been taken aback at first. The man had always seemed so big, so powerful, so in control of everything—a lot like Brand's own mother.

As he'd approached the bed, he'd had no idea what Holden's reaction would be to him. So when the man offered his outstretched hand and called him *son*, Brand had taken that large weathered hand and let Holden draw him closer.

They'd stayed like that, just looking at each other for the first time as father and son. To his surprise, a kind of wordless understanding seemed to pass between them.

Then the door opened again, and Holly Jo rushed in, calling his name, "HH!" Holden squeezed Brand's hand before Holly Jo reached his bedside. "You paid the ransom for me," she said, sounding near tears as Brand stepped back.

"Of course I did," Holden said.

"I thought maybe…since I don't like beef and I wasn't very good—"

"Don't be so silly," he said, reaching for her hand and drawing her closer. "You're family. I would have done anything to get you back. I'm just so glad you're safe." He glanced at Brand and smiled. "I hear I owe Brand and Birdie for getting you out of that house."

"They saved me," Holly Jo said in a rush. "The house was on fire. It was so hot and smoky, and the flames…" There was a catch in her throat. "But the horses are fine," she said, perking up. "Honey is fine. I missed her so much."

"I missed you," Holden said, his voice breaking.

The girl eyed him suspiciously before she said, "I promise to behave better from now on."

He laughed and pulled her into an awkward hug. "You be you, and I'll be me, and we'll work it out. Don't worry about the house. We'll build an even better one, and you can design your own room."

"Be careful what you promise," Elaine said as she came into the room. She glanced at Holden and seemed pleased. Then she smiled at Brand and mouthed, *Thank you*.

"I should get going," he said.

"When I get out of here…" Holden met his gaze. "Until then."

Brand nodded, turned and left the room, feeling lighter than he had since learning the truth about his parentage. It was over, behind him. Now all he had to do was figure out who he was. But even his footfalls were lighter as he walked down the hallway. He had a feeling that he was on his way to becoming the man he was supposed to be.

BIRDIE WAS UP, dressed and ready to leave when she looked up to see Brand come into her hospital room. Just the sight of him sent her spirits airborne. He had a bandage on one side of his head, but otherwise he looked wonderful—at least to her. Her heart kicked up a beat as he gave her one of his lazy lopsided smiles.

"The doctor said I can go home," she said as he stepped to her bedside. "But what are you doing out of bed? I heard you had a concussion."

He grinned. "Seems I have a hard head, so I'm going to be just fine."

"A hard head, huh?" she said and coughed. He was still coughing too from breathing in all that smoke. "How's Holly Jo?"

"I just left her visiting Holden. She's contrite for being a headstrong kid before she was kidnapped and promising to behave from now on."

Birdie laughed. "Did he buy that?"

"Not for a moment." He could feel her gaze on him. "So, you saw your dad. How did that go?"

"Better than I thought it would." He sat down on the edge of her bed next to her and must have felt her waiting expectantly for all the details. "You're going to be disappointed. Not much was said. He took my hand and called me his son."

"That was it?" She was definitely disappointed. "Do you think you'll see him again?"

"I do. Now, what about you?"

"If you're asking if I'm going to give up my quest for justice—"

Brand shook his head. "I know better than that."

She eyed him, surprised. The Brand she'd met would cross a raging river to avoid conflict, and yet he wasn't asking her to stop, even though it now involved both sides of his parentage? "I'm not sure how this is going to end. You might want to keep your distance from me."

He reached over to brush a lock of her hair back from her face. His fingers grazed her cheek, sending a shiver of desire through her. His blue eyes were intent on her. "Are you trying to get rid of me?"

She didn't want to hurt this man. "Seriously, I could end up hurting people you care about."

"I know. But I would never ask you to change who you are."

That made her smile. "You sure about that? I'm too impulsive. You have no idea what I will do next—and, truthfully, neither do I."

He shrugged. "That's just you. Comes with the whole package." He grinned. "Have I mentioned how much I like that package?"

"Brand—"

"Birdie, you called it right. I'm tired of playing it safe, being careful not to make ripples in the water, doing everything I can to keep peace in my family. Thanks to you, I'm ready to discover who I truly am."

"I already know who you are," she said and leaned toward him. She really enjoyed kissing this cowboy rancher. He must have liked it too, because he wrapped her in his arms and pulled her over onto his lap.

That was how the nurse found them.

"Looks like you're feeling well enough to go home," the nurse said as she pushed a wheelchair into the room. "The doctor signed your discharge papers." With a chuckle, she turned and exited the room as they both burst out laughing.

ELAINE DROVE HOLLY JO back to Powder Crossing, explaining that they would be staying in the hotel in town until their house could be rebuilt. Before they left Billings, they shopped for clothing for both of them since theirs had all been destroyed.

Holly Jo didn't care about school clothes. She just needed jeans, shirts and boots so she could get back to riding her horse. "Are we going to the hotel?" she asked as they drove into Powder Crossing.

Elaine glanced over at her and shook her head. "There's someone who wants to see you." Holly Jo frowned. "Out at the ranch."

"Honey!" she cried. "My horse."

"Your horse, but someone else."

When they drove in, Holly Jo tried not to look at the house. She blamed herself for getting kidnapped. If she hadn't, none of this would have happened. But when Elaine stopped the SUV by the stable and Pickett Hanson stepped out, she pushed the guilt aside and let out a cry of joy. He'd been teaching her to trick ride—until he fell in love with Oakley Stafford, took off, got married and went on a honeymoon. Holly Jo had been afraid he wouldn't come back—but here he was.

He grabbed her and swung her around when he saw her. Then set her down and looked at her. She'd been afraid he was going to mention the kidnapping and everything she'd been through. But he smiled and said, "I swear you've grown six inches since I've been gone."

Filled with relief, she hugged him tight, and he hugged her back.

"I've got Honey all saddled for you," Pickett said. "Thought you might want to go for a ride while I catch up with Elaine."

She nodded. She thought of crying herself to sleep while kidnapped, hoping to dream of Honey and pretend she was galloping through the pasture again. She ran back to the car to get her clothes so she could change. Sure enough, Honey was waiting for her and let out a whinny when she saw her. She hugged the mare's neck, brought to tears, then hurriedly changed and led the horse out to the pasture.

But it wasn't until she was in the saddle, loping across the ranch, her whole world before her, that she told herself she was going to be all right. She thought how when she closed her eyes she saw Darius on fire and pushed it away as she felt the wind in her face. Breathing in the scent of leather and horse, she told herself that she would survive this.

Even as she did, though, she knew she would never be the girl who'd walked over to a woman driving a pickup one morning. That Holly Jo was gone.

CHAPTER TWENTY-EIGHT

BRAND HAD ALREADY arranged for a ride back to Powder Crossing for them, Birdie realized. Still, she was surprised to see Ryder, Brand's younger brother, leaning against a Stafford Ranch club cab pickup, waiting for them.

After slightly awkward introductions, she insisted Brand ride up front. Ryder, who resembled the green-eyed, blond-haired side of the family, appeared quiet like his brother. But there was no doubt that he was more than a little curious about what his big brother had been up to—almost dying in the McKenna house fire at the top of the list. Birdie figured she too was on that list, somewhere near the top.

"I guess we're going to have to catch up," Ryder said and shot her a look in the rearview mirror as he drove.

"I would imagine you've already heard most everything," Brand said.

"Right, I get away from the ranch so much. Not to mention that I haven't seen you in days. Apparently, a lot has been going on that I haven't heard about." He glanced pointedly at Birdie, who kept her expression blank.

"I'm sorry to have left you with all of the ranch work recently," Brand said. "Wasn't my intention. I just got caught up in everything after I got the results of the DNA test I took." She saw him glance at his brother. "Don't pretend you haven't heard."

"You're my brother. Who can believe a DNA test, anyway," he scoffed, but Birdie could see that he was grinning. Brand reached over and gave Ryder's shoulder a quick squeeze.

"Anything I've missed in the past few days?" Brand asked.

"If you're asking about Mother..." Ryder sighed. "She's back to her old self, pretty much. Apparently, she took your DNA news hard, because she organized a search of area ranches for Holly Jo, offering a ten-thousand-dollar reward for anyone who found her."

"Doesn't sound like our mother."

Ryder nodded. "Exactly. She's scarier when she isn't herself, I swear," he said with a chuckle.

She sat forward in her seat. "You know I'm in the area to prove that your mother killed my father, Dixon Malone, right?" she asked.

"Oh, yeah," Ryder said. "Everyone in the county knows. What they don't know is what you're doing with my brother."

Birdie sat back, cutting her eyes to Brand, before looking out the side window. The pickup cab fell silent, which could have been her answer, because she didn't know what her and Brand's relationship was either. Lovers. Friends? More or less than either?

Ryder and Brand talked ranching the rest of the way to Powder Crossing. It gave her time to think about everything that had happened. She hadn't had time to really deal with her near-death experience or anything else. Maybe especially her growing feelings for Brand Stafford.

She knew she was avoiding dwelling on both as she turned her thoughts to what she'd come to town for in the first place—seeing that her father got justice. She concentrated on that, going over everything she'd learned, and was surprised when they reached Powder Crossing so quickly.

Ryder dropped her off at the hotel. Brand started to get out of the truck to talk to her, but she didn't give him a chance.

"We'll talk later," she said, hopping out to hurry into the hotel. Once inside, she glanced back to see him standing next to the pickup, a frown on his handsome face, before climbing back inside with his brother and leaving.

Birdie breathed a sigh of relief before going upstairs to her room, showering, changing and heading across to the Wild Horse Bar. A half-dozen regulars were already sitting on stools at the bar, even though it was early in the day.

She spotted Elmer and motioned him over to the table where she took a seat. The elderly retired ranch hand hesitated before sliding off his stool. His buddies were joking about her being too young for him. He looked a little flushed as he approached. She motioned to a chair, and he sat, looking like he might bolt at any moment.

"You're going to get me in trouble," he said.

She suspected a part of him enjoyed the attention. "I need a little more of your help." He was the only person who had told her about Charlotte Stafford getting a call and going over to the McKenna Ranch. "Who could have called Charlotte that night?" He shook his head. Maybe he didn't know. "Someone must have either overheard the call or saw her leave late that night after my father had been gone for a while, presumably having gone to the McKenna Ranch. How would she know that he went there?"

Elmer shrugged, but she could see this time he knew something. He'd put his hands on the table and was fidgeting.

"That you know this means someone told you," she pointed out. "Elmer." She laid a hand on one of his. "Please."

He glanced around, acting almost scared. "I shouldn't," he said, lowering his voice. "You need to talk to Boyle Wilson, Charlotte Stafford's ranch manager. He's a son of a biscuit-eating cactus. Don't tell him I told you." She nodded. "Best watch yourself around him, you hear?"

"Is he the one who told you?"

Elmer scoffed. "He doesn't talk to the likes of me. I worked under him for a while at one of the first ranches he managed. Meaner than a kicked rattler."

"Then who?"

He leaned closer and whispered, "Boyle brags a lot that he knows everything that goes on out there on the spread. Get him drunk enough and he really shoots off his mouth. Truth is, he's had his eye on Charlotte for years. Seems to think that someday he'll own that ranch because he knows so many of her secrets. Said she'd been out in the stables, got a call, said something about Dixon and the McKenna Ranch. Then she took off late that night in her rig. Didn't say it, but it would have been just like him to follow her."

Birdie's heart began to pound harder, stealing her breath. If any of this was true, Boyle Wilson might have seen her father's murder—and his murderer.

CHARLOTTE HADN'T GONE back to the hospital or tried to see Holden again after that first time. All that mattered, she told herself, was that he was going to live. She hadn't lost him from this earth. She could live with that. She had to, since that was all she was going to get.

She'd been so relieved when she'd heard that Holly Jo was safe—and so was Brand. That Brand and Birdie Malone had saved Holly Jo and had barely gotten out of that burning house still made her weak. She could have lost her son—if she hadn't already, she told herself.

Her first impulse had been to rush to the hospital to see him, but she'd talked herself into checking on his condition instead. Brand was being released this morning. Ryder had said he would pick him up, and Charlotte had thanked him.

She had something else to do that she told herself was more helpful than racing to Billings and showing up in his hospital room. It would take a lot more than that to heal the distance between her and her son.

Pulling out her phone, she made the call. "Elaine, where are you right now?"

"I'm at the ranch. I brought Holly Jo from the hospital. She needed to see her horse and go for a ride. Pickett is back. That definitely made her day. I'm sure he'll start the trick-riding lessons again."

"The house? I heard it was a total loss."

"It is, but you know Holden. He plans to build something bigger and better once he's released from the hospital."

"When is that going to be?" Charlotte asked.

"Not for a while yet. How are you doing?"

It was so like Elaine to think of her and ask. "I have

an idea I want to run by you." She glanced around her living room, feeling the silence like an accusation. She'd pushed everyone she cared about away. "I have this huge house over here that's pretty much empty. I'd like to offer it to you and Holly Jo and Holden and anyone else who needs a place to stay."

Charlotte took a breath. "It would be a lot handier for all of you than going back and forth from town. I would imagine you'd been planning to stay in the hotel," she said, rushing on before Elaine could stop her. "I was thinking I could use some time away, so the place would be all yours. Ryder and Brand have their own wing and are always off working on the ranch and never around anyway. You'll love my kitchen. Please, before you say no—"

"That is so generous, Charlotte."

"I really would love it if you would take me up on my offer. You can all stay as long as you want. It would be closer to the McKenna Ranch while the new house is being built. You'd have the place to yourselves. But Ryder and Brand would be around if you needed anything." At least, she hoped Brand planned to stay on the ranch. "It would give Holden a chance to get to know his son."

Silence. Then Elaine said, "Let me talk to Holden about it. I think it's a lovely idea. But where are you planning on going?"

"I haven't decided yet."

More silence. "I'll let you know."

Charlotte disconnected more determined than ever to make changes in her life. One in particular had needed to be made for years, she thought as she left the house.

THE TIMES BIRDIE sneaked onto the Stafford Ranch, she'd made sure that most everyone was away from the house or in bed asleep.

Even with Holly Jo safe back at the McKenna Ranch, she suspected everyone, including those at the Stafford Ranch, would be on the lookout for anyone on the property who shouldn't be. That would mean her.

But she wasn't going to the main Stafford Ranch house—or anywhere near Brand. She didn't need to ask him what he would think of her approaching his mother's ranch manager to prove that his mother was a murderer.

Before she'd left Elmer, she'd gotten the information she needed to find Boyle Wilson's cabin. It was in a spot where he had privacy and could come and go at will unseen. Which also meant he wouldn't have known if someone had seen him leave the night Dixon Malone was killed. He could have followed Charlotte to the McKenna house that night, since apparently he had a romantic interest in his employer. He could have witnessed the murder and kept it to himself to use later as leverage. According to Elmer, that was the kind of man the ranch manager was.

Boyle's cabin was on the other side of the dense stand of cottonwoods, far away from the house and some distance from the bunkhouse. There was a path out the back door to the stables, but the front door faced the mountains in the distance. Out his front window was miles of ranch land and little else until the pastures rose to foothills and higher.

Realizing how isolated the cabin was made Birdie hesitate. She considered herself brave, but not foolish to the point of facing down death. Elmer, who was clearly afraid of Boyle, had warned her. She didn't doubt that the man was as evil as the retired ranch hand believed him to be.

But this couldn't wait, she told herself. Tonight, she might find out the truth. Once she did, there was nothing keeping her here. She thought about Brand and the silence in the pickup after Ryder had asked about them. They'd been a novelty in Powder Crossing, something to gossip about. Even after all they'd shared, how could they be more than that?

The sun had long set behind the mountains to the west. Twilight had settled over the Stafford Ranch. Long dark shadows had formed under the cottonwoods. As she approached Boyle's cabin, keeping to the pockets of darkness, she heard voices. The closer she got, the louder they became. A man and a woman were arguing. At first she couldn't make out what they were saying— until she reached the front of the cabin.

Through a partially opened window, she heard the woman say, "Boyle, I didn't come out here to argue with you."

She crouched down so she could see inside the lit cabin. Charlotte Stafford?

Boyle, a rugged, surly-looking man with a smirk on his face, took a step toward her. "You think you came out here to fire me?" He laughed. "If that was true, you would have called me up to the main house like you usually do. Queen-of-the-manor-like. But no." He took another step. Charlotte held her ground. "You came down to my cabin for the very first time for a whole other reason, and we both know it." He reached out as if to touch her, but she slapped his hand away.

"I wanted to look you in your eye when I fired you, and I didn't want anyone else to hear this," she said.

"Didn't want anyone to hear? You mean family? Or staff. You don't think I've noticed that you've cut your household staff down to nothing and your young'ins have scattered to the wind? This ranch is in trouble, Charlotte."

"It's Mrs. Stafford to you, Boyle."

His head tipped back, and a roar of laughter came out. "Why don't you admit it? How long has it been since you've had a man in your bed? A real man, not Holden McKenna, the man who used you and dumped you how many times?"

Her hand came up fast. Boyle didn't have time to avoid her slap. The sound of it ricocheted through the small cabin. But he was fast enough to grab her hand and jerk her toward him. He caught her at her waist with his free arm and slammed her against him.

"You're going to find out what a real man feels like," he growled as he shoved her up against the wall, trapping her there with his body. Charlotte fought hard, but he already had one of her hands and grabbed the wrist of the other, trapping them both in his huge hand. Pinned against the wall, she struggled as he bent to kiss her.

Birdie had shot up from where she was crouched the moment Boyle grabbed Charlotte. She rushed to the door and threw it open as the ranch manager let out a cry and jerked back from the kiss. She saw that his lip was bleeding, his face a distorted mask of fury.

"You bitch!" He drew back, fisted his free hand and swung it at Charlotte's face.

But before it reached its destination, Birdie grabbed his arm and cranked it down behind Boyle's back. At the same time, she got a knee between his legs and brought him down hard on the wood floor. She knew she wouldn't be able to keep a man his size and strength down, though, so she quickly jumped back, expecting him to rise and attack as he started to get up from the floor.

Out of the corner of her eye, she saw Charlotte pull a shotgun down from the gun rack by the door. She swung around, ratcheted a shell into the chamber and pressed the end of the barrel against the back of Boyle's head before he could get to his feet.

He froze.

Birdie exchanged a look with the woman. "Let's call the sheriff?"

Charlotte seemed to think about that. "Or I could pull this trigger and save the sheriff the ride out here."

"And join your son in prison," Boyle groused from where he was sprawled on the floor.

"I'll call for help." Birdie pulled out her phone and dialed 911.

"You don't want to do this, Charlotte," Boyle said. "Who knows what might come out of my mouth once I start talking to the sheriff?"

Charlotte ignored him, seeming unconcerned. "I don't think we've met," she said after Birdie made the call and pocketed her phone again. "I'm assuming you know who I am. Charlotte. Charlotte Stafford." The shotgun was still pressed to the back of Boyle's head. She looked like a woman who knew how to use the firearm, and Birdie figured Boyle knew it, too.

"Birdie. Birdie Malone."

The older woman nodded. "Dixon's daughter. I believe I did hear that you've been seeing my son Brand,

and that the two of you saved Holly Jo." Her eyes narrowed as she studied her. "It looks like I owe you."

Birdie said nothing, but she knew exactly what she'd ask for if given a choice. Someone owed her the truth about her father's death. But was it Charlotte Stafford?

From the way the woman was looking at her, she suspected that Charlotte had already guessed what Birdie wanted from her—and that Birdie wouldn't stop searching for the truth until she found it.

CHAPTER TWENTY-NINE

BRAND COULDN'T HAVE been more surprised to hear the wail of the siren and see the sheriff's patrol SUV go flying past the house, headed in the direction of the ranch manager's cabin. He and Ryder and some of the ranch hands followed, all concerned.

The moment he reached the cabin, he saw his mother holding a shotgun barrel against the back of Boyle's head. He sent the ranch hands away. Ryder went with them as if whatever was going on, he wanted no part of it. Brand remembered when he would have felt the same way, especially since the sheriff had gotten out of his rig and was headed this way.

But seeing Birdie standing in Boyle's cabin with his mother and Boyle on the floor, he couldn't have walked away even if he'd wanted to. "I hate to ask," he said, pretty sure that Birdie was neck-deep in it.

"Then don't," his mother snapped. "We have this under control." She softened her words and her expression as she looked at him, then shifted her gaze to Birdie. "Fortunately this young woman came along when she did."

"Really?" he said, looking to Birdie for an explanation and getting nothing as the sheriff pushed past him into the room.

"Someone tell me what's going on here," Stuart de-

manded as he stepped in and gently removed the shotgun from Brand's mother's hands. Boyle started to speak
at the same time as he began to rise from the floor. "You
just stay down there, Boyle," the sheriff ordered.

"When I told Boyle that he was fired, he threatened
me and then attacked me," Charlotte said, rubbing her
bruised wrists. Brand saw dried blood on her lip and
couldn't help but wonder what Boyle had been thinking. "If Miss Malone hadn't come to my rescue when
she did," his mother continued, "he would have continued his assault and tried to rape me."

"Don't kid yourself. You wouldn't have put up much
of a fight," Boyle said with a laugh.

"Shut up, Boyle, before you incriminate yourself further," the sheriff said and turned to Birdie. "Is what Mrs.
Stafford said true?"

She nodded. "He was about to punch her when I
grabbed him and threw him down. Mrs. Stafford picked
up the shotgun before he could get up. He threatened
her, was rough with her before that. His intentions were
pretty clear."

"Sounds like it was a good thing you came along
when you did," Stuart said to her. "You seem to be making a habit of showing up where you're needed. Why
are you here this time?"

"I wanted to talk to Mr. Wilson about my father. I
understand he might have seen him murdered at the
McKenna Ranch."

Boyle snorted. "Maybe Mrs. Stafford would like to
change the story that she and this woman concocted
here." He turned his head to look up at Charlotte. Brand's
gaze went to his mother as well.

"What Miss Malone said is what happened, Sheriff.

And yes, I want to press charges along with getting a restraining order against my *former* ranch manager," she said.

"Big mistake, bitch," Boyle said. "You think I'm not going to talk? You better send your fancy lawyer down with a deal before you make the second biggest mistake of your life. Holden McKenna was the first."

"You have the right to remain silent." Stuart began to read the former ranch manager his rights as he hand-cuffed him and pulled him to his feet. "I'm going to need a statement from both of you," he said to the women before he led Boyle out to his patrol SUV.

"Are you both all right?" Brand asked unnecessarily, looking from Birdie to his mother. He felt a small jolt at the thought that the two women might be quite a bit alike.

"I'm fine," his mother snapped and stopped rubbing her wrists. "Would you please have someone clean out all of Boyle's personal things from this cabin? I want nothing of that man left." She walked past him and out the cabin door.

Brand turned to Birdie. "What about you?"

"What about me?"

He took a step toward her. "Boyle didn't hurt you, did he?"

"Your mother put the shotgun on him before he could. I got the feeling that she knew how to use it."

Brand chuckled as he pulled her into his arms, thankful that neither of them had been badly hurt. Boyle had always reminded him of a wounded animal; he'd never known what the man might do if cornered. He tried not to worry how much the ranch manager knew about his mother.

"Good thing she didn't have the whip she carries to kill rattlers when she's out horseback riding," he told Birdie. "Boyle was lucky it was just a shotgun to his head."

"Your mother told me that she owes me."

He pulled back a little to raise a brow.

"I think she's going to tell me the truth," Birdie said. "If Boyle Wilson really does have something on your mother about Dixon's death, he made it clear that he planned to talk. So why didn't your mother seem more worried about that—if she was the murderer and Boyle can prove it?"

Brand shook his head. He hated to see her get her hopes up. "For your sake, I hope the truth comes out, but are you sure you want to hear it?"

"My grandmother warned me that I might find out things I won't like about my father, but yes, I want the truth. Then I can finally put my father to rest."

He drew her close again. "I want that for you, Birdie." Even if it meant that she would leave the Powder River Basin, her job here done.

HOLLY JO HADN'T wanted to see a doctor, but HH had insisted. She'd been reminded of her promise to not cause trouble if she made it back home. So she'd gone. She liked Yvonne Shepherd, the young woman psychologist. Yvonne let her talk about anything she wanted. Most of the time, Holly Jo wanted to talk about her horse and her trick-riding ambitions to be the best.

But they also talked about other things that had been bothering her—like getting herself kidnapped. Yvonne said she understood how Holly Jo might feel guilty, but that she shouldn't. "If they hadn't grabbed you that day, they would have some other day. You did nothing wrong."

She wasn't completely sure that was true and told Yvonne how it seemed like everyone in the Powder River Basin knew her, but she didn't know them. It was why she'd walked up to that pickup to talk to the woman. How could she trust anyone now?

"You will in time," Yvonne promised. "The majority of people can be trusted."

She'd even had the nightmare about a burning Darius Reed chasing her less often. She felt herself getting stronger.

After one session, she had the courage to ask HH something. "That man who kidnapped me," she said, her voice breaking, "was he my father?"

HH looked upset. "No, of course not. He was a man who felt I had wronged him and his family. I had. It was many years ago, when I was just sixteen, not that age is an excuse."

"Then who is my father?" Holly Jo had seen the way people around Powder Crossing looked at her, wondering who she was, what she was doing on the Mc-Kenna Ranch, wondering if she was HH's daughter. She'd heard the whispers behind her back.

She'd told herself that it hadn't bothered her. Let them all wonder. She wondered too, but HH swore he wasn't her father. Not that she'd ever known her father. Her mother had only told her that he was gone, which she'd accepted until she was older. Then she'd wanted her mom to tell her what *gone* meant. "Dead?"

"Just gone, okay?"

"Gone where?"

"Holly Jo, stop asking me about him. It makes me sad."

"Because he isn't coming back?"

"Exactly."

HH looked sad now. "I honestly don't know who your father was. Your mother never told me. It wasn't Bobby Robinson, the man who married her after she became pregnant. She never told him either. I'm sorry. But you don't have to worry. I'm going to legally adopt you as my own."

"Adopt me? But what if he tries to kidnap me, too?"

"No," he said hurriedly. "I'm so sorry this happened to you. I'm never going to let anything like that happen to you again."

She knew he meant well. Just as she knew that was something he couldn't promise. She still blamed herself for walking over to talk to the lady in the pickup.

"I learned something from all this," HH said. "The way you treat other people…it matters. Be kind, do the right thing. I know you will."

She wanted to ask, *What if they are mean to you?* She couldn't believe he was telling her to just take it. She thought of Gus, who was afraid of his own shadow. She didn't want to be like that. "Can I go ride my horse?"

HH looked relieved and then concerned. "You aren't planning to leave the ranch, are you?"

She shook her head. "I never want to leave." That made him smile, but there was still sadness in his eyes. "Maybe tomorrow we can ride together, but today I just want it to be me and Honey." She wanted to feel the wind in her hair, experience that feeling of flying. Honey made her feel safe. Honey made her believe that one day she wouldn't be afraid anymore.

"Go, have fun," HH said, though she could tell it was hard for him. Would he worry now every time she left the house? "Elaine said she's still going to take you to Billings to buy what you want for your room when you're ready."

"Okay, thanks." But decorating her new room when the house was finished was the last thing on her mind. Which reminded her how much she wasn't that girl anymore.

"Holly Jo?"

She stopped at the door and turned back to look at HH. He too had changed. He seemed older, and she felt bad about that. Maybe when he healed more, he wouldn't look so afraid for her. "Yes?"

"Just…enjoy yourself."

She smiled her thanks, knowing he was going to tell her to be careful but had stopped himself. "There's Pickett," she said at the sound of a car horn. "He's taking me over to the ranch."

HOLDEN WATCHED HER GO, his heart breaking. He'd wanted to hug her to him, to not let her out of his sight, but she was too old for a hug from him, and that had never been their relationship even if he could have hugged her with his injuries.

He'd been given another chance—not just raising a child, but also establishing a relationship with her. He'd been afraid of making the same mistakes he'd made with his own children. Now he'd already jeopardized her life. He couldn't keep worrying about messing her up. He told himself that he'd already done the worst.

"She'll be fine," Elaine said, coming into the room as Holly Jo went out the front door of the Stafford house in her jeans and boots and Western shirt and hat. "Children are resilient. I would imagine that once you live through something like that, you grow stronger. At least, that's what I hope for her."

"We almost lost her," he said, voice breaking with emotion.

She nodded and stepped to him to cover his hand with her own. "We almost lost you as well."

He scoffed, hating to think how he'd let his temper get the best of him. It was a wonder he hadn't gotten the sheriff and Holly Jo killed. "Am I ever going to learn?"

"Are any of us?" She smiled down at him. "Maybe you are, though. You accepted Charlotte's offer. That seems like a huge step."

He groaned, remembering his reaction when Elaine had told him about Charlotte's offer. Live in the Stafford Ranch house? What had Lottie been thinking? His first impulse was to turn her down flat.

"You would be doing Charlotte a favor," Elaine had said. "She won't be there. I think she might be trying to make up for the past a little. Would you deny her that?"

He'd groused for a while, but it had been Brand who'd convinced him his mother had been sincere in her offer. "The house is pretty much empty and right next door to your ranch," Brand had said. "It might be a way of putting all that old animosity between the two families to rest. I really wish you'd take her up on her offer. Ryder and I will be around occasionally, but that's about it. She's let go of the staff."

"This is your chance to get to know your son, a working rancher like you," Elaine had said, and he'd finally agreed.

Lottie wouldn't be there, but he knew he would see her everywhere in the home her husband had made for her—the home the two of them should have had together. The first day he'd walked in after finally being released from the hospital, he'd been anxious. But to his surprise, he didn't see Lottie here like he'd thought he would. It was as if she'd left nothing of herself behind.

"Cooper called to see how you were," Elaine said now. "I told him you were getting crankier by the day. He said that was a good sign, and you must be going to live. Tilly's so happy that we accepted her mother's offer to stay here."

"She have any idea where Charlotte went?" Holden asked.

Elaine shook her head. "No one seems to know or how long she will be gone. She told me she needed some time away."

Holden realized that Elaine and Charlotte were a lot closer than he'd ever imagined—or paid enough attention to notice. It surprised him. "The way our house is coming up, we shouldn't be here long. How will you let Charlotte know we've moved out when that happens?"

Elaine shrugged. "I guess she'll hear about it somehow. I doubt she's worried about it." With that, she left the room, making him think the two weren't that close after all.

His Lottie. He wasn't ready to see her. Not yet. He wasn't even sure when he would be ready—if ever—to dig through the ashes of his house, let alone his and Lottie's tragic love-hate relationship. So much had happened over the years. He just wasn't sure they could ever find their way back to each other.

But even as he thought it, there was that damned sliver of hope that still burned inside him as if nothing could kill it. Not betrayal or lies, or even bullets.

BIRDIE CAME OUT of the hotel and stopped short as she saw who was standing next to her SUV, apparently waiting for her. She'd been upset when she heard that Charlotte Stafford had turned her house over to the McKennas and left town. She'd thought it was to avoid making good on what she'd said she owed Birdie.

So seeing her waiting next to her SUV came as a surprise. Birdie took a breath, straightened and walked over to her. She'd been waiting for this for a very long time.

"If you came here to get me to stop looking for my father's killer and her accomplice, you're wasting your time," Birdie said.

Charlotte shook her head. "I've heard about what a determined, strong woman you are. I wouldn't presume to try to change your mind. The only thing I want from you is honesty. Are you using Brand to get to me?"

It was the last thing Birdie had expected her to say. She frowned in surprise. "I love your son." She realized that she hadn't even admitted it to herself until that moment. "It has nothing to do with wanting to see my father's killer behind bars—even if it's you."

The woman rancher nodded gravely. Birdie saw her swallow and look away for a moment before she turned back. "I'm sorry about your father." Before she could respond to that, Charlotte said the last thing Birdie expected. "I'm sorry I married him. I'm sorry he died. I'm sorry I was the one to take him away from you. I've already called the sheriff. I'm turning myself in. If Holly Jo's kidnapping taught me anything, it's time to do what is right."

"You're telling me you killed him." She couldn't help being shocked to have Charlotte admit it. "What about your accomplice? Someone had to help you get him into that well."

The woman looked at her for a moment before she smiled. "You underestimate what I'm capable of all by myself, but if you must know, he's already in jail."

Boyle Wilson had helped her? No wonder he said he would talk if she didn't take back her statement and get him released.

She didn't know what to say, but Charlotte didn't give her a chance. Birdie watched her turn to get back into her SUV, too surprised to move. Had Charlotte Stafford just admitted that she'd killed her second husband? Birdie had expected to feel something more than she did right now. The finality of it rang hollow. There had to be more.

"Wait," she called. Charlotte had just opened the driver's-side door when Birdie stopped her. "Why do I get the feeling that you're covering for someone?"

Charlotte met her gaze. "It's over. Now you have to decide if you love my son Brand enough to let the past go and allow yourself to be happy. Or you can make the mistake I did and let the past consume you." With that, she climbed into the SUV and drove toward the sheriff's department.

CHAPTER THIRTY

IT DIDN'T TAKE long for the news about Charlotte Stafford turning herself in for the murder of her second husband, Dixon Malone, to sweep through the county. The only surprise was that Charlotte had admitted the truth and turned herself in.

No one was more shocked than Brand. Birdie had been about to drive over to see him when she'd found Charlotte waiting for her.

"I saw her this morning before she turned herself in. She wanted to know if I'd been using you to get to her."

He cocked a brow.

She stepped to him. She'd found him mending a stretch of barbed wire fence not far from the house. "I told her the truth. Well, not all the truth. I didn't tell her that I started falling for you that morning when you'd come out of the stable and dropped that rope over me and pulled me in. You were so hungover and yet so cute. I almost felt bad about throwing you down on the ground."

"Almost," he said, grinning at her.

"It's the grin," she said, narrowing her eyes at him. "I'm a sucker for your lopsided grin."

"I'll have to remember that," he said as he took off his leather gloves and stuffed them into the hip pocket of his jeans. "I'd hug you, but I've been working out here in the summer heat, and I'm pretty sweaty."

She stepped closer. "I'm sorry about your mother."

"I still can't believe she confessed," he said. "It's not like her."

"People change," Birdie said.

"Not my mother. I hate to say it, but she must have an angle. Maybe she thinks the judge will be more lenient with her because she turned herself in." He shook his head. "Without any evidence, she could have gotten away with it. Why confess now?"

Birdie had wondered the same thing. "Maybe she did it for us. To make things easier for us to be together."

He chuckled. "That doesn't sound like the mother I know."

"You're probably going to hate hearing this, but what if she didn't do it?" Birdie said. "What if she's covering for someone?"

He groaned. "Who?"

"Maybe your father?"

"Now, that really doesn't sound like her."

She closed the distance between them, looping her arms around his neck.

"You'll be sorry," he warned.

"I happen to like my cowboys hot and sweaty," she whispered before she kissed him. His big hands cupped her waist and pulled her to him as the kiss deepened.

She thought about what Charlotte had asked her. Maybe she'd started out hoping Brand would help her, but along the way, she'd fallen for him. Whether or not she stayed around Powder Crossing, though, well, that was still to be seen.

No one took the news of Charlotte's confession and subsequent arrest harder than Holden. "It isn't that I didn't know she had violence in her. I just never expected this," he said when he heard the news.

The doctor said he could be a little more active, but suggested he put off horseback riding for a while yet.

He debated going into town and seeing Charlotte. He felt responsible for her marrying Dixon Malone, afraid she'd only done it because of him. They'd both made so many mistakes, but he hated to think what would happen to her now.

Cooper had taken over the reins here on the ranch, proving what Holden had already suspected. He was the one to take over when his father was gone. Duffy was leaving. Holden knew he shouldn't have been surprised. Duffy showed up when Holly Jo had been found, the ranch house was gone, and the doctors said Holden should have a full recovery.

"I'm taking a job on an oil rig in Wyoming," Duffy had told him one day in the hospital before he'd been released. "I just need to get away for a while," his youngest son had said. "Cooper left for a couple of years, and you were okay with that," he'd added, as if expecting an argument.

Holden hadn't bothered to tell him that he hadn't been okay with Cooper leaving. He'd worried that his son wouldn't come back. "I think it's a good idea."

Duffy had looked both surprised and disappointed. "Is that what you told Cooper?"

"A man has to roam sometimes to find out where he really belongs. Cooper came back. Whether or not you do, I wish you the best. You'll always have a home here."

His son had scoffed at that. "The home's gone. Everything feels like it's changing." He had seen how unsettled Duffy was. He'd suspected part of it had to do with his best friend, Pickett Hanson, marrying Oakley Stafford. Holden thought Duffy might have cared a lot more for Oakley than he'd let on.

"If and when you come back, your home will be here," he'd assured his son, and then he'd shaken Duffy's hand and thanked him for letting him know. He hadn't seen him since, but he knew in his heart it wouldn't be the last time.

Holden pulled himself from his thoughts, anxious for Elaine to return. She had taken Holly Jo to Billings to buy some things for the house that was quickly rising from the ashes.

Holden couldn't wait to get his strength back. He doubted he would ever be the man he was before. But damned if he wasn't going to try. He found himself dwelling on the past all the time when he should have been counting his blessings and thinking about the future.

Cooper and Tilly had almost completed their new house. Holly Jo was safe and seeming more like her old self every day. Pickett was teaching her some new horseback-riding tricks. Oakley was helping. Newly-weds Pickett and Oakley were about to start construction on their house on the ranch.

Like the rest of them, Holden figured everyone worried about the girl. What Holly Jo had been through had to have left its mark. It certainly had on him. But then again, he was to blame for all of it.

There was no reason that they couldn't all start over. The worst, he wanted to believe, was behind them. He'd heard from Elaine that Tilly might be pregnant and just waiting to make sure before she told anyone. He loved the idea of being a grandfather.

He thought of Charlotte. Would she feel excited about being a grandmother? But now she might not get a chance to even see her grandchild. He couldn't bear the thought of her going to prison.

At the sound of a vehicle pulling up, he got to his feet. The doctor had given him a cane to use, but he hated it. Elaine would yell at him if she caught him without it, though. He picked it up and moved to the door as Elaine and Holly Jo came in. He loved seeing the excitement on both of their faces.

"Wait and see what we bought!" Holly Jo cried as she rushed past, her arms full of packages. "My room is going to be perfect!" With that, she was gone upstairs in a flurry of movement.

He turned to look at Elaine, who stood in the doorway, smiling. "Let me take those," he said, reaching for the packages in her arms.

"I have it," she said, stepping past him to set them down on the sofa before turning to look at him. "What's happened?"

For a moment, he was too surprised to speak. Was he that transparent? "I thought you might have heard. Charlotte turned herself in for Dixon Malone's murder. She's been arrested."

All the color drained from Elaine's face. "No." She slowly lowered herself into a nearby chair, and Holden did the same. Her shock surprised him. Practically everyone in the county had suspected Charlotte killed him.

"No," Elaine repeated, shaking her head. "Why would she do that?"

"I wondered the same thing," he said. "She'd gotten away with it. Why confess now?"

Elaine raised her head to look at him. Her gaze locked with his. "She didn't do it."

"You are probably the only person around who believes that," he said, wondering again about their relationship.

"No, she didn't do it," she said more forcefully. Tears filled her eyes. "Holden…" Her voice broke, and he felt a jolt an instant before she spoke again. The floor under him seemed to give way.

"I'm the one who killed Dixon."

CHAPTER THIRTY-ONE

THE SHERIFF HAD been floored when Charlotte Stafford had walked into his office and confessed to murdering Dixon Malone. Not that he hadn't suspected she'd done it. But why confess now?

It definitely seemed out of character. But then again, she'd been doing things lately that had everyone raising their eyebrows. No one had ever expected she would turn her house over to Holden and family after he got out of the hospital.

Stuart had had her sign a confession, questioning why she didn't want her lawyer present. He still couldn't believe she was sitting down in one of his cells right now after she waived her rights. Her attorney, Ian Drake, had shown up, but she'd refused to see him. At her bail hearing, she'd been given a young defender out of Billings, but refused bail.

Stuart couldn't help questioning all of it. He'd known Charlotte Stafford for years. She hadn't been the kind of woman anyone seemed to get close to—except for Holden McKenna, if the rumors were true. Which they seemed to be, given Brand's DNA results, he reminded himself.

Arrangements were being made to send Charlotte to Billings to await trial because Powder Crossing wasn't set up to house a long-term prisoner, and that was where the trial would be held. The judge had moved the venue, afraid that Charlotte couldn't get a fair trial in her hometown.

He'd accepted that she was guilty—until Elaine walked into his office.

"Charlotte didn't kill Dixon," she said. "I did."

He stared at her. "Let me get this straight. *You* killed Dixon."

"Yes."

"Why would Charlotte lie about it?"

Elaine sighed. "I'm not sure, but you know that Birdie Malone is in town looking for her father's killer. Birdie saved Charlotte from Boyle. Maybe she thought by confessing to the murder, she was paying Birdie back. I don't know. Who knows what makes Charlotte do what she does?"

She had him there.

"Maybe she also lied to protect me," Elaine said.

"Protect you? Why would she do that? I didn't even realize that the two of you were…acquainted, really."

"We're friends," she said with a lift of her chin. "I've been trying to get her and Holden back together for years."

The sheriff shook his head in surprise. "Maybe you'd better sit down and tell me how it is that you killed Dixon. Did Charlotte hire you to do it?"

"No," she said, frowning. "I just told you. We're friends." She took a seat. "Don't you want to record this?"

"Sure," he said and turned on the video recorder.

Elaine cleared her throat and began. The sheriff had heard this confession already from Charlotte, only in her story, Charlotte had done what Elaine was now confessing to. What the hell was going on?

"I was at the ranch alone that night when Dixon Malone came by. He wanted to see Holden. I told him he was out of town. He was very agitated, said he had to see him, that he needed money, he was leaving town."

Stuart waited while she took a breath, reminding him that Elaine would have been in her early twenties when this happened. Her mother, newly widowed, had taken the McKenna Ranch housekeeper job when Elaine was a baby, with Holden providing a home for both of them. Elaine had grown up on the McKenna Ranch and gone away to college, returning to the ranch when her mother got sick and taking over the housekeeping job. She'd been at the ranch ever since.

"Dixon had been drinking." She hesitated, tears pooling in her eyes. "He said he knew things that Holden would pay to keep quiet. He demanded I give him money, said he needed it to start over, just him and his daughter. When I tried to throw him out…" She looked away. "He got rough. Said he wasn't leaving without something. He grabbed me. I told him he was hurting me. He backed me into the wall by the fireplace. I picked up the poker and hit him. The first time only stunned him. I hit him harder. He went down hard, striking his head on the hearth, and didn't get up." She wiped her tears. "That's it."

"Not hardly," the sheriff said. "What did you do with the body? And how is it that Charlotte told this same story with just a few minor changes? Not to mention your statement that she might have lied to protect you. How about the whole truth here?"

Elaine swallowed. "I panicked when I realized I'd killed him. I…I called Charlotte to tell her what happened and ask for her help. We'd become friends when I tried to get her to forgive Holden and Margie. She and Margie had been such good friends before..." Elaine shrugged.

He knew where this story was going. "She helped you get rid of the body and cover up the crime."

"Yes."

"The two of you kept this secret all these years," the sheriff said. "So what changed?"

"I didn't know Dixon had a daughter who would someday come looking for the truth."

"Also, Birdie Malone saved Charlotte the other day," Stuart said. "I suspect that's why Charlotte confessed."

Elaine nodded. "And forced us both to finally face the past."

"Here's what I want to know," the sheriff said. "After you struck Dixon the second time, did you stay there in the room?"

"No, I went outside to make the call to Charlotte. I didn't want to go back inside by myself, so I walked down the road to meet her. Then we both went back to take care of him."

"Take care of him?"

"You know, wrap him up and dispose of his body. She'd brought a pickup. He was very heavy."

"Did either of you have a gun?"

Her expression was his answer, and yet he needed it on the video.

"A gun. No."

"You didn't shoot him to make sure he was good and dead? Charlotte didn't?"

"No." She looked horrified. "Why would we do that?

He was dead. There was so much blood…" She swallowed.

He read Elaine her rights, then turned off the video and had a deputy take her down to a cell.

Then he sat mulling over everything he'd heard from the two women before calling the county prosecutor and telling him that they had a problem.

BRAND CALLED BIRDIE the moment he heard that Elaine had turned herself in for Dixon Malone's murder.

He'd wanted to believe Charlotte hadn't done it, even knowing that she could have. He realized that he'd been waiting for the other boot to drop from the moment Dixon's body had been found in the well so close to Stafford Ranch property.

The coroner had said the body had been in the well for years—probably since the night Dixon had stormed out of the ranch house and was never seen again. At least, that had been his mother's story—that Dixon had stormed out, and that was the last she saw of him.

Right now, he was more concerned about what this meant for Birdie. She'd come here to get justice. It had appeared that she was finally getting it. But now her reason for coming to Powder Crossing was over. There would be nothing keeping her here.

He didn't want her to go, but he wasn't sure he could make her stay. When he mentioned it to Ryder, his brother laughed.

"Seriously? How long have you known her? A week?" Ryder shook his head. "Don't you dare tell me that you've fallen in love with her."

When Brand said nothing, his brother swore and said, "Wait until our mother hears about this. You could have any woman you want in the Powder River Basin. Enough of them have thrown themselves at you, and yet you want Birdie Malone?"

He swallowed the lump in his throat. His brother was right, but it didn't change anything. "I do. I want her." He'd never wanted anyone more in his life.

Ryder shook his head. "Why her?"

"There's just something about her," Brand said. "She's quirky, exciting, fun. I never know what she's going to do." He laughed. "And neither does she. She's impulsive, daring, and cares deeply about things that are important to her, like finding her father's killer. Being around her makes me feel happy and free and…I don't know… alive." He could feel his brother studying him.

"Oh, you have it bad. But if her reason for being in Powder Crossing was to find her father's killer, now that she has, exactly where does that leave you?"

Up a creek without a paddle, he thought, unless he did something to try to make her stay. He avoided his brother's gaze until Ryder swore.

"You love her, right? You've told her. No? So you're going to tell her that you love her in hopes that she'll stay? And if that doesn't do the trick?" Ryder demanded.

Brand found himself grinning. "I'm going to ask her to marry me."

His brother shook his head. "You're that sure she's the one?"

He met Ryder's gaze. "I know it seems improbable, the two of us, but yeah, I'm that sure. I can't imagine life without her."

TREYTON MCKENNA DIDN'T want to take the call from the Billings detention center, let alone pay for the charges.

He had a pretty good idea of why CJ Stafford would be calling him now. But he also knew that if he didn't take the call, he might be getting a midnight wake-up visit from one of CJ's criminal friends.

"Yeah, I'll accept charges," he said in a growl.

"You don't sound happy to hear from me."

"What do you want, CJ?" he demanded, even though he already knew. He'd been expecting this call. But that didn't mean that he liked it.

"It's time to get back into business."

Treyton rolled his eyes. "We would have been in business for months if it wasn't for you getting yourself arrested."

"You have the property. How soon can my associates start bringing in product?"

"The sheriff is suspicious that I might have already been in business with you in the past. He's threatened a couple of times to get a warrant and come search the premises."

CJ laughed. "Can't get a warrant without some kind of proof. Your job is to make sure he doesn't get it."

"I already know my job. I'm the one sticking my neck out. It's my property. The new split is eighty-twenty."

His former partner swore. "I'm the one who introduced you to the business, remember? You begged to be let in. Now you think you're running the show? Have you met me?"

Treyton fell silent for a moment, warning himself about the man he was dealing with. "Seventy-thirty or I sell the land. It's worth more now than I paid for it. I've been thinking about going to Texas. Buy me a place on the beach."

"Bullpuck!" CJ laughed. "Sand between your toes?

You're too much of a wuss. Sixty-forty, but only because I need money for a decent lawyer. When I get out of here, we'll renegotiate."

He just bet they would.

"You'll be hearing from my friends."

The call ended. Treyton swore. If CJ ever got out, he'd take over and have him killed. The best Treyton could hope for was that it would be quick, and they'd at least bury him six feet deep on his own property.

It would be just like CJ to hire an attorney who found a way to get him out scot-free. If that happened, Treyton wanted to be ready, which meant socking away as much money as he could.

If CJ Stafford was ever free, Treyton promised himself he'd head to some tropical island and see how he felt about sand between his toes.

"TWO WOMEN HAVE confessed to the murder?" the prosecutor demanded.

"I have both of their confessions," Stuart told him. "As for the original confrontation, it appears to be self-defense."

"Then they decided to get rid of the body," the prosecutor said.

"They both told the same story. I believe them. A jury would believe them. So, what are we looking at here as far as charges?"

After he disconnected, he called down to have both women brought up from their cells. Their lawyers were cooling their heels outside his office.

After he had Elaine's confession down and signed, he had Charlotte brought up to his office. "Ladies, would one of you like to explain how you both killed Dixon Malone?"

Charlotte shot Elaine an impatient look. "I have this taken care of."

"She's covering for me," Elaine said. "I killed Dixon. You have my confession."

"I have two confessions," he snapped. "Both basically the same story. What I want is the truth. How about one of you tell me what I want to hear?"

The two women exchanged a look that made him swear. "Did you check for a pulse?" he asked.

Elaine started to speak, but Charlotte cut her off. "I checked when I got there. He was clearly dead."

"So you didn't check for a pulse before you called Charlotte," he said to Elaine.

"I panicked and called Charlotte and begged her to help me."

Her friend groaned. "Why didn't you just leave it alone?"

"Because I'm not letting you take the fall for something I did," Elaine said.

"You made the call from outside and went down the road to meet Charlotte," the sheriff said. "You didn't go back inside to check to make sure he was actually dead."

"He was dead," Elaine said. "There was blood on the floor under his head. He wasn't moving. He looked… dead."

The sheriff nodded. "So, which one of you had the gun?"

"We didn't have a gun," Charlotte snapped. "Why would you even ask that?"

"Because the coroner believes one of two bullets fired from a .22 to the brain is what killed Dixon Malone,"

Stuart said and saw their shocked expressions. "One of the slugs was lodged in the man's skull."

"I didn't kill him?" Elaine said in a whisper and began to cry. "He was alive when I called Charlotte?"

The sheriff looked to Charlotte. "Did you bring a gun to finish the job Elaine started?"

"No, I did check for a pulse. He was dead," Charlotte said.

"I was with her the entire time," Elaine said. "Neither of us shot him."

"He must have regained consciousness after his fall," the sheriff said. "Elaine, you're sure no one else was in the house that night?"

She shook her head, looking as mystified by all this as he was.

He turned to Charlotte. "You didn't see anyone on the way into the ranch?"

"No. We didn't see anyone," she said.

Studying the two women, he would have bet his career that they were telling the truth—which was what he was doing. "But you did get rid of his body," he said. He pulled out their confessions, tore them up and dropped them into the trash.

Then he got out two new sheets of paper. He shoved one toward each of the women and tossed them each a pen. "Let's start over, but this time write down the truth, because you could both be facing prison time if the judge doesn't believe your story."

CHAPTER THIRTY-TWO

THE DAY HOLDEN'S lawyer called to say that Elaine was being released after Holden had posted bond, his ranch manager, Deacon Yates, asked if he could pick her up.

"I'd appreciate if you'd let me do it," Deacon said, turning the brim of what appeared to be a new Stetson in his fingers and staring at the floor.

Holden looked at the man in surprise. Deacon, who was close to Elaine's age, was dressed in his Sunday-best jeans, sporting a corduroy jacket and an agate bolo tie. His sandy-blond hair had been reined in, and his boots were freshly polished.

For a moment, Holden was at a loss for words. He studied him, seeing himself in the man. He'd been that bashful young man around Charlotte when they were teens, so smitten that he couldn't rope two words together.

"Sure," Holden managed to say. "Doctor told me to take it easy." It wasn't true, and he figured Deacon knew it, because he nodded as he raised his gaze.

"Thought she might be hungry. Might want to go to the café. But after that, I'll bring her straightaway."

"No hurry. Let her enjoy being free for a while," Holden said. His lawyer had told him that Elaine probably wouldn't do any time. Charlotte either. With luck, they would get a hefty fine and community service since this was their first brush with the law.

"Dixon said he knew things about Charlotte and was going to talk unless he was paid off," Holden's attorney told him. "When Elaine had tried to throw him out of the house, he'd decided he wasn't going without something for his troubles."

That Elaine had fought the man off didn't surprise Holden. What hurt was that, like the kidnapping, this was something else he'd brought on the people he loved. It all came back to him.

He'd sworn then that he'd do everything he could to make sure Elaine didn't get any jail time. Same with Charlotte, if she would let him. He would use his money and his power—just as he always had. But this time for good, he told himself. From now on, only for good.

Apparently, Birdie Malone, the deceased man's daughter, had asked for leniency for both women.

"Thanks," his ranch manager said with a grin and left, a hop in his step, leaving Holden smiling and at the same time a little sad. He missed that old sensation that Deacon was feeling and wasn't sure he could ever get it back again.

ELAINE EMERGED FROM the back of the sheriff's department, stopping to squint in the bright sunlight. She'd expected to see one of the McKenna Ranch vehicles, probably Holden's SUV. Instead, there was one of the ranch pickups, and it wasn't Holden leaning against it.

She glanced around for a moment, wondering why Holden had sent his ranch manager. Her gaze returned to the ranch pickup and the cowboy standing next to it. She saw something cross Deacon Yates's face. Disappointment, embarrassment? Some of both. Her heart clenched. She would never want this man to feel either of those.

Smiling, she headed toward him. As she did, the ranch manager removed his hat and slowly raised his eyes to hers. Surprised to see him, she didn't even have a moment to consider what he was doing here or what he might say when she reached him.

"I came to see if I could be of help," he said in his soft-spoken way. She'd known the man since the day he was hired back when they were both in their teens. He'd always been respectful but shy. A man who would have walked on hot coals for Holden. Like her, he loved the McKenna Ranch.

She couldn't help but smile at the sincerity in his expression. "Deacon, that is very nice of you, but I'm not sure there is anything that can be done."

She was touched the ranch manager wanted to help, but at a loss to see how.

"If it's money you need—"

"No," she said quickly. "Holden..." She didn't continue. You didn't tell one man that another man had already taken care of it. "You came to pick me up. Thank you."

"I thought after being in jail that you might be hungry. The café special today is a barbecued pork sandwich. Didn't know how you felt about that."

Her smile widened. "I would love one, thank you."

He nodded, smiling too, as he hurried around to open the passenger-side door of the pickup. She climbed in and watched him run around to slide behind the wheel. She'd never seen him nervous before. He knew his job on the ranch, was good with the horses as well as the livestock and worked hard, confident in his abilities.

As he started up the engine, she took him in, seeing how he was dressed. She caught the scent of his aftershave and had to smile to herself. This hadn't been Holden's idea, she realized. This was a...date?

She couldn't remember the last time she went on one. It had been years. She'd told herself that she was too busy at the ranch, that she had everything she needed in her friendship with Holden. But looking at Deacon, she was touched.

They talked about the ranch and the people they knew in common during their lunch. Deacon relaxed, and so did Elaine. The ranch manager could be charming, funny, too. She couldn't remember a lunch she'd enjoyed better and said as much to him on the way to the ranch.

"I wish I could help you more," he said. "I know Holden got the best attorney money could buy for you. I did have something else in mind." He cleared his throat and glanced over at her. "You could tell the sheriff that I was the one who killed Dixon. That you were covering for me."

She stared at him, stunned. That he would take the blame for murder for her... "Deacon—"

"Elaine, you're always doing for others. I'd do anything for you."

She reached over and touched his arm. "I can't tell you how much that means to me. Thank you, but no. It's going to be all right no matter what happens."

He grew silent for a few minutes. "I know I'm not your first choice."

Her heart ached. "Deacon, you're any woman's first

choice if she got to know you. Promise me that when all of this is over, we'll spend some time together," she said. He glanced over at her in surprise. She nodded, smiling. "I'd love to go on another date with you."

He blushed to the roots of his hair but said nothing as he drove. After a few minutes, he said, "I'd like that. I've wanted to ask you out for years, but…" He shrugged and glanced at her, then back at his driving. "I thought you might be in love with Holden."

"We're just friends. You know he's never really loved anyone but Charlotte. I've been trying to get them back together for years."

He was surprised to hear that, and it showed in his expression. He seemed less nervous, more like the capable ranch manager he was. "So maybe…you and I…"

"I don't see why not."

"I'd wait for you to get out of jail."

She thought of Deacon being there when she was released. "I'm not going to hold you to that, but I would love it if yours was the first face I saw."

He grinned over at her. "Count on it."

"In the meantime, while I'm out on bail, maybe we could go for a horseback ride together."

"'Speck we could," he said.

"All this time we've known each other, I realize we don't know much about each other," she said.

"Not much interesting to tell on my end."

"Oh, I'm sure that's not true," Elaine said. "It's too bad we're just now getting to know each other. I could probably use a few letters while I'm locked up."

"I could do that, though I wouldn't say much for my penmanship."

"Don't worry. Bet I won't have any trouble reading your letters."

He looked over at her. Their gazes locked for a moment.

"You have beautiful brown eyes, Mr. Yates."

HOLLY JO WAS glad to run into Gus one day in Powder Crossing. He was outside the feed store, kicking rocks in the alley, no doubt waiting on his father. She was waiting on Elaine, who was running errands.

"Hey," she said as she approached him.

He brightened at once, then dipped his head shyly. "Are you okay?"

"I'm fine. Being kidnapped was nothing." She definitely didn't want to talk about it. "So, how about you?"

Gus looked up and shrugged. "I was afraid Tana had taken you."

She shook her head. "I would have gotten away from her without any trouble," she boasted, hating that her kidnapping was going to be the subject everyone wanted to talk about. "You should ask your dad if you can come over to the ranch and ride horses with me sometime."

"Sure," he said, although he didn't look like it was anything that was going to happen. He was peering at her now. She could feel the intensity of his gaze. "You seem different."

"Different how?" she asked, sincerely curious.

"You always were crazy brave, but now…it's like after what happened, you're not afraid of anything."

She wished that was true.

"No one is going to bully you ever again." He kicked another rock. It skittered across the alley and came to rest next to the supply store. "Maybe I need to get kidnapped."

She knew he was kidding, but she hated to hear him say it. "You're great just like you are," she told him. She didn't think he believed her.

She wasn't the only one who'd changed. Gus was getting taller. He looked stronger. She suspected he'd been working hard this summer at the ranch his dad managed. Soon he would be taller than his father.

On the way back to where Elaine had parked her SUV, Holly Jo spotted Tana and her group of friends coming up the sidewalk. For a moment, she panicked. She didn't want to see them, not now, maybe not ever. But they'd already seen her, and she wasn't about to let them think she was afraid of them.

Tana slowed as she approached, almost looking afraid to pass her on the street, even though her friends were with her. Holly Jo waited, unsure what was going to happen, feeling anxious, but almost curious.

To her surprise, the girl stopped and said, "Hi. Glad you're okay." Some of the others echoed her words in mumbles. "I like your short hair. It's cute on you."

Her hand went to her hair. She was still trying to get used to it. She realized it was the nicest thing Tana had ever said to her. "Thanks."

"Guess we'll see you in school. Summer is going way too fast. Sucks." More agreement from her friends.

Holly Jo nodded. "Sucks."

"Well, see ya around," Tana said, and with a little wave, she and her group walked away.

She watched them go, feeling thrown off balance. She'd understood the old Tana. This one confused her.

When Elaine came out of the post office, she asked, "Those girls weren't giving you trouble, were they?"

"Nope." With that, she climbed into the SUV, leaned back and just breathed. Gus was right. She was different. She wasn't sure how she felt about it, but then realized she felt okay. The thought made her smile.

Elaine climbed behind the wheel, studied her for a moment, and then started the engine and headed out of town.

CHAPTER THIRTY-THREE

THE FOURTH OF JULY party was Holden's idea. "I think we're due a celebration after everything that has happened."

Elaine looked skeptical. "It's just that…" She shook her head. "Why not? You're right." Just as Holden had suspected, Elaine had gotten off with a fine, time served in jail and community service. Charlotte had gotten a lesser sentence and had been able to leave the county. Or maybe she'd left the country. Holden didn't know.

When former Stafford Ranch manager Boyle Wilson had heard that Charlotte had been exonerated, he'd been furious and began to talk. While telling everything he knew about her, he'd mistakenly dug his own grave by admitting that he'd overheard her on the phone and beat her to the McKenna Ranch. There he found Dixon—bleeding but alive.

He thought he finally had Charlotte where he wanted her—but only if Dixon was dead. He couldn't stand the man as it was, so he'd shot him, thinking that he would plant the .22 at her house if she ever crossed him—or, worse, tried to fire him.

"We could do it over Fourth of July weekend," Holden said, determined to start over. "I'll buy lots of fireworks." She made a face. "Maybe not too many, given that we've just moved into the new house after the other one burned down."

He changed the subject, the fire and how they'd almost lost Holly Jo still too fresh on everyone's mind. "You haven't heard from Charlotte, have you?" She shook her head. "I feel bad about how I left things the last time I saw her. If you hear from her..."

"I'll tell her you want to at least talk to her. How would that be?"

He smiled. "Thank you. I'm not doing this in the hope of bringing Charlotte back to Powder Crossing. It's a chance to bring the families together. To put the animosity to rest."

She cocked her head at him. "One word. *Treyton.*"

"Yes, he won't attend the party, I'm sure. Hell, Bailey might not even show up, and Duffy's down in Wyoming. Cooper and Tilly will come, though. Pickett and Oakley, too. Maybe you should see if Holly Jo would like to invite a few friends." Again, Elaine looked skeptical, but said she would ask. "Ryder will probably come, don't you think? Be sure and invite Deacon, too." He saw her face heat for a moment. "I'm delighted that you two have—"

Her look made him choke back whatever else he'd planned to say.

"I'll invite everyone," she said as she started to walk toward the kitchen. "Let's leave it at that."

"Why is it that my love life has always been fair game?" Holden said under his breath, but loud enough that she could hear.

She didn't take the bait, and he was almost relieved. The truth was, he didn't have a love life and hadn't for years. Who was he kidding? He was lonely and missed Lottie like a lost limb. He'd give anything if she showed up for the party, but he knew better than to hold out hope.

BRAND HAD NEVER been this nervous in his life. He'd decided to ask Birdie to marry him at the Fourth of July party at McKenna Ranch.

As fireworks exploded all around them, he looked over at Birdie, instantly charmed by her expression. She was staring upward, eyes wide in awe, as if she'd never seen anything like this before. Maybe she hadn't. Holden had gone all out, even though Brand had heard that Elaine had tried to dissuade him from buying too many.

All Brand knew was that he wanted to snatch a star out of the sky and give it to Birdie. Anything to see that wonder in her eyes when she looked at him.

She glanced over at him, her gaze softened in the lights bursting around them. He felt anchored to the spot as she reached out to cup his cheek, before she leaned in and kissed him. Drawing back, she whispered, "Thank you."

He had no idea what he'd done other than invite her to the party—just that he wanted to do whatever it took to make her happy for the rest of his life. He pulled her to him. "Let's take a walk." He held her hand, and they wandered away from the barbecue area some distance from the new house and into the darkness of the thick cottonwoods along the Powder River.

Drawing her to a stop, he pulled her close and said, "I don't want you to leave." He rushed on before she could speak. "I know I probably wouldn't be your grandmother's choice for you, but I…I…" He swallowed the lump in his throat. "I love you. Marry me, Birdie Malone. Make me the happiest cowboy this side of Chicago."

She looked so serious for a moment that he feared she would turn him down. "You're wrong. Nana would have loved you, Brand. Just like I do."

Sweeping her up in his arms, he kissed her hard, then drew back to just look at her as he slowly lowered her to the ground. After his mother's disastrous relationships, he'd had no plans to ever marry. But then again, he'd never been in love before. He'd never handed over his heart, not sure it wouldn't get crushed or that he might never get it back.

"I love you," he said again. "Heaven help me, but I love you more than my next breath. So, was that a yes?"

Birdie laughed. "You sure about what you're getting into?"

"Not in the least," he said and laughed, too. "But I can't wait to find out. There's never a dull moment with you, Birdie Malone. It should be one hell of a ride."

"Then yes. I'll marry you. Saddle up, cowboy. This is going to be fun."

THE SHERIFF HAD been invited to the big shindig out at McKenna Ranch. Holden himself had called with the invitation.

"I don't think I ever thanked you for saving my life," the rancher said. "Thank you. You're a good sheriff. Better than your father."

The compliment had taken him by surprise in more than one way. His father had been kind of a legend in the Powder River Basin. "Thank you, Holden. But I'm afraid I can't make the party unless I have to break up a fight or haul someone off to jail."

The rancher had laughed. "I understand."

Stuart had thought about it, but the Fourth usually came with its own challenges for law enforcement. He was back to just two deputies and couldn't leave them alone tonight.

He leaned back in his office chair as he finished the last of the paperwork on Boyle Wilson's confession to killing Dixon Malone. Wilson had been transferred to the Billings detention center. Still exhausted from everything that had happened, Stuart couldn't have felt more relieved—or surprised—to finally be able to wrap up the case. Holly Jo was home, Holden McKenna was going to live, and Darius Reed was no longer a threat.

From the ashes of the McKenna Ranch house, a new structure had emerged. "It will be bigger and better than before," Holden had said, and Stuart had heard it was. The fire had to have destroyed a lot of memories since it was the original portion of the homestead that had burned—the part Holden's grandfather had built more than a hundred years ago.

Holden, though, had seemed to have taken it in his stride, as if almost glad to have some of those memories gone. Stuart wondered where that left Charlotte, who'd exited town after paying her fine for helping Elaine dispose of Dixon's body.

Charlotte and Holden were just full of surprises, like offering her house until Holden's was rebuilt—and Holden accepting—let alone her leaving town. No one seemed to know where she'd gone or if she'd be back.

His cell rang. "A woman's been mugged right outside the bar." He recognized the voice of the female bartender, Patty LaFrance, who worked the night shift at the Wild Horse. "She didn't want me to call you, but

I think you'd better come down here. It's Bailey Mc-
Kenna. A couple of cowboys ran after the person who
attacked her."

That sounded like trouble. Holden had good reason
to worry about his daughter, it seemed. "I'll be right
there."

A few minutes later, he pushed open the door into
the bar and saw Bailey in a booth with Patty, who was
clucking over her like a mother hen.

When Bailey saw him, she rolled her eyes. "I told
her not to call you. I'm fine and I didn't get a good look
at the guy, so no point."

She didn't look fine, Stuart thought. She was holding a bloodstained cloth to her temple. He could also
see that her hand holding the cloth was trembling. As
he took her in, he saw that her arm was also scraped,
the sleeve of her blouse torn. But it was what he found
in her blue eyes that told him she wasn't as fine as she
was trying to get everyone to believe. She was scared,
a look he'd seldom seen—if ever—on her face before.

Bailey McKenna was fearless, stubbornly independent and secretive. The sheriff had been wondering for
some time what was going on with her.

"What happened?" he asked as he slid into the booth
across from her.

"It was nothing," Bailey said, eliciting a rude response from Patty.

"It's something," the bartender said as she opened
the first aid kit on the table in front of her. She pulled
Bailey's hand and the cloth away to press a bandage
over the wound.

"Thank you, Clara Barton," she said pointedly to the

bartender. "I'm *fine*." Patty mugged a face and, taking her first aid kit, went back to her real job behind the bar.

"Okay, we're alone now," Stuart said. "What happened?"

Bailey met his gaze and seemed to relax. She even forced a smile. He wasn't buying that she was fine, and she must have realized it, because she looked away and said, "I don't know what happened."

"You don't remember?"

She rolled her eyes again. "I don't have a concussion or amnesia. It just happened so fast. I was leaving. I crashed into someone."

"He tried to take her purse," Patty called from behind the bar. "She was lying in the doorway, determined not to let him take it, and him just as determined to get it away from her—even if he had to drag her out into the street."

Bailey groaned. "It wasn't that dramatic."

"Did you get a look at him?" She shook her head. He turned to the bar. "You get a good look at him, Patty?"

"Wearing one of those damned hoodies. Plus, that front light out there is worthless, even if he wasn't doing his best to stay out of it," the bartender called back.

He looked to Bailey again. Her large purse was on the table next to her. He knew she carried it everywhere. "Mind if I have a look in your bag?" He reached to look inside, but her hand dropped over his to stop him.

"He didn't get anything. My wallet is inside. I already checked."

"What about your phone?"

"He didn't get it."

"Your laptop's in there too, isn't it?"

"It's fine. Everything is fine." She picked up the purse and swung it onto her shoulder with a grimace.

"You sure you shouldn't have a doctor look you over?"

"Yes, I'm sure. I'm a little sore, that's all." She met his gaze again. "I'm fine."

He nodded, studying her. Her blue eyes were deep as a bottomless well. There was more to the story, and she knew that he knew it. "Wish I knew what's going on with you," he said quietly so Patty and the rest of the people in the bar couldn't hear. "But if you ever want to be honest with me, you know where I live."

That made her smile. "There's nothing going on," she clearly lied. "But if there ever is, I'll stop by again." She dropped her voice to a whisper. "I've missed you."

He shook his head, rose and walked away while he could. He feared the day would come when he could no longer walk away from Bailey—either because he'd finally admitted how he felt about her or because whatever trouble she was neck-deep in had gotten them both killed.

At the bar door, he turned to look back. Just as he'd suspected, she was watching him leave, the fear in her eyes almost as glaring as her stubbornness. He hated to think how scared she'd have to be to come to him not just with the truth—but for help.

He hoped she didn't wait too long.

* * * * *